I0677795

PRAISE FOR

"Gruesomely romantic, *Spit Back the Bones* pulls you in as surely as the bog does. Gripping, ethereal, and ultimately hopeful."
—HANNAH WHITTEN, *New York Times* bestselling author of *For the Wolf*

"Beautiful and impossibly filled with the stench of stagnant water and loamy earth, *Spit Back the Bones* is a slurry of pain, rage, and hope. In her haunting debut, King exposes the horrors of coming home to the ghosts we never really bury and the pervasive rot of regret."
—TANYA PELL, author of *Her Wicked Roots* and *Cicada*

"Emotional and atmospheric, *Spit Back the Bones* is dripping in heady bog water. You'll never look at black flies the same way again."
—SARATOGA SCHAEFER, author of *Serial Killer Support Group* and *Traditional Wife*

"*Spit Back the Bones* is at once grotesque and hauntingly beautiful, exploring grief, rage, love, and of course, power—those who take it, and those who reclaim it. A monstrous debut that yanks at the heartstrings so well it hurts."
—AMANDA LINSMEIER, author of *Starlings* and *Six of Sorrow*

"Teagan Olivia King's debut tears through you like a scream and shows how home can be a place that holds you and haunts you all at once. Mila's dedication to her family will speak to anyone who has a sordid past they just can't shake—but can't bear to let go. Small-town religious corruption, a rekindled romance, and a bloodthirsty bog culminate in a story that will creep you out as much as it will lovingly embrace you."

—Isa Agajanian, author of *Modern Divination*

"*Spit Back the Bones* will consume you. King's world is nightmarishly beautiful; her setting will claw beneath your skin and settle deep in your bones. Beyond its delectably dark prose, this debut offers a deeper exploration of love and loss and the monstrous form one's grief can take in the dark."

—Skyla Arndt, author of *Together We Rot* and *House of Hearts*

"Lush with dread and steeped in folklore, *Spit Back the Bones* is a spellbinding fever dream of grief, rage, and the monsters we inherit."

—Lindy Ryan, author of *Bless Your Heart*

"Grief, family legacy, and religious trauma make for a truly authentic American gothic, this one possessed by the grasping hands of a living bog. *Spit Back the Bones* is equally gruesome as it is beautiful."

—Dawn Kurtagich, bestselling author of *The Thorns*

TEAGAN OLIVIA KING

SPIT BACK THE BONES

KEYLIGHT
BOOKS
AN IMPRINT
OF TURNER
PUBLISHING

Keylight Books
an imprint of Turner Publishing Company
Nashville, Tennessee
www.turnerpublishing.com

Spit Back the Bones

Copyright © 2025 by Teagan Olivia King. All rights reserved.

This book or any part thereof may not be reproduced or transmitted in any form or by any means, electronic or mechanical, including photocopying, recording, or by any information storage and retrieval system, without permission in writing from the publisher.
This is a work of fiction. All the characters and events portrayed in this book are either products of the author's imagination or are used fictitiously.

Cover design by M. S. Corley
Book design by Ashlyn Inman

Library of Congress Cataloging-in-Publication Data
Names: King, Teagan Olivia author
Title: Spit back the bones / by Teagan Olivia King.
Description: First edition. | Nashville : Keylight Books, 2025.
Identifiers: LCCN 2024048124 (print) | LCCN 2024048125 (ebook) | ISBN 9798887980744 hardcover | ISBN 9798887980751 paperback | ISBN 9798887980768 epub
Subjects: LCGFT: Horror fiction
Classification: LCC PS3611.I58624 S65 2025 (print) | LCC PS3611.I58624 (ebook) | DDC 813/.6—dc23/eng/20250325
LC record available at https://lccn.loc.gov/2024048124
LC ebook record available at https://lccn.loc.gov/2024048125

Printed in the United States of America

This book contains content such as: vomiting, murder, gore, body horror, Evangelical religious trauma, missing loved ones, mom trauma, blood, mucus, fly swarms, portrayal of alcoholism, recreational drug use, drowning, brief homophobic comments, and portrayal of an abusive relationship. Please read with care.

To Jeddy, who never truly left us

But God appointed a worm when dawn came the next day.
—Jonah 4:7

In the bog, sound is muffled. It plays tricks. Leads you to believe the ground is solid, that if you place your foot against the mud seeping from between peat and cattails, it will remain sturdy and carry you forward.

But the bog is a lover. And lovers like to lie.

It will lead you deeper into its murky depths with promises that brush your skin like featherlight kisses, and it isn't until it opens its dark, drooling mouth and swallows you whole that you realize it was all a fleeting romance, this dance across the bog. And you will slip down to join so many others who brushed lips with the water and tasted only death.

But tonight, the bog plays host to something more than muffled footsteps and doomed liaisons. Tonight, it opens its gaping maw, gnashes murky teeth, and spits out something wholly unmade. Something hungry. A monster bred from a love turned so sour it now reeks of hate. It twists up from the water, pale against a blackened sky, and slinks, dragging its humanoid form toward the shore where a man stands, a Styrofoam cooler locked in one hand. The monster's tongue caresses the roof of its mouth, feels the raw pink flesh, and can almost taste the man, taste his *soul*.

The thing it has craved since the very beginning.

The thing that will make it immortal.

The young man's skin thrums, and his blood bubbles and pops with the alcohol swimming sick in his stomach. He is lost, wandering aimlessly through the shallow reeds of the lapping water. The man is numb, cold, and should not be out here alone, away from familiar faces, and yet he stares in wonder at the night looming above. At the many stars that crowd the blanketing black.

The bog wavers beneath the yellow half-moon, reflecting the light off its foul, shimmering surface. The roots below the glassy waves tangle and undulate in a dance laid in shadow and buried deep in putrid water. So deep, in fact, one might think the roots do not feel the thing slipping through the mucky shallows on the forest's edge. But one would be mistaken.

Here, between the clumps of gathered reeds and the half-dead pines protruding from the water like charred rib cages, the bog feels everything.

The bog *is* everything.

It senses the tremors of footsteps, the ache of groaning earth, the piercing of bloody claws upon its peated soil. And it wants to cry out from the pain, but there is no one to listen. Not anymore. The cabin on the shore lies in ruins now.

And the man standing at the muddy bank does not have much longer.

The moon passes through the clouds above, and a single shaft of light illuminates the figure creeping through the shallows. Its arms—long and stained with decomposition—writhe through the water as it slides closer to the muddy bank and contorts like a water snake in the shadows. Weeds and bits of rotten foliage hang from its slick skin.

The bog shudders with its heaviness of the horror walking through its waters.

It knows this monster and the others like it. The ones who came before. The bog has watched the creatures bury bodies in its soil, felt the hollow ache of sinew and flesh drifting to the depths. And the bog has done what it was told to do: to swallow and spit out the bones.

The deal was done many years ago—between boy and bog and bitter heart—and the waters are tired. Exhausted beneath the weight of souls drowning in its inky blackness, rotting in limbo between sky and distant, ancient earth. The bog aches for release, and so it will call on the one who made the deal. Or what is left of her—the pieces on this earth of the girl who dipped a finger in the water and spoke the first curse still holding the monster in an icy grip.

Moonlight crosses through clouds, and the beast looms *up, up, up* from the water, silence on its lips. Cold claws wrap around the neck of the young man on the shore. The wretched screams do not last long; they twist into the air like sawn-off limbs, stunted as the monster presses its mouth against the man's lips and draws out whatever it is that makes humans mortal.

Its long, corded fingers linger over the man's chest, lifting his feet from the mud until he is splayed out, hanging in the air like a crooked cross. A sound cracks through the darkness. A squelching of crimson and bone. The man's chest flays open, and the monster drinks his soul. And the young man can no longer cry, as the blood pours from his eyes in rivulets.

The bog pulses with pain, carrying this torment—the spoilt witchery—to the town beyond the woods. Its waters are nothing but poison now, seeping deep and taking root in the people who call the town home.

A pestilence plagued by murder and blood.

The monster wipes a claw across its slimed face and revels in the green-budding taste of life—the very thing the first cursed soul taught it to take so long ago. It lets the body splash to the water and rolls it over. Blood drips from the wounds like fishhook tears, and red hair lolls in the shallows.

The bog does not like the taste of the body. It is a metal taste, filled with anger, and the bog knows what the monster has done. What the monsters have been doing for so many years now.

Killing for a chance at eternity.

A crack of wind breaks through the dead pines, and the creature looks up, eyes like pallid pools in corrugated skin. Its face—now lipless and flat—tears at the edges with what might have once been a smile, but is now nothing more than a rip of flesh. The monster takes the body in its supple arms and rolls it deeper into the water.

And the bog does what is expected, what it has done for so long now.

It *swallows*.

It curls dark, ice-water lips around the flesh and drags the body deeper until it rests against a pile of timeworn bones. And the bog wishes it was alone. That no one—save the monster—knew the secrets of the graveyard in its depths.

But it is not alone.

The swallow is *felt*.

Another pair of eyes watches from a neighboring shore, human and whole and altogether filled with a fear so thick, the air seems to swim with it. If the bog only looked, it would see those eyes and remember them.

Know them.

But instead, it focuses on the monster. On the sickness seeping up from the peat.

The monster watches the body sink beneath the rippling, dark surface, and then—after its skin is sewn back together—it slinks off into the shadows beneath the trees, thinking it is done, that the deal between boy and blood and bitter heart is secure. That it is one step nearer to eternity.

But the bog aches, and so, it sends out a voice. A single, forlorn sound to the whisper-wind wings nestling in the trunks of trees and breeze-kissed leaves.

Find the girl, it instructs the nesting insects.

Find her and warn her.

He is coming.

1

THE LIAR

I wrap white knuckles around the worn leather of the old Ford's steering wheel and try to keep from looking out the window. Farther down the road, where the black tarmac chews itself into gravel, a cargo train bites along the rickety tracks, and red siren lights blare at me to stop. But I don't want to. The last thing I need is time to pause, to think, to have an opportunity to turn back, to glance over my shoulder and see the damned thing.

The bog.

The clock on the dashboard blinks 2:45 p.m. I'm late and the train isn't helping. Tires crunch when I bring the truck to a halt, and the bell rings in my ears. My neck throbs as invisible hands wrap around my throat, trying to pull my eyes toward the acidic water, but I can't. Not now. I still need time.

Dammit, you've had enough time, Mila, a voice whispers.

My voice—I'd know if it weren't. Would recognize dead prattles from the bog. I've spent most of my measly twenty years picking out the difference, separating my own voice from those of the mingling dead and fitting them into neat, straight lines. So, on occasion, when the two do cross, when they get mixed up in my brain and I can't decipher reality from those murky, gray depths, at least I have a page of scribbles to refer to. To pull me up and out of the water.

Metaphorically speaking.

Metal, I remind myself. The taste of death in my mouth is metal.

The one thing separating my words from those of the dead. My therapist thinks it has something to do with blood—the taste of metal. Blood from the body. She doesn't listen when I tell her the body was drained.

My fingers grip the wheel tighter, and I grind my teeth together. Fear catches up to me, turning sour in my stomach. The train takes for-fucking-ever and I sit here, like a goddamn idiot. No one should be afraid of something that isn't even *alive*. Not really. Sure, the voices talk, but they're dead. Just a bunch of bodies rotting in the tar-black water, bloodless, floating somewhere in the liminal spaces.

I take a steadying breath and look up at the clattering cars blurring past—rusty red and brown, stained by a hundred years of iron-ore dust. Even my own lungs are probably tainted with the stuff. Maybe that's what will kill me dead.

Or it will be the guilt.

It pulls on the left side of my neck again, the tendon greedily pressing against my skin, like a finger through nylon.

Don't look, I tell myself. *You can't look.*

But I don't have to face it to recall the bog's appearance from memory. It has been burned into my brain for the last year. Every inch of it. There are hundreds of bogs across Michigan's Upper Peninsula, but this one is different.

Angrier.

Deadfall pines sticking up like exposed spines. Stagnant water like stomach acid sparkling in the midday sun. Water snakes licking through the gray-green algae choking the shores and creeping through the reeds. Clumps of cattails and dry rushes luring you with the promise of sturdy ground, a foothold, only to give way beneath your weight when the bog opens gaping jaws to swallow you whole.

My body hums. No, I don't need to look to remember. To know the truth of what lies beneath that glittering surface.

All those bodies.

It isn't needed when I can still *feel* it. My skin swims and the lights on the track stop whirling. The gate lifts and I press the gas—gravel flying when the truck screeches over the tracks.

It's easy—*too* easy—remembering the way the body felt beneath my skin. The cold, the squelching wet, the dead and murky gaze despite the voice being very much alive.

He had no eyes.

I shove away the words—try to, anyway—but my mind has been playing them on repeat ever since last summer, and I haven't been able to stop. Four words, over and over and over, and I think they'll make me insane.

Maybe they already have. I reach over and flick the blue hair tie on my wrist. Once, twice. My skin stings.

He had no eyes.

Three, four, five.

I turn the truck onto another gravel road, this one marked by a simple black-iron sign: Thomas Road.

Fuck me, I think. *Fuck me.*

I've chosen the worst way home without even realizing it. Just a gut reaction. My body remembering how much I used to love this drive.

Before.

The white house appears first, a sign skewered into the perfectly manicured grass. The red and black letters are peeling away, but I've driven by them enough times to know what it says by heart.

Go to church, or the devil will get you.

No one knows who put it in Reverend Byron's yard all those years ago, but he has never bothered to take it down. His truck is missing from the driveway—he's probably out healing the town's sinners—but the space isn't empty. Simon, his oldest son, lies beneath the underside of a beaten-up, baby-blue Ford, brown leather boots sticking out. I slow my truck and roll down my window.

"Hey, asshole!" I holler over the sound of clinking wind chimes.

There is a crash of forehead against metal before he swings out from beneath the truck and starts spitting words that would curdle the stomachs of Credence Hollow's most devout. His eyes narrow in on me, and another string of expletives leaves his mouth.

"Hello to you too." I lean over the bench seat. Hot air billows in through the open window.

He is as tall, thick, and grotesque as I remember him. All muscle and reaching hands, lingering and hungry eyes. I do fast math in my head.

At twenty-one, he is the typical all-American boy who has never had to fess up to anything in his whole life. Never had to take the blame or the responsibility.

The poster child for everything wrong in this world.

We love to see it, Simon Byron, you absolute shithead.

He reaches his fingers up to the crown of his head and they come away sticky with blood.

"Didn't know you were coming back to town, frog-face."

I roll my eyes. *Seriously?* The best thing he can come up with is the stupid nickname he gave me in grade school?

I shove aside thoughts of the bog and wiggle my eyebrows. "Surprise, surprise, motherfucker!" Then I flip him the bird and peel out of there.

I know not to stick around too long after Simon has had some blood spilled. The last time it happened was when his brother, Roe, punched him in the nose after Simon called me a word I will not be repeating, thank you very much. I had never seen anything like it—the look that came over Simon's face once he realized he was bleeding. Shadows gathered beneath his eyes, like ink-blotting paper, and I thought for sure Roe would be dead by morning.

I swear, Simon Byron is going to kill someone one day.

Gravel and dust sprays out behind my ripping tires. The trees turn into nothing short of tangled limbs, creating a dark canopy over the road. I crank the music louder, letting the iron rhythm steel my nerves. It is loud and screeching and fury-filled, and I settle into it. Because maybe those things are exactly what I have become. So very angry.

Maybe that's what happens to a girl who raises a body from the bog.

Maybe that's what happens when she's so scared, she puts the body back.

Three shrill beeps replace the rock and roll coming from the radio, and a staticky voice spills from the speakers.

"This is a special news bulletin. Police in Leo County today are still searching for local missing person, Owen Shelby, last seen the evening of June fifteenth by friends in a wooded area just outside Credence Hollow."

A sharp sliver of ice inches its way between my ribs.

"Sheriff Lowell is asking that if you have any information concerning this case to please call the offices..."

A phone number follows, but I'm not paying attention. Not to the voice coming from the radio, not on the way sweat is slicking my navel, the creases of my palms. No, I'm focused on my heart heaving in my chest. I count the quickening beats and pray I don't have a heart attack at the ripe old age of twenty and crash my dead grandmother's trusty, well-loved pickup truck.

I switch the radio off. Abandoned in my own wretchedness, I only stop when I spot the trailer. It is parked a way off the road, surrounded by year-old poplar growths, messy logging, and ruts in the mud. If I didn't know better, I would think it was abandoned.

But I do know better.

The curl of black smoke gives it away. It coils from behind the gray-brown aluminum, licking up against the clear blue sky. It doesn't take long for the scent to carry through the AC unit of the old truck—burning pine logs, ash, the sweet tang of weed. It is a welcoming smell, a comforting one, and for a moment, I let myself believe coming home for a few days won't be so bad. Maybe it can be like all the years before I left last summer.

But it's a lie. Everything spilling from between my lips these days seems to be. Lie after lie after lie. And deep down, it's stupid, *so stupid*. Nothing can be like what it was before.

Before the body.

Before I touched it and its eye sockets snapped open.

Before I killed it and sent it back to the bog.

The scent of smoke sours, and I press on the gas. I don't want to see him anyway—the boy in the trailer. Because the last time I saw Roe Byron, he was helping me put that body back in the bog. My nerves twitch and sharpen with the memory: the cool-like-butter surface of the still-ripe skin, the blackened lips, the cavernous hollows in its skull. And the voice. God, I remember the voices more than anything else.

He had no eyes.

They were all saying those words.

A chorus of the dead.

The voices are not strangers. I've been hearing them since I was a little girl with braids and a smile too big for this world. Since the day I almost drowned in the bog and Grandma Ruby fished me out. She wove strands of my hair together between her leathery fingers and said:

"It's a gift, Mila-May. One that takes a near-death experience to gain. The swamp is in us, and we are in the swamp. We must use our talents to help the poor souls trapped there. To give them peace."

I turned around, one hand on the floral cotton of her dress, angling my eyes to peer into hers. There was so much torment in the shadows above her sunken cheeks, pain masking the truth. The truth of what, I didn't know—still don't—but I think she understood what was coming.

She realized our family was cursed.

My older brother Jed admitted it first—the family curse. Saying the words, over and over, like the call of a loon on a midsummer night.

I'm a curse, Mila. There's something stuck inside me. Something I can't just pull out. And I'm scared one day it's gonna hurt somebody.

I'm a curse.

And I think, maybe I am too. Perhaps I can't help people. I can only do the opposite. Can only hurt them. Especially the ones I love. Isn't that why I'm coming home? To make up for all the hurt I have caused? To atone for running away when it all got too heavy, when I stared into the face of death and didn't like my reflection?

My sister's message beats like a tattoo in the back of my mind. *I'm leaving for college at the end of July. Would be nice to see you before I leave. Unless you're too busy...*

Something cold and miserable spreads across my chest, and a laugh bubbles in the back of my throat like bile. Right. *Too busy.* Too busy living a few towns over. Too busy working a dead-end job at a gas station, just to scrape enough money together to pay rent to a man who smells like cheap cigarettes and cat piss. Too busy pretending the past doesn't exist.

So now, here I am, forcing myself home to make amends.

Or, at least, to try.

Not that this is home. Nowhere feels like home anymore.

My insides churn like tar in the hot sun, and I crank up the AC. The cold blasts me in the face, waking me up. The trees stretch taller the farther I drive down the old dirt road. Outside grows chilly with air from the swamp. I smell it—the muddy tang, the spicy-sweet of cedar and black earth. When I roll my window down further, the breeze sweeps in and brushes yellow curls off my slick skin.

It's hot, even for June. A sort of thick, chewy atmosphere settling around the bones and warning of coming rain. I swallow and the sides of my throat turn to glass.

Jed disappeared on a day like this.

The wet heat hung in the air, like cobwebs threatening to choke me, while I watched him walk deeper into the cedars and never come out. He told me he was just going for a walk, but when he didn't return for Grandma Ruby's homemade ice cream and the chocolate birthday cake she promised, I knew he wasn't coming back. We searched the swamp for the next three days, my hands wrapped tightly around the wire handle of a Coleman lantern until my palms blistered. But there was no sign of him.

I caught our grandmother swirling her hands in the water on the last night, begging the bog to tell her where Jed was, but it gave nothing up, not even a voice. And she screamed things at it. Things that made no sense. When I asked her what she had been doing down at the bank, she lied, told me she needed peace and quiet to figure out her thoughts.

Lying must be an inherited trait in this family.

When I was little and my mom would bring us to church, people used to whisper, saying my grandmother was a witch. Even the former Reverend Byron gossiped about her, bent over his pulpit like a frostbitten fern. He wished she would come to church and save her soul. And when I would tell Grandma Ruby this and wonder at why she didn't just come with us, she would scoop my sun-kissed hair up into her calloused palms and whisper:

"The bog is my church, Mila-May, the water my god."

And it was enough for her.

But it isn't for me. The bog took Grandma Ruby three weeks after Jed went missing, and I've despised it ever since. Hated the way it can crawl into my brain and whisper things to me. The way it takes and takes and only gives death.

Sometimes, I block them out—the voices—if I catch them quick enough. My therapist reminds me they aren't real and can't hurt me, but I think she says it more for her own benefit than for mine. To help her feel like maybe, just maybe, the world can fit into the explainable, scientific bubble she wants it to.

But they're real. I *feel* their pain.

A mailbox comes into view on the side of the road. If not for the rust and lichen clinging to the metal, it might have once been white. There is a single word scratched along it in peeling blue paint: *Thomas*. I take a deep breath, hold it for a few seconds, just like my therapist taught me, and remind myself of all the things I can control.

Literally nothing.

Literally, absolutely fucking nothing.

I turn into the driveway, pine cones crunching beneath my tires. The family cabin winks through the branches: dark-stained logs, bubbled-glass windows, the screen door with butter-yellow curtains swinging in the breeze, an ancient grapevine spinning serpentine from the porch rafters.

I should feel happy to see the house. It's where I grew up, where all my core memories took place. But it just sits there, staring at me with its dark-window eyes and whispers, *You don't belong here, Mila-May. You don't belong anywhere.*

Two bikes—one blue and one a rusted orange—lean against the uneven wooden stairs leading up to the door. Agatha, my sister, must be home; her girlfriend, Camille, with her. I let my nerves settle. Agatha will forgive me. She is the only person who hasn't totally written me off as a lost cause. But the truth is, she might know about the voices, but I never told her about the body.

The memory of that voice whispers in my ear.

He had no eyes.

I park my truck and try to wash away the image of the corpse I pulled from the bog. It wasn't just his eyes that were missing—it was his whole goddamn chest. I picture the open gash, the way the blood had coagulated black around its ripped flesh, turning to tar in the water. My palms dewy with sweat, and I wipe them on the worn denim of my shorts.

Roe trembled beside me in that moment, begging me to notify the cops, to tell anyone. *Please, we have to tell someone.* But I refused. I was scared of whatever my touch had done to reanimate the thing. Scared of who might have put that body in the bog and what the cops would do if they found them.

Terrified my brother was the one with blood on his hands. Worried his curse had made him a killer.

I swallow my guilt, the taste of it metallic on my tongue. Grandma Ruby used to say we were given the gift to help people, to bestow upon them peace and allow them to move on. That the gift wasn't meant for *us*. But then she died, and so I told myself her words were just lies too.

My fingernails sink into the worn fabric of the bench seat while I look at the cabin through blurry eyes. My coworker at the gas station, Denise, told me it was stupid coming here. That I didn't owe anyone shit. Her voice rings in my ears.

You don't have to go, honey. You know that, right? You have nothing to prove.

But she's wrong. I have everything to prove. I have to show my mind the lies I tell myself are true. That... The thought crumbles in my throat. Jed is alive, and he's not a murderer. He is not the one putting bodies in the bog, only for me to find and put them right back.

I lean my head on the steering wheel, staring at my palms. My vision swims and bleeds with salt water.

Everything is a lie here in the bog. We bury our secrets in the mud and the water, keeping them submerged until we can go down to join the rest of the dead things.

People used to call my grandmother a witch. But me?

Well, they just call me a liar.

2

GONE GIRL

The worst part of summers in the bog is the bugs. Almost immediately after jumping down from the truck, I'm fighting off a swarm of black flies—*buzz, buzz, buzzing* around my bare arms, my ears, biting any open skin. They're insatiable. Just like everyone else here in Credence Hollow.

But instead of blood, human beings swarm to feed on gossip, on other people's pain, on the self-pride high they feel when they say, "There, there. It must be awful now that he's gone. I'll pray for you," and then walk away and never do a damn thing. It's so easy to say, "I'll pray for you," and forget your prayers and promises at the moment you turn your back.

It is half the reason I left. That and all the dead bodies piling up around me.

I stretch my arms up to the sky bleeding blue through the leaves overhead. It's a long drive from Marquette to here, the edge of the world, and my bones ache. I twist around to reach inside my truck for my wallet, and that's when I see it.

The reverend's shiny truck.

A familiar rush of adrenaline courses through my body, and I chalk it up to righteous anger. You know, it's funny how the man claiming to live off the donations of his congregation is the same man who owns the newest car in town. And believe me when I say, Credence Hollow is no Beverly Hills. So, *obviously*, the church is putting its donations to good use.

I curl my lip. Typical.

But also, why the hell is he here? I study the reflective metal of the vehicle's red outer shell, glinting like a pool of freshly spilled blood in the sunlight. Mom stopped going to church when she found more solace at the bottom of a Smirnoff vodka bottle than she did on her knees.

And when the reverend called off their on-again, off-again affair.

I grab my bags out of the back seat and slam the door shut.

The air around me is sticky with heat, and hot bugs screech in the tall grass on the edge of the lawn. Last year's pine needles crunch and crackle beneath my feet as I make my way toward the cabin. Thelia moss grows along the shingles and between the logs like mortar. Grandma Ruby's rocking chair is still in its place on the front porch, all these years later, and for a moment, I let myself imagine her there, rocking back and forth with a cup of green tea in one hand and a knowing smile on her face. She was always open to the voices, had heard them since she was a little girl.

"Almost died at birth, you know," she told me once. "The voices used to sing me lullabies."

Grandma Ruby had a different relationship with the dead than I do. I shift one bag higher up on my shoulder and climb the steps to the cabin's front door. I mean, if I really had my way, I wouldn't have a relationship with the dead at all. They still find a path in, but it's usually just a breath, a desperate inhalation, before I block them out and tell them to go find someone else to listen to their pain. I've got enough of my own, thanks.

The front door is open, so I fling back the screen door and step inside, letting it slam behind me. The cabin remains untouched, like the swampland surrounding it. My childhood home has only grown dark, tangled, and rooted to the ground it stands on. Dust filters down through the rays of sunlight peeking beneath the lemon-checked curtains above the kitchen sink. The basin that, when I look closer, is overflowing with dirty dishes.

I drop my bag to the floor and kick my green Converse off beside it. A blister rubs on my heel, and I wince when I walk across the worn floorboards. The downstairs is empty. And an absolute mess. The dining room table is covered in bills. Mostly unpaid, if I had to guess.

The living room gapes open before me, nothing more than a cracked leather sofa, two overstuffed chairs, and a stone hearth. I don't remember the last time a fire was lit inside. Probably the time the power went out for a whole week and we cooked stew in a cast-iron pot on the bed of coals Jed made. I smile at the memory. The house got so cold one morning, Agatha and I made a blanket fort and swore we were never leaving.

Three quilts are tossed haphazardly on the lumpy sofa, their only company a squadron of overturned Smirnoff bottles.

Well, guess we know where Mom's been sleeping.

Careful not to kick the glass, I inch through the living room and poke my head in the bathroom. Nothing. Just a yellow toothbrush in a glass and a tube of toothpaste at least three years old.

Dammit, Mom. Why does she refuse to throw anything of Jed's away?

I twist the hematite ring on my finger—the only thing Jed ever gave me. He had found the chunk of metallic gray rock in an old mining pit and fashioned it into two rings and a necklace. Jed kept the necklace for himself and gave the rings to Agatha and me. I haven't taken it off since the day he gifted it, so maybe I get it. Maybe I *do* understand why Mom refuses to throw away his yellow toothbrush and instead chooses for it to just sit there, collecting dust. Because it would be an admittance, the final nail in my brother's proverbial coffin.

I try to hold back the tears pounding on the backside of my eyes and twist the ring harder.

He's not dead. If he was, I would hear him. And I would let his voice in.

Instead, a different sound hits my ears. A voice that curdles my blood. I draw my fingers into a tight fist.

The Reverend Byron.

Of course. I just saw his truck parked outside. But I didn't really think about seeing him until just now. His words filter in through a glass sliding door leading out to the deck. I can't make out what he's saying—honestly, I probably don't want to—but I inch forward. Floorboards creak beneath my feet as I press my ear closer to the glass.

Two Adirondack chairs point out toward the cedars towering on the edges of the sloped lawn. A table sits in between them, two mismatched mugs of coffee steaming in the late afternoon sunlight. Tendrils of Mom's thinning gray-blond hair rest against the back of one chair, slipping down from a mussed bun. Reverend Byron is sitting beside her, leaning close, probably telling her everything happens for a reason. Yes, even a dead mother and a missing son.

Bullshit, I think.

Just another excuse for people to feel like they've done their duty before forgetting about it.

I'm about to sneak past the glass and make my way up the stairs, probably to find Agatha hiding, when the reverend turns his eyes toward the house.

Well, fuck.

A somber smile cracks across his lips when he sees me. And I fight the sudden urge to smack it right off his face. But the last thing I need right now is to start off my visit throat-punching the town reverend.

Instead, I smile back and turn to go up the stairs, but he's already standing, and when Mom's head swivels around to look at me, I know something is wrong. Something past the empty Smirnoff bottles or the unwashed dishes piling up in the sink. Mascara runs in black streams down her pale face, and her eyes are puffy and red.

My stomach drops to the soles of my feet, like I'm being launched into space with nothing to catch me. The familiar claws of dread hollow out space between my ribs, and the room begins to spin. I grab hold of the doorframe, just to steady myself as the reverend comes to open the door.

The spice-sweet air of the swamp hits me before anything else, and I let it ground me, allow it to fill me up with familiarity before whatever the hell is about to come next. I swat at a fly buzzing in my ear.

"Mila. We didn't know you were coming home." The reverend's deep voice echoes around the inside of my head like a swinging pendulum.

A headache is already blooming across my temples.

Goddammit.

He says the word *home* like he knows exactly how I feel. Like he anticipates the word will sink its dagger-sharp teeth into me and suck my soul dry. The bastard.

"We were just talking about you."

I turn to look at him—Reverend Titus Byron. His salt-and-pepper hair hasn't changed much since I was a kid, but the lines around his mouth have grown deeper, digging trenches into the gray-stubbled skin on his jaw. He wears his usual outfit of a button-down shirt and slacks; sweat stains seep under his arms and around the collar. I pull at the neckline of my own white T. It suddenly feels like a million degrees outside.

"Agatha texted me a few days ago." I try desperately to swallow the lump forming like cotton at the back of my throat. "Asked me to come home for a bit."

The reverend wears a pained expression. I've seen it before, the kind of look he wears when something bad has happened and he's trying to show an ounce of sympathy.

"Mila."

Mom's voice is like distant wind, thin and feeble and yet so far away. For a moment, I decide it isn't real. *None of this is real.* Whatever they're about to drop on me is all some messed-up dream. The reverend takes a step closer and puts a hand on my back. I wince and pull away.

"Why don't you come sit down by your mom? There's...well, there's something you ought to know."

Panic rises in my chest, crashing and breaking against my ribs, like I'm on the brink of death. I dig my nails into the soft flesh of my palms and bite my tongue.

Don't give in, don't give in, don't give in.

I've been having panic attacks since I was a kid, but only recently did I figure out what they are. Three months ago, when I couldn't breathe and Denise found me on the bathroom tile at work, gasping and crying and shaking and sweating, all at once, she made me book an appointment with a therapist the next day. My therapist is great—actually, she has helped me more than anyone ever has in my entire life—but right now, the calming techniques she taught me are doing absolute jack shit.

The reverend leads me over to the empty chair, and it takes everything within me just to breathe, to remember to let the air out of my lungs for as long as it takes to draw it in. This is not going to be good. It's obvious. A million worst-case scenarios flood my mind, but one starts playing on repeat like a broken record.

Jed's dead. They found his body. Jed's dead. They found his body. Jed's dead. They—

Mom leans forward and laces her fingers between mine. "Mila, whatever he tells you, you must listen to him."

Listen to who? The reverend? Like hell. But from the tone in Mom's voice, I know something is wrong. Very, very wrong. My throat swells, and tears puddle in my eyes.

Stop crying, you idiot.

There's no reason to cry, not yet. They haven't even told me anything.

Owen. That's it. It must be about Owen Shelby. I try to make my body relax, but it doesn't work. Because from the way Mom is looking at me, this is about something so much more than the missing local guy I went to high school with.

Reverend Byron wraps thick fingers around the back of my chair, staring down at me with that "Don't worry—it all happens for a reason" face.

And now I really want to reach out and hit him because, whatever is coming... Well, there is probably no good reason for it at all. That's one thing I've learned about this world. There isn't a reason for everything. Sometimes, bad things just happen; sometimes, people are just cursed.

I'm a curse, Mila.

And I think, through choked tears and shallow breaths, maybe I am too. Perhaps this entire family is. This whole goddamn town.

I shift my gaze to Mom, studying the harsh lines sprouting from her eyes. She didn't look this old last summer. When was the last time I even talked to her, let alone saw her? I spent most of last summer in Roe's trailer and—

I push the thought away. Mom's graying hair is tangled and knotted, escaping a black rubber band. Her cardigan slips over one shoulder, and her skin looks sallower and paler the longer I stare.

"What is going on, Mom?" I'm barely able to get all the words out, my throat choked by my own saliva.

She looks like she's about to cry or maybe swig from whatever half-drunk bottle is lying around. Her fingers shake against mine, and I take a deep, steadying breath, holding her hands tight. I am always the strong one, the one to swallow my own fear and anxiety and absorb someone else's. This time, I blink my own tears away.

"Mom, tell me what's wrong."

A lie. I don't want to know. I'm terrified of what she is going to say.

She opens her mouth and then collapses back in her chair, body shaking. Tears spilling down her sunken cheeks.

My whole world is spinning. The trees blur gray and brown and green, and the scent of the swamp presses in from all sides. I want to be angry—at my mom, at the reverend—furious at myself for not being able to hold my own family together. Or hold anything together, really.

Breath in, breath out, I tell myself. *Breath in, breath out.*

The reverend comes around my chair and kneels in front of me. For as much as I hate him, his hands are warm when they grasp at mine, and I don't pull away.

"What's—what's going on?" I ask, barely recognizing my own voice as it spills from my lips. Another fly buzzes around my ear.

The reverend sighs, pulls his glasses off his face, and massages the brim of his nose.

"It's your sister, Agatha," he says. "She's missing."

3

GOOD TROUBLE

Words turn to ash on my tongue, clog my throat and settle somewhere deep in my chest, choking me, squeezing my lungs until I'm sure they'll never taste oxygen again. I pull away from the reverend, his damp hands and bitter breath. Anxiety creeps along my spine, and I sink my fingernails into the wood of the chair's armrest.

Something shimmers just above the surface of my skin. It isn't fear or shock or anger. It just *is*. And I can't explain it. Can't explain the sensation currently snaking its way through my body, threatening to shatter me into a hundred pieces.

Reverend Byron says my name, but he sounds miles away, like there's a fog wrapped around me and I won't get out. Will never feel the sun on my face again. His thick fingers tighten around my shoulder, and it's only then I realize I'm shaking—when he tries to steady me.

"Mila? I need you to look at me."

But I can't. Because every time I look into Reverend Byron's eyes, I get gut-punched with two emotions I can't handle right now, on top of whatever it is I'm already feeling—rage and guilt. The memory starts playing out before my swimming vision...Roe and me, the bark of a pine digging into my back, the smell of something dead.

"Get off me!" I jump up from the chair, nearly knocking him over.

My fingers rake my arms, the skin prickled and cold. I can't inhale, can't even *think* about breathing. A noise rings in my ears, shrill and broken. I close my eyes and cover my ears, almost dropping to my knees.

Not now.

Not the voices. I squeeze my eyes tight and try to focus on anything else.

Not Agatha. She can't be missing. They mean Owen, right? Agatha is fine. She is probably just upstairs or biking with Camille to Phil's Corner Store for beers and bags of Swedish Fish. She's at that age now, right? God, how old is she? Eighteen? She just graduated high school, so that would make sense. I try to add the math up in my head, let it distract me from the gaping hole carving itself in my stomach. The noise turns my brain to soup.

The dead voice breathing against my skin.

"No." I thread the words between my teeth. "No, I'm sure she's just with Camille." I try to lighten the mood with a laugh, but it comes out sharp and stunted. "You know, probably drinking beer and smoking cigarettes in the swamp."

But it is another lie; both their bikes are slumped against the porch.

A look passes between the reverend and Mom. She peels herself off the back of the chair, wipes at the tears on her cheeks with the cuff of her sweater, and reaches a shaking hand toward her coffee mug, which, if I'm guessing right, is probably more vodka than coffee.

The reverend clears his throat, and I steel myself for a lecture on alcohol, even though the person who actually needs the talk is currently bottles-deep in the stuff already.

"Mila, Camille is the one who told your mother."

The noise filters deep into my bones, ringing until the headache flowers out across my forehead and grows roots behind my ears. I shake my head, taking a step forward, every inch of me wanting to hit him. To hit *something*. But I don't. I bite my tongue and try to breathe.

"No," I repeat, feeling stupid. It seems to be the only word I know how to say right now. "No, that's impossible. Those two are inseparable. They've been dating since Christmas."

The reverend flinches, and that urge to smack him only grows.

I've known about Agatha and Camille even before they did. Last summer, before I left and they started their senior year, there was just *something* between them: gentle brushes, longing gazes, sharp inhalations when they touched. And it made me glad Agatha was finally coming into herself. Not something anyone else thought she should be, but exactly and wholly just *her*.

It's hard to find yourself when half the people who are supposed to love you are either dead, missing, or running away. I was so happy for her—*am* happy for her—but this is how I know something is wrong. If Camille says Agatha is missing...

I wrap my fingers around the deck rail, dragging the humid air into my lungs. The voice presses in from all sides, making my head throb, but I won't let it in. Not now, not yet. I strengthen the ward, my iron gate.

Breath in, breath out, I tell myself. In, out.

I snap the band on my wrist. "Where's Camille? Her bike is still outside."

Who the hell has both their siblings disappear? It's not fair, and I want to scream about how exactly unjust it is, but the reverend would just give me the usual "Life isn't fair. It all happens for a reason" bullshit and right now, that's the last thing I need.

The reverend crosses his arms over his broad chest. "She came by in the early hours and dropped both bikes off before going home."

I blink at him.

"You let her go home?" The words cut sharp and angry across my tongue. "She, what? Comes and tells Mom that Agatha is missing and then you just let her go?" A laugh cracks from my throat. "Has anyone bothered to maybe, I don't know, call the cops?"

"We haven't gotten that far." Mom's voice is just as weak as the rest of her. Her knuckles whiten around her mug. "It's not even been a full day, and Reverend Byron thought it might be a good idea just to wait it out. You know how Agatha can be."

Blood kisses the surface of my skin, and sweat breaks out along my brow, even in the shade of the cedar trees. Owen has only been missing for two days, and already, the police have a bulletin out. But no one is making excuses for him. No one is saying, "Oh, you know how Owen can be." I run clammy fingers through my hair.

"You've got to be fucking kidding me."

I say it more to the trees around us than anyone else, but Mom spins in her chair, nearly dropping her coffee from sloppy fingers.

"Mila-May, language."

And that's what does it. What makes all my edges turn to sharpened steel. Not the reverend and his useless one-liners. Not the fact my grandma is dead, my brother has been missing for the last three years, and now my sister has vanished too. Not the reality that the last time I saw the boy down the street, he tried to kiss me, and the stench of something dead made me pull away. No, it's the fact my good-for-nothing alcoholic mother is scolding me for my language.

It takes me two steps to cross the deck, bend over, and stick a finger in her face.

"You know what you are, Mom? Nothing. Absolutely nothing." The words are bitter on my tongue, but I spit them out anyway. "You just sit around and drink and pretend to be a mother, and all the while, you're just rotting away, forgetting you even have any damn kids, and defaulting to someone who couldn't even love his own son."

The reverend stiffens.

Mom's hazel eyes—tinged yellow at the edges—widen, as if she's some animal being attacked. And frankly, screw that. She's no victim. Mom does not get to play this role. I laugh again, the sound cracking in half when it leaves my throat.

There are a million things I want to tell her, starting with the fact she's half the reason I ran away. She told me I was corrupted by anger and kicked me out of the house. But instead, I straighten and stare down at her while she folds in on herself. I should have pity for her, but I don't. Not a single inch of me feels anything but anger toward my mother.

"You're pathetic," I say.

Silence hangs in the air. Nothing but the steady droning of hot bugs and frogs from the swamp. I wait for her to respond, to tell me what an ungrateful asshole I am. To bring up stuff from years ago she's still holding onto. To remind me I'm a curse too. But she just crumples, and I turn my back.

The reverend opens his mouth, but I meet him with a middle finger before brushing past him and going into the house. I don't stop until my shoes are on my feet and slapping on the boards of the front porch. My fingers curl into fists, and I push a silent scream from between my lips. A headache splinters through my skull, and my mind explodes with frantic thoughts. Owen, missing. Agatha, missing. All these people I know and love, gone.

I have to do something.

If no one else is going to figure this out, if no one else is going to get off their ass and go to the police, I will. I clench my teeth. Just another case of me having to do the work. Me sticking my neck out.

But it's Agatha. She is blood. And that might mean nothing to the reverend, but it means something to me.

I leap down off the porch and cross the lawn to my truck. The rusted hinges groan. I jump up onto the seat and jam my keys into the ignition.

Mom won't notify the police because the reverend says not to? Well, fuck him. I'll go to the authorities myself. I whip the truck into reverse and slap at a black fly buzzing around the cab.

Damn bugs.

I am halfway out the drive when I remember the last time I went to Sheriff Lowell's office. My throat turns jagged, and I swallow.

Three years ago—when Jed went missing and everyone let his case go cold.

I slam the gas pedal to the floor, peeling out of the drive and back onto the dirt road. Sheriff Lowell got away with it then, marking Jed as a missing person and tacking his face up beside so many others who walked into the bog and never came out. People who Credence Hollow has slowly forgotten about.

But no one is going to forget Jed *or* Agatha. Not if I have any say on the matter.

I drive back past the Byrons' house, not stopping this time to flip Simon the bird. His truck isn't even there anymore, just a vacant driveway and an empty house. Not that the house was ever full to begin with. There's something about houses that make them feel alive, like they have a soul.

Even in the shadows of the cabin, Grandma Ruby lingers. She's in the crackling beeswax candles on the stone hearth and the tangy breeze blowing in through open windows, rustling the curtains.

But the Byrons' house? It doesn't have a soul. It's as dead and empty as a corpse.

My hair tangles in the wind rushing through the open window. I turn down Main Street, and my stomach drops.

Nothing has changed much in the last year or so. Same old half-abandoned buildings, same pigeon shit strewn across the sidewalks, like leftover

Fourth of July parade candy, same familiar faces coming and going from Phil's Corner Store and the crumbling dive bar where Roe washed dishes during summers in high school.

I press harder on the gas. The faster I can make it down the street, the quicker I can figure out where the hell my sister is.

I slam the truck into *park* in front of the police station and jump out, heels smarting on the asphalt. My breath comes in shaky gulps, and my eyes burn while I stare up at the sand-colored tile, half the letters missing from *Leo County Police Department.*

God, I haven't been here in three years. The air is stale and hot and my stomach feels hollow. I palm my keys, the metal biting my skin.

In, demand something be done about Agatha, and get out.

Should be easy.

I take a steadying breath and throw open the glass door.

The familiar scents of reheated Folgers and sweat has me grasping for some semblance of calm. A ripple of movement at the front desk makes me suck in another breath of hot air.

"Well, look what the cat dragged in." Flo Higdon, the secretary, sits crumpled over her desk, nursing a mug of some unidentifiable substance. Her hair is dyed an unnatural orange, the roots cropped close to her head and feathering white. Pink rouge smears her cheekbones, and I swear her eyeliner is 3D-printed onto her face, it's so thick. Her lips pull apart in what I suppose is a smile, but looks more like a sneer, with yellowing teeth poking through.

"Hey, Flo," I say, trying to act cool and collected and feeling anything but.

I shuffle across the linoleum. If I can just get to her desk before she yells what she always does, if I can just distract her until—

She stands up. Too late.

"Sheriff, your favorite Credence Hollow runaway is back to say hello," she calls through a doorway behind her.

My stomach drops to my feet, and I clench my keys tighter in my fist. Fucking Florence Higdon. I plaster on a smile and grit my teeth.

"I can just see myself back there, Flo." I try to wind my way behind her desk toward the sheriff's office, but she and her overpowering gardenia body spray are suddenly standing in my way.

"Oh, sweetie, you know the rules. Can't just go busting back there and interrupting his important work." Her lips spread further, and she flicks a speck of dust off the sleeve of my shirt.

I back up, sneakers slipping on the slick floor. "Right, sorry. I'll just wait here. I—"

"Mila-May Thomas."

Sheriff Lowell leans against the doorframe, his badge just as shiny as the balding spot on the top of his head. His pudgy hand clutches a coffee mug that reads *Yooper Flip-Flops*, with a pair of snowshoes etched in black ink. I fight the urge to smack it out of his meaty fingers.

"Hey, Sheriff, I was hoping I could talk to you about something."

He shares a wary look with Flo, but then steps back in the doorway and motions me through.

Well, that's a goddamn freaking miracle.

The hallway is made of paneled wood straight from 1975. A few fish corpses on plaques line the wall, only broken up by the odd deer head or stuffed squirrel. Sheriff Lowell leads me to a door at the end of the hall and into a room filled with more taxidermized carcasses and an entire section plastered with missing persons posters.

My stomach sours. I grab ahold of the doorknob just to steady myself. Jed's eyes strike me immediately. His sandy hair; his funny, lopsided smile; the collar of his jean jacket ratty and worn, just how he liked it. That picture was cropped from a photo of the three us: me, Jed, and Agatha. Grandma Ruby took it after showing us how to paddle the old cedar canoe across the bog.

I try to imagine what Jed might look like now. The same blond hair, the same crooked grin. But maybe deeper shadows beneath his eyes. Scars. The ones seen *and* unseen.

Like mine.

Sheriff Lowell slumps down in his leather chair and mistakes the nostalgic smile on my face for total and complete healing. Because of course he does.

"Glad to see you looking happier, Mila. The time away has done you good, eh? Finally decided to let the past stay in the past."

That's all it takes to snap me out of the memory. I close the space between us in two sharp strides and slam my fists onto his desk.

"The past doesn't stay in the past, Sheriff, when the same shit keeps happening."

He puts down his coffee mug and flexes his muscles, popping joints in his shoulders and elbows. "Mila, I think it best you take a deep breath and—"

"I don't need to take a deep breath. I need someone to find my sister."

He hesitates, like he's calculating his words, formulating the right sentence to help me calm down and be less of a problem. But I like being a problem. "Look, Mila. Your sister has only been gone for a short period of time, and with these kinds of situations, knowing the kind of girl she is—"

I inhale, breath jagged in my lungs. My throat burns. "You already know? What, the reverend called you but told you to keep it a secret? And don't give me that *what kind of girl* bullshit, Sheriff. I know for a fact that if Simon Byron was missing, the whole force would be out there right now, looking for him."

Sheriff Lowell takes a deep breath and another swig of his coffee. "Well, that would be because Simon isn't one for...trouble. He's a good kid, following in his daddy's footsteps and going into the church. And honestly, after what happened to your brother, we all know Agatha can be a little *dramatic*."

"Dramatic?" The only thing keeping me from punching this man in his face is the idea of getting slapped with a felony. Instead, I let my fingernails curl into the soft wood of his desk. "Look, you've got two missing people on your hands, Sheriff. Three, if you count Jed, which I do. And one of them is still a kid. Doesn't that look bad? Don't you want to figure out where they went and"—I wave at the other posters on the walls—"I don't know, wash your hands of it?"

"Mila, Mila, Mila." He says my name like a disappointed parent after finding out their child cheated on a math test. It's a tone I'm used to hearing, unfortunately. Even though the last time I took a fucking math test was three years ago.

I point a finger at one of the posters. It's older than some of the others—rolling corners, the photograph starting to fade. Dani Chartier. Camille's older sister. She went missing after being crowned Blueberry Queen at a church picnic.

"Dani disappeared near the bog five years ago, and you never found anything. Jed, two years after that, not that there weren't others between them. And now Agatha and Owen?" I turn back to the sheriff, hoping he sees the fire burning in my eyes. Praying it ignites him too. "How many people are gonna have to go missing in this damn town for you to do anything about it, Sheriff?"

Instead of the reaction I'm hoping for, he furrows his brow. "How did you know Owen went missing by the bog?"

His words slap me into silence, my mouth dropping open in disbelief. *That's* what he wants to know? Not, "When was the last time anyone saw your sister?" Does he think *I'm* a suspect?

"I heard the news bulletin. People go missing in the bog all the time, I just assumed—"

Sheriff Lowell pushes himself to his feet and leans over the desk until his breath is moist and bitter on my face. "Look, Mila, go home. We're looking for Owen, but other than that, I can't comment on active cases. We'll keep an eye out for Agatha too. Most likely, they both got a little too drunk at a party and are just out in the woods, doing what stupid kids like to do."

"Agatha is dating Camille," I say. "Owen isn't her type."

"Well, maybe that's half her problem, then." Sheriff Lowell crosses his arms over his broad chest, and my fingers itch to tear his face right from his bones.

"Do you have an issue with who my sister is dating, Sheriff?" The words are flint on my teeth, poised to spark. "Because if that's the reason you haven't investigated the fact that she's fucking missing, maybe you shouldn't be sheriff. Maybe you should, I don't know, go to hell."

He only glares harder. "Go. Home. Mila. Take care of your mom and leave the investigating to those of us who can actually function as responsible adults."

I open my mouth to argue, but the sheriff pushes past me and leans out the door. "Flo, could you see Ms. Thomas out?"

My vision pitches from side to side while I try to blink past my anger. Clearly, I am getting nowhere. I grip my keys and push out into the hall.

"I can see myself out. Thanks for nothing."

I march past the rainbow trout, its marbled eyes watching me, and the turkey head poised and ready to peck at my skin until I am nothing but bones. Flo waits for me in the lobby, her fists jammed into her hips.

"Causing trouble again, are we, Mila? Seems as though adulthood hasn't taught you much."

I stop and bite my tongue. At this point, I could be nice, tell her to have a great day, and hope she doesn't choke on her coffee cake when she gets home. But I'm done playing nice. I have played nice for three years, and it has gotten me nowhere.

"Your hair looks like shit, Flo, and if you don't remove that stick that's currently shoved up your ass, it's gonna come out through your mouth."

Three black flies follow me from the station and into the cab of my truck. I smash one against the window, guts and red blood smearing like lipstick on the glass. Rain begins to pepper the windshield.

"Where is my sister?" I ask the crimson, not expecting an answer, just watching it dry on my palm.

You know where, it answers. *Listen to him.*

THE SHOWER

When I stumble into the kitchen, I don't wait for a confrontation with Mom. It won't do any good. She believes the reverend, just like Sheriff Lowell. Agatha is simply one of *those* girls.

Bullshit.

I run up the stairs, bare feet pounding on wood, and don't stop until I'm face-to-face with my reflection in the bathroom mirror. After grabbing a towel off a shelf, I wad it against my mouth to muffle the sounds of my scream. It doesn't do a bit of good, but I can't stop. There's too much pain built up over too many years. My body feels like a compost pile—grief, anger, loss, all compounding a skeleton of bones, blood, and sinew that doesn't feel like my own anymore.

I rip my phone from my pocket and pull up a new message to Denise.

FAMILY EMERGENCY. NOT SURE
WHEN I'LL BE BACK. COVER FOR ME?

My eyes go blurry with tears while I wait for her response. I'm half terrified to lose this job because I need the money. Needles prick the back of my neck, and I blink. A tear splashes on my screen as Denise begins to type back.

SURE HONEY. LET ME KNOW IF YOU
NEED ANYTHING.

What I need is to find my sister. I slam the phone down on the sink and take a deep breath.

"Where the fuck are you?" I whisper.

And that's when I feel it—the cold. It blooms across my temples like frost and licks my spine. It's a voice. A dead one pushing its way through to be heard. The absolute *last* thing I need right now.

It echoes in my ears, swirling through my head like an icy fog. I try to ignore it, shedding my clothes and hopping into the shower, but that doesn't stop it. The breathing only intensifies. Like my entire body is being battered with hot bugs, all burrowing and bleeding their shrieking song into my brain. One. Two. Two hundred. Two thousand.

I want to scream again. But I slip my face beneath the warm running water. It helps drown out the words.

I haven't had an attack like this in years. Not since...*Fuck*. No, don't go there.

Not since the night Jed disappeared.

But it wasn't his voice I heard. It was Dani's.

He had no eyes, Mila.

No eyes. The memory of the words joins the voice breathing cold fire against my skull.

You know how to fight this, I tell myself, letting the shower run hot on my back and the aching muscles of my legs, neck, and arms.

And I do. It's simple, really. Just like turning a light on and off. A simple flick of the switch. But now the voice is changing, the breaths coming together to form sounds I don't think I can hear. Not yet, not now, not when Agatha is missing.

I tip my chin up to the water, letting it slip around me like a veil. A smell fills my nose—decay and green, wet things. My stomach swills when something cold brushes my toes. Clammy as dead skin.

Mila.

I look down slowly, breath leaving me in gasps.

Mila Thomas.

Something bubbles up from the drain, dark and strangely familiar. A lump forms at the back of my throat when I bend low and brush a finger against the blackened matter rising through the pipes. It squirms and I yelp, wiping water from my face.

It's algae. From the bog.

My fingers scrabble with the shower curtain and a towel, but I am too wet, and the floor is slick. I go down, teeth clacking together against the tile.

Mila.

The dead voice intensifies, and words begin to cloud my brain. *Fuck.* I turn over, eyes to the ceiling. It's too late. I have to block the voices before the breathing becomes words. And I didn't. Maybe it's a punishment. The ice settles deep in my spine, the droning piercing my bones. A wave of nausea ripples through me, and then the voice cuts through, hard and crystal clear.

Mila, can you hear me?

My heart stops in my chest, and my eyes go wide. My back arches, and I can't breathe, can't even open my mouth. I cling to the towel wrapped around my chest.

He has no eyes, Mila. He has no eyes.

I gasp for air, my own eyes rolling into the back of my skull. The voice says the same words over and over and over. Its timbre cuts through my body, spilling viscera as it goes.

He has no eyes, Mila. He has no eyes.

Who? I want to ask. Who has no eyes?

But I can't. I'm unable to even press my tongue against the roof of my mouth. My body seizes, the muscles going tense and rigid. The droning drills into my teeth, shaking them against the thick red flesh of my gums. Every part of me vibrates while the silky words spill through me like oil. And I can't make it stop. It's relentless. I try desperately to claw the towel, to make any kind of movement I can.

Just to breathe.

And it's over, as quickly as it began. I let my body relax—as much as it can—and sink back against the cool tile, not moving until I know the voice is gone. Until I'm sure. I wipe at the sweat beading on my brow, check my pulse, which I'm pretty sure will be through the roof. It is. I try the breathing technique my therapist taught me.

In. One, two, three, four. Hold. Out. One, two, three, four, five.

I repeat it over and over until my heart slows and the panic in my chest has turned to a dull throb.

"Hello to you too, dead guy," I mutter under my breath, sitting up and planting my bare feet on the bathroom tile.

I gather my hair at the base of my neck and let out another shaky exhalation. That was the worst attack I have had in three years. I drop my head to a sweat-slick palm and focus my eyes on the floor beneath me. Sure, there have been plenty of other voices that came in between. Monstrous ones screaming for deliverance.

Monsters aren't real, I tell myself, over and over and over.

But people are. There are so many who, when you peel back their skin, are twisted and shrunken and rotten underneath. They're the *real* kind of monster.

The human kind.

I cross to the sink and switch on the faucet, splashing frigid water on my face. The cold centers me and steadies my breathing, even though the dull ache in my chest has turned to a sharp fluttering. My therapist tells me it is all anxiety, but damn, does it feel like I'm dying sometimes.

I press my hands on either side of the sink basin, porcelain cool against my hot skin. Up until now, I decided I could handle the voices on my own. But I'm not so sure.

Why is it always the same words?

I look back at my reflection—the pimples breaking out on my chin, the sunburn flares on my cheeks, the gray-green eyes—and then I stop. I blink. A sharpness twists in my chest.

No. It wasn't the same words, not this time. I mean, I might not be a genius, but I know the difference between past and present tense.

He has *no eyes.*

Present. Now. Current.

A shiver works its way up my back, curling around my neck and whispering in my ear. *Has.*

I close my eyes and focus on the way my teeth rattled around in my skull, how the voice sat at the edges of my consciousness before pushing its way through. Doing the one thing I have sworn not to since Jed disappeared. The one thing I have been keeping myself separated from. I respond to the dead.

Who? my thoughts whisper. Just the one word—the one, simple word.

I tighten my grip on the sink and wait for the reply I know won't come.

The voice is gone, just like every other person who has died in the murky water of the bog. Grandma Ruby never taught me how to talk with them, just how to listen. And to be honest, I haven't had a reason to speak with them until now. I haven't wanted to let them in and hold a conversation.

I shake my head to clear the thoughts. Grandma Ruby might be dead, but Jed and Agatha can't be, no matter how much Mom might think they are.

Unless they didn't die in the bog.

The thought spins cold threads of nausea through my body. Grandma Ruby used to say the women in our family, our souls, are connected to the bog. We only hear the voices of those who died in its waters.

So, if Jed and Agatha *are* dead...they've just died in a place where I can't hear them. The thought sends spider-vein cracks through my skin.

I sink to my knees and press my cheek against the floor. The algae swimming at the mouth of the drain taunts me.

No, *no*. I won't let myself believe it. Jed disappeared into the swamp. I saw him go. And Agatha...she was always in the swamp, even as a kid. If there is any place she disappeared to, it's there. And maybe, *maybe* someone saw something, deep down there in the water. Maybe something with dead eyes saw whatever piece seems to be missing.

I inch my fingers along the tile, reaching out to center myself, to remind myself I exist in this world. And goddamn, isn't that a beautiful thing? That I get to live in this fucked-up world, with its fucked-up people trying to just breathe on a bathroom floor? The pain twists deeper in my chest and crawls up the back of my throat. And that's when I decide—come morning—to go to the one place I've avoided since Jed disappeared, the one place I witnessed my grandmother hold a conversation with the dead.

The one place maybe I can too.

The bog.

5

THE HAND

Come morning, as soon as my foot hits the bottom step, I know I've made a mistake. Mom is standing in the living room, arms crossed, a glass of something clear and viscous sloshing in her hand. I raise my eyebrows when I see it, and she gives me one of those don't-you-dare-judge-me looks. She has perfected those.

"Kind of early for the good stuff, hey, Mom?" I try to move past her toward the kitchen.

She steps in front of me, her face gray and hard. "You embarrassed me in front of Reverend Byron yesterday."

I roll my eyes when I reach the door and pull on my Converse. "You embarrass yourself enough. I don't think you need my help."

The sneaker rubs at the blister, and I wince, debating going barefoot. Damn it, I should have grabbed a Band-Aid. I choose the blister and turn toward the screen door.

"You're a sad girl, Mila-May." Mom has moved into the kitchen now, her words slurred and sloppy. "With all your bitterness. It's gonna come back and bite you some day."

I heave a sigh. She is relentless when she gets drunk. It wasn't always this bad, back when Agatha's dad, Niall, was still around. But I can *see* it now. Dried and peeling nails, yellow skin, wrinkles around her eyes that weren't there last time I was home. And you know what? I should say nothing at all. Maybe even give her a compliment. But if the last three years have taught me anything, it's that sometimes, bitterness just *tastes* good.

"Says the woman I haven't seen sober for the last three years, after she *gave up on her kids.*" I let the words slip slowly from my lips so, when they reach her, they have turned to sharpened points.

From the look on her face, my vitriol hit its mark. It feels good to speak the truth. Tears bubble in her eyes, and her bottom lip quivers. Again, I should feel bad. But I don't. I just feel anger.

"I'm going to go find your *missing* daughter. Enjoy your vodka. Maybe call the cops." I slip out into the heat and let the screen slam shut behind me.

Midmorning in the swamp is quiet. The sun burns the top of the water, skimming the mist off so it hangs thick and heavy in the air. Even just walking is exhausting. Every inhalation coats my lungs in moisture. I'm regretting the fact I decided to wear my shoes. The top layer of skin has peeled away from the blister, and the wound is raw, red, and angry. I take a moment to crouch and slip my shoes off, not minding the prickly under-brush meeting the bare soles of my feet.

When you're as silent as the bog, no one can find you.

The trees are tall here. Lithe trunks reaching up toward the sky. Crows call overhead, and a breeze cracks between the limbs of jack pine and ce-dar and birch. I take a deep breath, tasting the loamy scent of the swamp. The water hasn't even come into view yet, but already, the ground at my feet has turned softer, spongier. Somewhere up ahead, the beating of heavy wings fills the air, and my heart thuds in my chest, freezing me in my tracks.

In, out, I tell myself. *In, out.* "Just a heron"—though the words don't stop my heart from racing in my chest.

I jump down from a small ridge of sandy earth, my knees cracking when I land in a pile of last year's leaves. The impact kicks up the scent of autumn—dead and molting foliage—and I smile wryly. Strange how the smell of death can sometimes be beautiful. I pass beneath a copse of twisted poplars, their bark more black with rot than white, and am met with a gust of suddenly cool air.

The heat of the day melts away when the water of the bog comes into view. The trees growing from the marsh are slim as blades, their trunks and limbs void of leaves. The tangled tamarack pines hang like gallows, their needles all dead, branches draped with ropes of brown moss. Saw grass and goldenrod stand quiet in unusual calm. No wind blows down from the switchback stands of cedar and paper birch along the far ridge.

Golden drips of sunlight filter from the sky to kiss the water pooling around the trunks of trees, and when I break through the line of brush, I spy the blue heron far to the south side of the bog. It wades through the shallows—the places its instincts say are safe—dipping its beak to search for minnows.

I stand on the last patch of firm earth and spread my arms wide, taking in a deep breath of the thick, heady air.

I've missed this.

These waters and moss-laden trees...I kept myself away because I didn't want to hear the dead, didn't want to be weighed down by the voices reaching toward me from the murky depths. Didn't want to be touched by their bitterness and pain, when I was so full of my own. They are a constant reminder Jed is gone. That he could be a killer. But when the sun dapples across my skin and wavers through the trees, all I can do is breathe and listen to the wind in the leaves and the steady drone of frogs in the water.

I drop my arms and look to the west, where the trees grow closer together and the water turns darker. That is the most dangerous part of the bog, and it is where I need to go. I take a deep, steadying breath, holding it in my lungs before I let it slip out between my lips.

It has been three years since I walked the paths to the west with Jed. I hope I can remember them now.

They are tricky things, the paths. If you don't know them—and know them *perfectly*—one wrong step could put you at the bottom of the bog. My skin suddenly flares ice-cold, the tiny hairs prickling on the back of my neck. A vibration in the earth trembles against my feet and spikes up my legs. I want to turn back, to check the line of trees for something— *someone*. And even though the feeling in the pit of my stomach tells me not to, I tip my chin over my shoulder, searching the wet and hungry air.

The bog is still behind me, frozen against its backdrop of hazy yellow sun. Nothing moves but the shadows, undulating in, around, and through the trees, branches, and undergrowth of mottled dead wood. The breeze has stilled, and the heat is rising again. It licks along my skin, and when I return my focus to the bog before me, a streak of shadow dances along the roots of an old willow. A shiver brushes up my spine.

It's just the bog, I tell myself. *You're seeing things.*

And hell, I can hear the dead. A bit of shadow shouldn't scare me.

I square my shoulders, take a deep breath, and step one shaking foot out onto the layer of peat floating on the surface of the marsh. It sponges beneath my weight, the water pooling against my skin. It feels delightfully cool against my blister, but before I lose myself completely, I jump to the next pedestal of land. The paths are marked by the cattails. Out here in the bog, the slender stalks are the only thing with roots long enough to sustain human weight for even a fraction of a second. Otherwise, I'd be sinking to the bottom already.

I leap from one snag of mossy earth to another, not staying long enough for the water to reach my ankles. The sky off to the west blooms with soft, gray clouds, and already, there is a heaviness in the air. The scent of the bog has turned damp. Rain is approaching.

The way through becomes second nature as I cross the water. Grandma Ruby taught me and Jed these paths; she grew up in the bog. The remnants of the old cabin still lie half sunken in the murky shallows beneath the cedars on the northern edge. No one talks about what happened to make the family move to the cabin farther into the forest—not even Mom—but I have my assumptions.

The dead got too loud.

The town tells stories of the old cabin, of ghosts living in its walls. How, on especially cold winter nights, wisps of smoke still echo from the chimney.

People in town don't know how close they are to the truth. But the dead have no need for warmth.

I shift my weight on my back foot and leap to the next clump of river sedge, my bare toes skimming the bog. For a moment, the peat remains stable. The roots tangled in the water hold the force of my landing. I expel the air from my lungs and steel myself for another jump, but catch the scent of something wrong.

Something dead.

I flare my nostrils and fill my lungs until I think I might pop like a blood-bellied tick. The scent reminds me of the algae in the shower drain—decay and things left green too long. I scan the bog. My heart races into my throat. I turn and take a step forward, forgetting the bog does not take kindly to those who wander from the path.

The shock of the voice hits me first.

It starts off thin, just a weak echo of someone long dead and gone. I *feel* it in my bones again before it slips into my mind, rattling my rib cage against my lungs. The steady stream of consciousness floods against my own thoughts, and I close my eyes, trying not to panic.

Ruby.

The name almost stops my heart. I haven't heard my grandmother's name uttered in a long time.

It comes again, somewhere out of the murky depths.

Ruby.

My teeth begin to rattle around in my jaw. The cry intensifies, comes closer.

Ruby.

Water pools between my toes. I search frantically for the nearest jut of land. Something to hold onto while my body shakes with the cries of the dead thing calling out from the water. My eyes land on a clump of decaying cattails only a few yards away. I take a deep breath and jump.

The outcropping catches me. I weave my fingers through the feathering grass to steady myself, attempting to block the name calling toward me from the depths.

Ruby.

Why is it calling me by my grandma's name? I stumble on my next jump, catching myself on my palms and cutting my skin against a sharp reed.

"Fuck."

Blood drips from my hand and sends ripples across the bog. A silence rings in the air, but my head is filled with dead things. Grandma Ruby never taught me how to communicate with them, only to let them in and listen, but maybe...maybe if they think I'm her...

The water threads through my toes again. It takes me three more leaps to reach the western shoreline. The trees here are older, their limbs knotted and stained with the acidic water leaking up from the bog. The long wisps of cedar branches tease the surface, and the air hangs heavy with the threat of rain. I inhale two deep breaths, steadying myself on the firm earth beneath my bare feet. My palm stings, and the blood runs diluted down my arm. I reach up for the green bandanna tied in my hair and wrap it around the wound. Hopefully, it will stop the bleeding.

This is where I watched her do it.

Three years ago, only a few days before Jed disappeared, I followed Grandma Ruby out to the western edge of the bog. She had been acting funny all day—easily distracted and wringing her hands. It was strange for her. She was usually calm. So, I'd followed, tiptoeing through the shallows, skirting around the water's edge while she jumped from one cattail clump to the next. She bent down once she reached the western edge, pressed one palm against the murky surface, and closed her eyes.

I decide to do the same. The cold sand of the shore bites into my knees. With my unbandaged hand, I touch the glassy surface and close my eyes. A shiver races across my skin, but I am no stranger to the cold. I press my hand deeper into the water and open my mind.

I'm here. I'm ready to listen.

The silence in the bog is deafening. It rings in my ears and presses against my skin until I am almost suffocated. The gentle plops of the evening rain kiss the inky surface of the water. I try to empty my mind, to forget any thoughts of Jed or Agatha. Even the shame roiling around inside my belly when I think of Roe. I press past my anger and the bitter taste on my tongue, ignore the smell of dead and dying things slowly starting to seep into my nose.

Please. Please talk to me. Please, tell me my sister is still alive. That my brother is still alive.

A chill ripple of wind sweeps through the swamp, swinging the thick ropes of moss hanging from the broken pines. Even though my eyes are closed, I sense the clouds above begin to cover the sun. The temperature drops, sending a shiver down my spine.

Ruby.

My skin spits electricity, and I jolt forward, water surging up to my wrist. *Yes. I mean, no. I'm not Ruby. But can you hear me? Can you talk—*

Ruby.

The voice is unknown. But it's male. It's a gravelly, tin-textured sound ringing in my ear, like winter wind carving out a hollow space in my mind.

"I'm not Ruby."

Ruby.

The voice slinks closer, whipping through the waves like a water snake. There's a crack of twigs and underbrush behind me. I spin, eyes searching the shadowed places beneath the trees.

Nothing.

I turn back. Thick, fat raindrops hit my skin.

I'm not Ruby. My name is Mila. Mila Thomas. My grandmother was—

Ruby.

I want to fucking scream. I plunge my hand deep into the mucky shallows.

"My name is Mila!"

The water starts to churn, slowly at first, like a spoon through tea. But by the time it is sucking me in elbow-deep, the water has turned to a maelstrom. A scream rips from my throat before I can stop it, before it is swallowed by the swamp. Icy fingers wrap around my wrist, dragging me forward and pulling me under.

My scream turns to a strangled choke when the water fills my mouth, my lungs, my belly. I try to keep my eyes open. There's nothing but murky water. I thrash my legs. My lungs burn. I try to scream again, but the only things leaving my lips are bubbles of air.

Ruby. My Ruby.

The name sluices through the water like a knife. It cuts angry across my skin. Whatever has the voice and the cold fingers drags me deeper.

My heart pounds against my chest. I wrench my arm, but the water makes me slow, like I'm stuck in a dream and my bones have turned to molasses.

Mila, Mila, Mila, I think.

But if the dead voice can hear me, it doesn't seem to care. The light is quickly disappearing.

I shake my head, nostrils flaring with anger. No. No, I will *not* be drowned by a ghost with my grandmother's name on its lips.

I kick with my feet, angling toward the surface. My free hand reaches up, up, up, and then a shadow crosses through the dwindling, cold light, slicing through the water. Fingers—warm fingers—twine through mine. My shoulders burn, and I am pulled in two different directions: the ghost, and whoever waits above for me. Another scream curdles in my throat, and I wrench myself toward the top.

Ruby. The voice cuts cold, and the grip weakens on my wrist. *Ruby, I've missed you. I've waited so long to drag you down.*

You're gonna have to wait longer, bitch.

I kick at the darkness below, thrashing my way until I break the surface. The air is cold and damp on my tongue. Warm hands drag me up out of the water until I am gasping and heaving in the mud of the shallows. My heart thrums wildly, and veins pulse in my neck. I turn over on my back, shielding my face from the sun.

"Didn't know you were coming home."

At the sound of the words, I'm drowning again. Maybe that fate would be better. The breath rushes from my lungs, and I struggle to sit up. I lock eyes with the person who pulled me from the water.

Well, *fuck.*

The last time I saw Roe Byron, he was helping me hide a body.

6

THE BOY IN THE TRAILER

The memory comes into my mind fully formed and bleeding. It's the image I have been trying to push away and forget for the last year, but it all comes rushing back. Roe and I in the bog, my back pressed against a tree, his hands on my hips. And then the smell—the overwhelming scent of something dead, rotting in the acid muck.

I can still picture it perfectly. The body half sunken in the bog, brown corpse finder mushrooms sprouting across what little was left of the torn and jagged flesh. Roe insisted on telling the police. And me...

Me brushing a finger against the corpse and watching its shredded lips part and take in air. Its chest contracting. Me grabbing the nearest rock and silencing the thing. Its skull cracking like an eggshell beneath my hit. My fingers skimming its rotten flesh. Sending it back to some semblance of peace.

Roe gasping. Me lying, telling him it was dead.

It was already dead.

I didn't kill it.

I swallow the shame and guilt currently crawling up the back of my throat and scramble out of the muck. Muddy water and weeds drip from my hair. I face Roe with a mouthful of words I want to use but don't know how to.

"I didn't think you'd be coming home this summer," he says with a kind of nonchalance that makes me want to hit him.

Hit him and then smash my lips into his until we stop breathing.

I wring my hair, coaxing out as much of the gray water as I can, and stare at him, noticing all the details I have tried to forget. He looks more tired than he did last summer. Deeper circles under his storm-slate eyes, a hollow ache above his sharp jaw. Bloodstained bandages wrap around his knuckles, so he's obviously still punching things.

The air around us swims with tension, like if I open my mouth and say anything, it will come sweeping in between my lips to choke me. But my own guilt is already doing that. Regret over what we did last summer clamps icy fingers around my throat. I open my mouth and say the first damn thing I can think of.

"I missed you."

As soon as the words leave my tongue, I want to take it back, but it's too late. A wry smile quirks the corners of his lips. He bends down at the water's edge, filling a green five-gallon bucket up until it sloshes to the brim with muddy bog. He straightens and shovels a hand through his ashy-blond hair.

"What are you even doing out here, Mila?"

I bite back the anger quickly replacing my guilt. So that's how we're going to play this, huh? No *I missed you too?* Or *Sorry I never texted you back?* Or the fuck-it-I-just-want-to-kiss-you kiss my body is currently craving?

I think I've loved Roe Byron since we were kids, knees and elbows deep in bog water, Grandma Ruby screaming at us to get out. *That bog's a funny thing,* she'd say. *It will eat you up, gnaw you right down to the bone.*

She hated when we swam in the swamp. But maybe she was right. Everyone talks about it, how the bog acts strange in Credence Hollow. How it licks an acidic tongue across skin and turns you to a slurry.

Maybe that is what is wrong between me and Roe: I've spent too much time away, and the bog is eating him from the inside out. I stretch my fingers, the muck cracking on my skin while it dries.

Fine. Fine, if he wants to carry on and play the bitterness game, I can do that. Hell, I'm a pro. I squeeze more water out of my hair and search the shallows for my discarded Converse.

"The bog is as much my family's land as it is yours," I say, which feels like a stupid comeback, but right now, it's all I have.

He snorts and hoists the bucket up with those bandaged fingers. I watch him from the corner of my eye. He shifts the bucket higher in one fist, and the hem of his ragged cutoff flannel rises to expose a slice of tanned abdomen. My cheeks flush hot. I wasn't supposed to have fallen in love with him. But I did anyway. A small part of me believes I was always meant to, like the bit of bog stuck in me matches the sliver of it burrowed deep inside him.

Grandma Ruby always warned me about the Byron boys, told me of their wandering hands, eager eyes, and wayward betrayal. But ever since we were kids, with red fruit punch rings around our lips, there has been something different about Roe.

There it is, even now, sitting behind his soft anger and sunken cheeks. The kind that comes from being reminded over and over that you'll never matter to much of anyone. Never good enough for his father or his brother, or the wooden pews he was forced to sit on every single Sunday. The kind of soft anger that comes when your father kicks you out of the house and all you have left is a rusted-out trailer in the swamp.

Dammit. I swing my sneakers out of the mud. *We're just kids.*

Forced to grow up too soon. Kids with adulthood thick in our throats, choking on all the ways it doesn't fit and chipping away at whatever innocence we have left. But it doesn't matter, not in this place. The bog swallows whatever the hell it wants, no matter how old you are.

And then it comes back to me, the whole reason I came out here in the first place. Guilt rips through my gut.

Agatha.

I look at Roe from where I'm still crouching in the shallows and squint my eyes against the sun.

"Your dad was at my house yesterday."

Roe's expression ferments into vinegar, and his fingers tighten around the bucket's wire handle. I get to my feet.

"I guess..." The words taste like ash on my tongue, and I'm so afraid, if I speak them out loud, they'll turn out to be true. "Agatha is missing."

The look on his face melts, and the bucket slips from his fingers, water spilling out.

"Shit, sorry," I say, scrambling forward.

He holds out a hand, and before I can stop myself, I reach out and grab it. Roe's eyes widen, and his jaw goes slack. He stumbles back as if I punched him, eyes welling with sharp, hot tears. I jolt but don't let go—I *can't* let go. The separation will hurt more if he doesn't process what just hit him. Tears well in his eyes, and his breath starts crashing.

And I hate it because there is nothing I can do.

I might be able to hear the voices of the dead things in the water, but Roe Byron can *feel* them. It started when we were just kids, barefoot in the bog, swimming along the sedge grass when Grandma Ruby wasn't looking.

"They're angry, Mila," he whispered. "All those dead people down there."

Whatever was dragging me down into the bog's depths just minutes ago is still present on the hand it was holding, and Roe can *feel* it.

I let him relax beneath my touch and his body goes soft again.

"What the hell, Mila?" Roe pulls his hand away and dries it on his jeans. "You've pissed off enough of the living, thought you might start pissing off some of the dead too?"

His words are cold and cutting. I wrinkle my nose. "What are you talking about?"

He picks up the bucket and presses it down into the shallows until it fills again. Roe is careful to not let any of the water touch his skin, even though the spirit is long gone by now. If it was close, I would hear it. And right now, only the sound of blood pounds in my ears.

"Whatever it was that was dragging you through the water... It's pissed." He shudders in the deepening sunlight. "It wanted to kill you."

I cross my arms over my chest and level him with a look. "I could tell that by the fact it was trying to *drown* me."

A funny smile cocks his lips, but then his face is serious again.

"You said Agatha is missing?"

"Yeah. Camille showed up at my mom's yesterday morning saying that she couldn't find Agatha. So your dad came and sent her home. I thought—" I gaze down at the water lapping near my toes. "I thought that maybe I could see if they know anything, the dead. Grandma Ruby used to be able to talk to them, you know, hear them like I can. And would ask them questions. But they—well, I guess they just want to kill me."

Roe shakes his head. "Agatha is probably just off doing whatever she wants. I haven't seen her around much lately, come to think of it. Not since the night of Olive's party."

A bitter sweetness churns in my stomach. *Olive Denton.* My childhood best friend and Simon's on-again, off-again girlfriend.

A question lilts on my tongue and presses against my lips. I try to bite it back. Half of me is scared to ask it, and the other half is afraid of the answer. But I ask anyway because, at this point, what do I have to lose?

"You can't feel her, can you? In the water?"

I asked him this question when Jed disappeared. He said no then, and I whisper a quick prayer he will say no now.

His shoulders heave with a sigh, and he places the bucket back down on the ground. Roe unwraps one of the bandages on his fingers, exposing the dark blood dried in the cracks on his knuckles. When you carry as much of the world's emotion as Roe does, there is only one way to get it out.

Punching.

I fight the urge to reach forward and wrap my fingers around his, to try and take some of the pain away and carry it myself. When we were little, when he'd come through the bog to my house, bruises lining his arms like ants on a log, I'd fit my palm over the painful places, and he would tell me all about it. About how the reverend raised his fists and called it the hand of God, about Simon's fits of anger and how they both took it out on him. But I don't let myself do it now because I have so much of my own pain cramped up in my veins. If I touch him, I'll only make him hurt worse.

Instead, I take a step back, creating even more space between us.

"What night was Olive's party?"

Roe scrubs the space between his eyebrows with a dirty thumb and squints up at the darkening clouds. "Three nights back, I think."

I do the math in my head. Three nights ago was June 15—the night Owen went missing.

A clap of thunder rips the sky in half, and Roe flinches. He looks warily toward the clouds again and then down at the green bucket at his feet.

"I don't think the weather is gonna hold much longer. Do you want to come back to the trailer? I made coffee."

The question sends heat through the far reaches of my stomach. I want nothing more than to go with Roe to his trailer, to curl up on the old mattress and watch black-and-white movies like we used to. For everything to be how it once was—that carefree, wild kind of living we had when we were just two kids on the brink of exploring what it meant to be in love with someone we had known our whole life. Before...

I can't stop myself from opening my mouth and asking something I shouldn't. "Do you ever think about the body we found last summer, out here?"

Roe looks me dead in the eye, and that soft anger comes over him. He shifts his weight from foot to foot, grabs the bucket, and turns around.

"Let's go," he says.

The walk through the marsh is quick and dry. The bog turns solid more swiftly on the north side than it does in any other direction, and almost as soon as we leave the shallows, we find ourselves beneath spindly pines and sandy blueberry patches. Roe's bucket sloshes in front of me, and by the time we reach the trailer steps, a third of the water has escaped. The scent of campfire smoke fills the air, and I take a deep breath. It reminds me of so much: hot summer nights, parties in the swamp, roasting marshmallows with Agatha and Jed when we were little.

Roe walks around the end of his trailer, and I follow. From the way his shoulders hunch up around his ears, I know he doesn't want to talk. He is still processing the emotion of the thing from the bog.

A pile of sawn logs smolder inside a ring of charred stones, and above them, an old cast-iron pot swings on a chain. Roe hoists the bucket in his bandaged hands and pours the muddy water into the pot. It sizzles and spits, and he stokes the fire. Black smoke curls up into the clouds.

The silt filters from the water, and bubbles line the top. I have half a mind to dip my fingers into it, just to get a taste of the sweetness now it has been purified. Folks in this town talk about how the bog used to be fresh, sweet. How you could dip your palm into it and take a sip that gave a lilt of honey on the tongue. But then something happened. Maybe it was the iron mines dumping slag further upstream, or maybe the flow of the water changed, and the bog grew stagnant.

Whatever it is, it eats the bodies faster than it should. Turns them to piles of bone and mire.

A crack of thunder shreds the sky, and a shiver runs up my spine. The clouds have a texture like cotton balls dipped in spring mud. I have always loved storms—something about the way they cool the air and make the whole world smell like magic and damp—but right now, the storm is the last thing I'm worried about. The trees around us creaking in the strengthening winds.

Where is Agatha? I listen for the gale to whisper her name, to lead me to wherever she is. But there is nothing. Just the deafening silence of a storm rolling in.

I can only picture her now, hiding in the crevice of some rock, trying to stay out of the storm. Or worse, her corpse splayed out in the swamp, brown mushrooms growing along her supple limbs. How long has she even been missing? How long has Mom sat on her ass and drowned her self-pity in bottles? How long has she listened to the reverend telling her to wait? The thought makes my stomach swim and sway, and I fight the urge to spill my guts out on the cracked pine needles at my feet.

"Mila?" Roe is leaning against the end of his trailer. "You coming inside?"

With one look back at the tree line, I follow him into the place he now calls home. I've been here before—hell, I've spent nights here—but each time I see it, it makes me somehow sadder. It's an old trailer, the carpet stained orange with age and mildew. A small sink sits beneath the largest window, brimmed with too many half-filled coffee cups to count.

I smile. Hence, the bucket of water. Roe refuses to hook up to any real water system. He does his dishes in the pot outside and boils his drinking water twice. Roe has never told me why, and I've never asked. I don't have to.

Beyond the acidic tang of the swamp water, Roe is like me: connected to the land our families have lived on for almost a hundred years. He *feels* the pain of those who have died in the bog, but he also senses the despair of the trees, the swamp slimed in oil from the mines upstream, the animals choking on plastic bottle caps. And so even if it's not much, he refuses to add to the pain of the very earth itself, as best he can.

I peel my shoes off and toss them against the door, then slump down on the torn vinyl bench. My knees almost hit the table. I run a finger down a crack in the green, fake marble surface. Roe takes two mugs from the cupboard above the sink and fills them with coffee from a glass pitcher. He hands one to me.

It's not warm, not really, but the bitter taste sloshes against the insides of my mouth in a familiar way, and I relish in the comfort of something I know. Roe sits opposite me, and we stay there for a while, silent. The rain pings against the metal sides of the trailer.

He is the one to speak first. "Before we say anything else, I want you to know that I haven't told anyone about...about what we found last summer. About what...you did."

Bile floods my mouth, and I try swallowing. "Neither have I."

He chuckles and takes a swig from his mug. "Obviously."

I'm waiting for him to say, "Who do you have to tell anyway?" But he doesn't, and I'm grateful he somehow knows my pain before I've even mentioned it.

"Were you there?" I ask, over the rim of my own mug. "At Olive's party?"

Roe stares out the window for a moment and then nods. "It was mostly just people home from college for the summer. A handful of kids who stayed. But, uhm, yeah, I was there briefly. You know me."

I *do* know him. How much he tries to stay away from people as best he can. He rarely goes into town if he can help it. Three years ago, when his dad kicked him out of the house, Roe dropped out of high school too. I think he still works shifts down at the bar, washing dishes. Maybe even mixing drinks, though I doubt it. There is too much pain in this world for Roe Byron, and he knows if he tries to face it, it will tear him apart.

"Why did you go at all?"

His shoulders tremble. He finishes off his coffee and reaches for the glass pitcher to refill his mug. Roe holds it up to me, but I shake my head. There's only so much black coffee my heart can take before it threatens to spontaneously combust.

"I feel like if I tell you, you probably won't believe me."

I stare at him incredulously. Says the guy who *feels* the dead to the girl who hears them.

"Try me."

He shifts in his seat. "The bog told me to."

7

THE BODY

I've always thought the bog might be alive, but more in the kind of way a tree or a hedge of roses is alive. They don't have a consciousness, not really. Not enough they can communicate. They are creatures of water and earth and all the things that have emptied themselves into it.

But the more I think about it, the more I believe Roe. Hell, that bog is full of dead people who somehow talk to me. Why wouldn't the bog itself be a being? I swig the last of my coffee from the mug and fix Roe with the most serious expression I can muster.

"I believe you."

He blinks twice, purses his lips, and drums his fingers on the tabletop. "You're lying."

Shame rolls across my skin, bringing me right back to where we found ourselves last summer. I set my mug down and reach across the table for his bandaged hand. He flinches when our fingers connect, but doesn't pull away.

"Do you feel that, Roe? I believe you. I have always believed you, okay? About this, about how you feel things, about your dad being an absolute fucking asshole to you practically from the day you were born." I search his eyes for any sign he's hearing me, for any hint he believes *me* right now. "Roe, I'm on your side."

The skin around his eyes turns red, and glassy tears cloud his stormy irises. I only hold his hand tighter, curling his scabbed fingers through my own.

"I know. It's just—fuck, I don't trust you." He pulls his hand from mine then, rubbing the skin where we connected.

His words drive iron spikes into my heart. Of course he doesn't trust me. Not after...not since...

"This is about last summer, isn't it?"

I pull back when he stands up from the table, nearly knocking into it with his knees, and slams his coffee mug down beside the other dirty ones. He stares out the window at the rain pelting the remnants of last autumn's logging. Tears slip down his face, one after another.

"It's not *just* about the body." His voice cracks like old glass. He turns to face me. The pain is breaking him inside, eating away underneath his skin like maggots.

I want to reach out, to gather him up and run my fingers through his dirty blond hair. Tell him it will all be okay. But that would just add to my list of lies.

"Then what is it about?"

His jaw slackens, and he falls back against the wall, sliding down until he's resting on the carpet, his head in his hands. I stare stupidly at him, torn between wanting to comfort him and half terrified my own pain will send him over the edge. Roe's shoulders shake, and the rain beats softer against the window.

I throw my feet over the bench and slip down, sitting on the floor opposite the boy whose agony courses through him like a hundred violent thunderstorms. I fight the urge to place a hand against his knee.

"Roe?" My voice is quiet, a simple whisper against the torrent shaking him. "Roe, what is it? What did I say? Did I do something?"

He looks up, and the despair in his eyes almost breaks me. It pulses in his pupils, so palpable, so thick, I could dig it out with a spoon.

"You don't get it, do you?" he asks, his voice choked with tears. "What last summer did to me? You don't understand."

I reach out, but he pulls away. "Help me understand, Roe."

His pale skin stretches taut across every bone and muscle in his body, as if his own soul is trying to push out the pain.

"Why didn't you let me tell the police about the body? We could have—I don't know—saved it." Saliva gathers in the corners of his mouth, and his fingers peel at the cut sleeves of his flannel shirt.

The memory floods me like white-hot heat. My fingers brushing against the pliant dead skin. The way the empty eye sockets tore open and the tongue lolled out with words I couldn't understand. How fear put a rock in my hand and had me bash the skull in, killing whoever it was. For the second time.

"I was afraid." I shift my position on the floor, inching closer. "I was afraid that if the police found out, they'd...they'd only think it was Jed. Or think he was a murderer. Or that I was. It might have been dead at first, but whatever I did—" I shiver. "I wasn't ready to feel all that pain on top of everything else."

I fall back against a cabinet, suddenly overwhelmed, like the air has been sucked out of the trailer and all that's left to breathe is smoky heat.

"Fuck. Agatha is missing, and your dad has somehow convinced my mom that we need to wait." I slam a fist onto the table. "What is with this town and letting people just disappear?"

For a moment, the only noise is the rain on the window and the wind cracking through the trees. I stare across the small space between us, at the broken boy who used to have the most beautiful smile. Our knees are only moments from touching, but even the slightest brush will crack Roe in half, and I might never be able to help him piece himself back together. I pull my legs up to my chest and study the feelings swimming so vividly across his face, wanting to wipe each one away. Hold each one and set them out to sea so he never has to feel them again.

But I can't. Just like he can't bring my brother back—or my sister, it seems. I turn my chin over my shoulder and look outside at the brightening sky.

What the hell am I doing here when she's out there, *missing?*

"I touched it." Roe's voice breaks the silence, sluicing through like a jagged knife through meat.

I turn back to him, a spark in my chest. "Touched what?"

"The body, that day in the swamp. After you...with the rock." He shovels a shaking hand through his hair, and his legs seize with the anxiety bucking through him. "I didn't mean to. It was an accident. I knew I shouldn't touch it—I was terrified it would be Jed—and it was only briefly, but I felt it all."

Heat prickles my skin, and the familiar taste of fear floods my mouth. I reach a hand across the carpet, stopping just short of his. The air between us seems to grow lungs and breathe, and a silence rings in my ears so violently, I'm afraid they might explode.

"Was it Jed?"

The look he gives me could crack the world in half. But then Roe shakes his head. My body fills with cool relief.

"Why didn't you tell me?" I ask, not angry, just...tired. "If you'd have just told me, we could have avoided all this"—I flap a hand in the air—"all this weirdness between us."

"Because I felt Jed *on* it, Mila. On the body."

The cool relief instantly changes to heat and wraps fingers around my throat to choke me.

I'm a monster, Mila.

A monster.

"But I felt the pain, Mila. The fear, the unbelief. It was like looking into a great black void and realizing that nothing makes sense anymore." His body shakes again, and his finger brushes against mine for only a moment. Roe pulls back as if stung. "Like everything is a lie."

I swallow, my throat lined with nails. Maybe everything *is* a lie. Perhaps nothing is real and everything is made up. Wouldn't that make life so much easier? But it's not. People bleed. Humans are consumed, and you never see them again. The pain burrowing into your skin like wood borers will eat away at you until you're nothing but a shell. I've watched it happen to my mom, and I'm scared it will happen to Roe.

Maybe that's even what has happened to Jed. To make him...to turn him into...I push the thought away.

No, my brother is *not* a murderer. He can't be. The boy who held my hands during thunderstorms, who sang lullabies in his scratchy voice while the wind shook, isn't a killer.

Before I can think about hurting Roe, my hands are on his, and I'm pulling him to his feet. He shakes against me, but I don't stop. I wrap him in an embrace. His hair teases my shoulder, and his arms slide around my waist.

"I haven't been able to get rid of the pain, Mila," he cries into my hair. "Not being able to talk to anyone, you know, it just gets all bottled up."

The sting of guilt rakes across my ribs, but I only hold him closer. "I'm so sorry, Roe. I didn't even think about that. I was...I was only thinking—"

"You were only thinking about your brother." He pulls back and wipes at his face.

No, I was only thinking of myself, but I let him assume better of me.

Roe's chest heaves with the need for air, and he lets it out slowly. He reaches to the counter above me for a bandanna, and I catch his familiar scent—black coffee, pine sap, the sharp tang of weed. It brings a kind of comfort I didn't know I needed. He drags the creased fabric down his cheeks and blows his nose before tucking the cloth into his pocket.

"Thanks," he says.

My breath catches. "For what?"

The corner of his lips twinge, and he knocks a loose curl from my face. "For listening."

I nod and fit my hand into his. Even though I caused the pain he's been feeling for the last year, I'm happy I can be the one to take it from him too.

"Always." I exhale all the breath from my lungs, like I'm breathing out my own pain and misery into the air around us, willing it to just float away.

We stay that way for a moment, standing elbow to elbow against the trailer's counter. The sun breaks through the window, and the rain turns to mist in the cooling air. I wish we could stay this way—just the two of us, with nothing between except the natural world outside. But there is something still tearing me from the inside out.

"Did you see Agatha?" I blurt out stupidly. "That night at Olive's party. Did you see her at all?"

Roe regards the carpet at our feet. He's trying to remember, to piece together something that will make sense.

"I left the trailer as soon as I heard it, the bog. It was almost like a tremor in my bones, a pull, I guess. Like, even if I'd tried to stay home, I wouldn't have been able to." He looks up at me. "It was like the bog was in pain and I could *feel* it."

I raise my eyebrows. "How can a bog feel pain?"

He shrugs. "Everything alive feels pain. Some things just aren't as good at showing it."

I drum my fingers absentmindedly on the counter behind me. There's something here I need to know, something I'm missing. A familiar cold tingles at the nape of my neck, and I try to push it away. Roe must notice the look on my face because his hand slides over my own.

"If this is too much, I can stop."

A bitter laugh coats my tongue. "Says the guy who just fell to pieces on the floor because I made him keep something inside for a whole year." I shake my head and try to push the dead voice away. "No, keep going."

Roe's thumb strokes the top of my hand. "I could hear the party before I even saw the light coming from the bonfire. They'd set it up on the northwest side, near the shallows behind the old Thomas cabin. When I got there, I saw Agatha and Camille sitting next to the fire, talking with Olive. And then—"

His face twists, and for a moment, I think he's not going to say anything else. He shudders.

"And then we heard shouting."

My pulse quickens. "Shouting? Who was shouting?"

Roe closes his eyes, trying to *feel*. Attempting to know. His bandaged hands are flitting at his sides like flightless birds. I reach forward for one of them, trying to steady him, to ground his wild mind.

"Take a breath, Roe."

His chest heaves again, and his eyes pop open. "I gotta go back out there. It's all muddled, that night. I need to go back out into the bog."

The ground beneath us is soft and supple, like we're stepping on layers of warm flesh. Roe leads me hurriedly through the marsh, cutting through the trees until we find ourselves along the southern edge. I squint my eyes, searching the landscape for any sign of a party. The sun is hanging low in the sky now, and the bugs are even worse than they were earlier.

Where are you, Agatha?

Cold prickles the back of my neck and arms. A dead voice presses against me, willing my mind to let it in. But I block it out. Refuse it.

My sister is not dead.

I close my eyes, building the mental barricade I have learned to put up time and time again. But this voice is desperate. It almost aches to be heard, and it terrifies me. Roe squeezes my hand, and I look up at him. There's a soft smile on his face, and the redness in his eyes is beginning to fade.

"You good?" he asks.

A twig behind us snaps, and we both whip around, searching the tree line for something breathing. But there's nothing—just shadows and cooling, watchful air.

"I'm fine." I turn back to the water. "Can you remember now? Who was shouting?"

Roe drops my hand and rubs his temples. "I had a smoke and something to drink. I remember that. Agatha offered me something from a glass bottle she and Camille were taking swigs from. It burned."

I huff out a breath. "She probably found Mom's high-end stash she only brings out for special occasions. You know, like Tuesday nights." I turn on him, a grin on my face. "Wait, so what you're saying is, you got drunk?"

His face reddens. "What? No. I didn't—"

I click my tongue and start inching my way along the shore toward the cabin. "What will people think? The reverend's son, drunk?"

It's the wrong thing to say, and I know it as soon as it leaves my lips. Roe's face hardens, and his feet stay planted. I turn back.

"Shit, Roe. I'm sorry. I didn't mean—"

"It's fine." He blows past me, carefully avoiding the lapping water.

I scramble after him, chastising myself as we go. The amount of times I have opened my mouth and inserted my damn foot is becoming astronomical. He moves quickly along the mucky shore, stepping over downed tree trunks half rotten in the water. A small flock of ducks paddles away from the reeds when we approach the western edge. I grimace at the mud there. The dead voice still presses against my mind.

Roe moves away from the shore and climbs up a bank, stopping in the center of a ring of cedar trees. Beneath the thick limbs, the air is even colder and wetter, and I shiver against it.

A pile of charred wood rests with half a dozen tree trunks around it. The ground is gouged with tire marks and bike tracks. A white Styrofoam cooler sits tipped over on a patch of moss, and Roe curses under his breath when he goes to pick it up.

"It's this kind of shit that really pisses me off." He reaches toward the cooler.

As soon as his fingers touch it, though, he shoots back, as if the Styrofoam is electrified. My chest clenches.

"Roe?" I say, jogging toward where he now crouches on the ground, breathing hard.

I bend down beside him, but he pulls away, gets back to his feet, and fills his lungs up with air.

"Could you pick that up?" He gestures to the cooler. "I—fuck—I can't touch it."

I don't ask questions. Whoever left it here has enough emotion coursing through their veins, even the rain couldn't wash it off the last thing they touched.

I scoop the cooler into my arms and look around the clearing. "All right. Can you think of anything now?"

Roe crosses his arms over his chest. "The voices were coming from behind Simon's truck, which was parked over here."

He walks forward to where deep ruts are cut into the soft ground, collecting rainwater. Roe leans over and drags a finger through the mud. I wait for the reaction, not realizing I'm holding my breath until my heart rattles against my sternum like a caged bird. Roe wipes the mud on his jeans and stands up.

"Anything?" I ask.

He shakes his head. "No, not really. But can't you feel it?"

I crinkle my eyebrows. "Feel what?"

Yeah, actually, I *can* feel a lot of things right now: fear, worry for Agatha, a crushing headache while I try to block out the voice not taking no for an answer. I grind my teeth.

Roe gestures at the trees around us. "Something's angry out here. Even the ground is upset. It's weird. I never felt the bog like this when we were kids, like it's *alive*, like it has a soul."

Anxiety settles like a noose around my neck. "Okay, well, I'm usually one to tell you that's fucking weird, but right now, I think I'll listen to anything to figure out where the hell Agatha is." I look across the bitter, stagnant water. "Can you tell where the anger might be coming from?"

Roe passes a hand down his face and sighs. "You're the one who can hear the dead, Mila. But yeah, probably."

It is a mistake to ask him, I know. Just like it was an error to not let him tell anyone about the body I revived last summer before bashing its skull with a rock. Or reminding him his dad is a total dick. Or asking him to feel the spirit in the water that tried to kill me a few hours ago. But I *have* to know. Is Agatha still alive?

Roe leads the way back through the trees to the water, stopping every now and then to run his finger along a charred trunk or to pause and press a thumb against the leaf of underbrush. With each touch, I wait for him to snap, to be stung, but he only seems to grimace and bear it. We inch closer to the water's edge. My Converse sink into the thick sand on the shore. Still barefoot, Roe inches into the water, pain on his face. I don't know what to do, and the helplessness makes me feel stupid and selfish.

You're doing this for Agatha, I remind myself. *You're doing this for your sister.*

Roe stops ankle-deep in the bog, sinking fast. Already, the rolled cuffs of his jeans are stained with muck. His eyes are closed, and his jaw punches out against his skin. I drop the cooler on the shore and kick off my sneakers. If he's going to do this, if he's going to *feel* the whole of whatever is wrong with the bog, I'm going to be there with him, even if I can't understand it. The water is cold, and the mud sucks at my toes. I creep forward.

And then it hits me.

Out of fucking nowhere.

A scream rips from my throat, and I fall knees-first into the shallows. The cry is deafening, piercing my mind like iron spikes. Pain sears across my forehead, boring into my bones. I can't see, dammit. I can barely breathe. Roe is somewhere beside me, but it feels like he's miles away, like some kind of black void separates us. The voice cuts through the darkness, flushing my skin so hot, I might burn to ash right here in the water.

Mila.

Another cry teases my lips, and I try desperately to swallow it.

Mila, you have to find me.

No. I shake my head, tears burning my cheeks. Saliva collects in the back of my throat.

A man's voice. It has been all along.

No.

It cracks against my skull, the impact like a car crash. I fall sideways into the water, my entire body seizing and releasing there in the mud of the bog.

Mila, please. Find me. Open your eyes.

I can hear Roe somewhere above me, feel his hands like wisps of smoke on my shoulders, my face, tangling in my hair.

The voice is familiar. I try desperately to string words together. *Who are you?*

And for the first time in my entire life, the dead thing responds. The words flood my mind, cold and sharp and wholly familiar.

I'm the one everyone is looking for.

"No!" The scream rips from my throat with the strength of talons. I heave up, shoulders trembling. My fingers scramble through the muck at my sides. I can feel it—*everything.*

The bog beneath me. It's boiling. God, *I'm* boiling. My eyes blink wildly, and I look around for anything to focus on, to ground myself with, but it's all just a blur of green and gray and blue.

"Mila, you have to breathe."

Roe's voice drifts toward me. He is crouching beside me, his hands resting on my shoulders. There are tears in his eyes and coursing down his cheeks, rimming red against his blond lashes. I push myself away from him, my fingers peeling at my own skin.

"No, you can't touch me," I warble, my words thick with my own spit. "You can't touch me."

Every instinct in my body is screaming to let Roe comfort me, but I can't. He's already felt the agony currently shredding me in two, but his grip only tightens.

"I'm not letting go of you, Mila. Whose voice was it?" he asks.

I close my eyes and shake my head. No. No. If I say it, that makes it true. If I say who the voice belonged to, that means...

"Jed's," I croak. "I think...I think it was Jed's."

Without a second thought, Roe reaches forward and pulls me to his chest. His arms prickle at the grief coursing through my veins, but still he holds me. I shake against him, tears hot on my face, and I don't stop until the breath catches raw in my throat. When I wipe at my eyes and have regained my breathing, Roe stands and pulls me to my feet.

He brushes a thumb across my cheek. "We're going to figure this out, Mila, okay? You and me. We're gonna find Jed and Agatha and figure out what is happening to this place. But you gotta breathe first."

He sounds like my therapist. *Breathe, just breathe, Mila.* And hell, sometimes all I *can* do is breathe. I straighten my shoulders and inhale deeply.

"All right," I say, my voice cracking. "Did you... What did you feel from the bog?"

Roe twists and squints in the direction of the cabin sitting ramshackle on a small spit of land behind us. "It's coming from over there." He points. "Whatever is making the bog angry."

I take another shaking breath and plunge forward, the putrid water up to my ankles. "Let's go."

We make our way toward the cabin. The water sucks at our feet, and with each step, Roe takes gasping breaths. The closer we get, the worse it becomes. I slow down, wait for him to catch up, and then hold his hand in my own. We're in this together now, whatever the hell it is. Roe and I feel the same pain, the same grief, just from different sources somehow all connected to this place. I squeeze his hand, and he returns the gesture.

I got you. Not letting go.

When we reach the outskirts of the cabin, Roe stops, like he's been frozen in time. His eyes search the reeds and then focus on something. I turn to see where he's looking.

A body lies bloated in the water, pale flesh purpling at the edges. It's a boy on the cusp of manhood, flat on his back, one eye turning to soup in his skull. His jaw cracks to the side, tilted unnaturally, as if someone broke the bones while he lay screaming.

But it's his chest I notice. Or the lack of one.

Surrounded in folds of ruined apple red fabric, a hole gapes where his heart should be. The sedge grass on the other side of it sticks through the jagged flesh like porcupine quills. But it isn't the body making my blood run cold. It isn't the disfigured face, the shredded flannel, or even the blood blackening the water.

No, the thing stopping my heart beating is the hematite necklace clenched in the remaining fingers on the corpse's hand.

The bog regrets nothing. There is no room for remorse when the deepest, blackest sin sinks beneath its waves and threatens to swallow it. Yet, when the little lost girl falls into the water beside the body, the bog feels the grief issuing from her lungs. She *had* to *see*. She had to see so she would listen. So she will do what those who came before could not. Her blood made this curse; her blood can unmake it.

The bog is heavy and sick with burden. The bodies pile in its inky depths. It aches, yearns to cry out, to expel all the years and all the sadness. The bog can no longer live under the weight of the monsters stalking its shallows at night, feeding flesh and bone to the water and thinking no one has seen its sin.

But people have.

Another girl has seen, and *she* knows what's coming. Knows so deeply, anger coats her bones like oil. She hides among the sedge grass, plotting vengeance. This one does not want to hear the cries coming from the shallows. She can only feel the bog beneath her, instructing her, making her its soldier. Its avenging angel. And now that the bog has its infantry, it needs a general.

The bog ignores the shrieking cries of the little lost girl in the shallows and the shaking wrath of the girl in the grass. It reaches up into the skies, trees, and plants scattering its blistering hide. It licks the crystalline wings of the insects.

Go, it says. *Bring him to me.*

8

THE SINGING BOG

The noise is faint and shrill and out of tune. It pierces my ears like the silence after a bomb goes off and it takes everything inside of me not to press my palms to either side of my head and scream. Roe sits next to me on the clapboard porch, one arm slung around my shoulders, tears plaguing his storm-at-sea eyes yet again. Three cop cars sit in the driveway, collecting yellow pollen. The people in uniform disappear into the trees, a single black body bag between them.

Jed is dead. It's his body we found, I'm sure of it. And my sister is still missing. Yet the one thing boiling my blood is the cops didn't turn off their fucking sirens when they left for the bog.

I try reciting facts to ground me to the present: the porch steps are brown, the quilt on Grandma Ruby's rocking chair is peach and cream, the cedar branches are green, the sky is blue, my name is Mila-May Thomas, I am twenty years old, and my brother is *dead*.

The sirens screech through the yard, ringing out into the trees and pressing against my very bones. I want to block them out, to put up walls, just like I do with the dead voices so I don't have to hear them, but even that didn't work for me today. Even Jed was able to find his way in.

I'm the one everyone is looking for.

I sag against Roe's shoulder, pressing my elbows into his knees. Fresh sobs wrack my rib cage. Honestly, I'm surprised he's still here. Mom called the reverend before I wrenched the phone from her grip and dialed 911. He's inside with her now, probably feeding her that everything-happens-for-a-reason bullshit and quoting verses that will only make her more numb. Roe's fingers reach up, brush my hair, and gather it into a clump. My skin tingles when he makes contact, and I lean in closer. Hungry.

What are we coming to? Weren't we just kids catching frogs in the creek behind the church and stealing candy bars from Phil's? Dammit, we're *still* just kids.

I peel my face away from my palms and lift my gaze to meet Roe's. He's clearly feeling everything I am tenfold, his eyes red and shot with veins. It's not just from the joint he smoked out between the cedars when he thought no one was looking. He pulls the bandanna out of his pocket and offers it to me.

"It might not be Jed," he says, his voice cracked and frayed like a broken guitar string.

I wipe my face with the bandanna and hand it back. Try to inhale a deep breath. "It's Jed. I heard him in my head, asking me to find him."

Roe shoves the cloth back into his pocket and opens his mouth, but before he can let his words out, another car engine adds its noise to the shrieking sirens. It skids to a halt at the end of our drive. I scramble to my feet, standing on tiptoes and looking past the black-and-white cop cars to the burned-orange Honda pulled in behind them.

A figure emerges. A Black girl, softly tossed curls gathered into a bun at the nape of her neck, a green cardigan tied at her waist. Eyes swollen from crying.

Camille.

I leap from the porch, across the pine needles scattered through the yard, and throw myself at my sister's girlfriend. Her arms wrap around me, and suddenly, we're both crying. My guts are all twisted, and I'm sure Camille feels the same. Like the whole world has tipped on its side and everything inside us is turning to ashes and mud.

I pull away, keeping my hands in Camille's. "We found Jed." The words feel flimsy on my tongue, but they're all I have.

Except, I haven't heard him. That voice in the bog, it didn't *sound* like him.

I'm the one everyone is looking for.

It could be anyone. People wander into the bog and drown all the time. Drifters, drunks, strangers no one will ever miss—a whole slew of faces pinned on the sheriff's office wall. I pick at the thin skin of my lips;

it flakes away between my fingernails. The bog can take a body and, in a matter of moments, turn it into something unrecognizable. Bloated flesh, waterlogged lungs... The acidic water gnaws everything away, so even if you were pulled out the next day, your loved ones might not be able to identify you from all the rot and slurry.

The bog is sick.

Camille throws an arm over my shoulder and leads me back through the screeching cop cars to the porch. Roe moves over, and we squeeze in beside him. He offers Camille a sad smile, and she presses a gentle fist to his shoulder.

"Hey Roe-Roe," she says.

Camille is the only one I've ever heard call Roe by something other than just his name, and he loves it. He wipes the tears from his cheeks.

"Sorry 'bout Agatha," he says.

I think it's more to help himself feel better than anyone else.

Camille leans her head on my shoulder. Her breathing and heartbeat align with mine. I twist my right hand through hers and my left through Roe's. It was always like this when we were kids. Us together. Ragged pants and scuffed knees and skin dirty with muck from the bog. We didn't care about the gaps in our ages. We were all different, marked as other by a town that saw our feral hearts and turned us away. So, we crowded closer in together. Then Jed was gone, and I was exiled. Now another member of our merry band of misfits, our company, *our army*, is missing.

We sit like this for a long time, watching the tree line, waiting for the cops to come out with Jed's rotting corpse. The sirens only grow shriller. Mom is crying inside the house, and though I can't make out what he's saying, the reverend's voice spills into the evening air. It sends angry, slimy ripples through my body.

For as long as I can remember, he has always been here. In and out of the house, making sure a single mom with three kids was taken care of—had her "spiritual needs" met. What we needed was more food on the table and someone to help pay the electricity bill. My palms go damp at the memories.

Always the reverend. Even when his own wife and kids were eating dinner in their grand, white farmhouse on the top of the hill, he was here, filling Mom's head with promises of a better future while doing shit-all to help.

Camille picks her head up first, spinning toward the cedar stand west of the house. Roe and I follow. Five people in uniform carry the black mass between them. It drips wet, and clumps of algae and weeds cling to the nylon fabric. My stomach lands somewhere in the soles of my feet, and even though my body wants nothing more than to sag against Roe and burst into a thousand pieces, I force myself up.

"Mom!" I scream toward the house. "They're back."

Almost immediately, the screen door slams, and Mom pushes between Camille and me. She sloshes down the stairs and across the lawn. There is a kind of bitterness in the air that follows her, and it's more than just the alcohol. Something seeps from her soul.

The reverend stands on the porch behind us, his arms crossed over his broad chest, avoiding his son's piercing gaze. His jaw is a tight line, and sometimes I wonder if he isn't just poisoning souls with half promises instead of saving them. Catching them like fish, bringing in their tithes, praying for their futures that may never come.

I narrow my eyes at him. *I'm onto you.*

Mom's cry turns my attention back to the yard, and before I know what I'm doing, my bare feet feel the crushed pine needles again. I'm running toward where the cops are loading the body bag into one of their cars. Mom's fingers scramble at the black nylon, pulling it toward her, reaching for the zipper. Sheriff Lowell has his hand on her shoulder, but she's wrenching away, the vodka thick on her breath.

"Let me see him, Asa. Let me see my son." Her voice is a needle, sharp and thin and piercing. She pushes Sheriff Lowell, but he's stronger than a broken drunk of a woman.

Mom crumples on the ground at his feet, her body shaking, face like a tragedy mask. Her fingernails dig into the sleeves of her blue cardigan, and she starts rocking back and forth, waiting for the earth to swallow her, to eat her just like it has her one child.

Maybe two.

I push that thought away before it can take root.

Here I am, the only one left, and there's nothing I can do. I stand stupidly while they load the body into the trunk of the sheriff's car. It's like watching the world through slow-motion glasses, as if everything is moving at a speed so miniscule, movement turns to heady blurs.

I don't have to be an empath to recognize the grief boiling off Mom in waves. It cuts against my own skin too. The knowledge the rotted corpse in the black bag could very well be the brother who used to read me bedtime stories. The brother who kept a fire going in the hearth on cold winter nights. The brother who made sure his two sisters had food before he would even take a bite. I swallow hard, the flesh on my throat sharpening to steel edges.

The brother who walked away because he was scared he would hurt us all.

I fling myself at the sheriff, the hunger coming on swiftly. The need to have my brother back. To touch him. To see, just to make sure. I stretch my hands out, arms rigid, and reach for the zipper.

Sheriff Lowell curses, and then his hands are on my wrists, but I won't let him do this. I won't let him take my brother from me. The zipper slips through my fingers when Sheriff Lowell grips my elbow, but I send it flying into his measly guts. The *whoosh* of air from his lungs assaults the back of my neck.

Swamp water spills from the opening in the bag, and when the nylon pulls back, I see the face. If you can even call it a face. Dirty hair falls over a patch of flesh speckled with old blood. I hear Mom somewhere behind me, but I'm already crashing to the ground beside her.

My hands scramble desperately toward the fist of the corpse, my stomach splitting. My fingers rake the cool, gelatinous skin. I don't stop until I find what I'm looking for—the necklace. The hematite necklace Jed used to wear around his throat every day, even when I watched him disappear into the bog. I rip it from the rigid, dead fingers.

And then I stop.

Still. Half frozen there in the dwindling sunlight.

The sheriff yells something. Doesn't see one filmy eye pop open, staring at me.

The breath catches in my lungs.

That fucking eye is brown.

Jed's eyes are as blue as cornflowers.

I touch the candle wax flesh again, and the eye clouds over. Dead again—at peace, I hope. Just like Grandma Ruby used to say.

My fingers scramble toward Mom and claw up her arm, pressing against her jaw to turn her face toward me.

"Mom, look at me." I can barely say the words, can barely breathe while I try to pull her attention to what I desperately need her to hear. "Mom, it's not Jed. It's *not* Jed."

Her face is like a bleating lamb stretched out for sacrifice. The sweat leeching from her temples smells bitter and sick, and I nearly gag on my own saliva. The air swims around me, not only with her scent, but with the sudden sharpness of the rotting body. I don't know why I didn't notice it before, but now, even the oxygen I'm dragging into my lungs is thick with it—the putrid, razor-edged tang of dead flesh, bog water, and sun-sick algae.

Everything comes up at once—the fear, the worry over Agatha, the feeling of the dead thing gripping my body in the water, the way the bog is beating against Roe, against me. My palms hit the grass, and my stomach churns, shoulders wrenching. I spill a line of milky sick onto the lawn.

Roe and Camille are at my side in a matter of seconds. His hands thread my hair, but I pull away. I don't need both of us puking our guts out in front of half the town. I struggle to my feet, Camille's hand on my elbow, and face the sheriff.

"That's not Jed," I say, my voice weak and shaking. "That's not my brother."

Sheriff Lowell swears, zips up the bag, and slams the trunk shut. He motions to his deputies to get into their cars, then turns to face me, arms crossed over his chest.

"Look, Mila. We've been dealing with your brother's missing person case for three years now. Emotions are high—"

"You're damn right my emotions are high!" I fly toward him, barely able to contain my own strength, but Camille has a strong grip on my arm.

Sheriff Lowell's eyes narrow in on me, testing me. I want to punch him. Want to land a fist into his big, doughy face, maybe even break his nose in the process. Camille's fingers tighten on my skin.

"Not now, Mila," she whispers.

But I'm sick of it. I'm sick of the *not-nows*, and I wrench from her grip.

"What are you doing about my sister, huh? Oh right, nothing. Because he"—I whip around and point at the reverend still standing on the porch—"told us to wait!" I spin back. "What about Owen? Dozens of missing people over the years can't look good for the department, *Sheriff.*" I spit the last word out like poison, spittle flying from my lips toward his sleek, black-shined boots.

His eyes sharpen to darts, and he takes a step forward, a single, pudgy finger shaking toward me. "Now, you listen here—"

"I think it's time you left and got back to the station, Asa." The reverend steps in front of me, blocking whatever bit of sun is coming through the clouds and pine trees.

I move to push him out of the way—I do *not* need this man fighting my battles—but Camille's hand is on my shoulder, and she's pulling me back. And I go, not because I'm beaten, but because there's nothing else to be done. Not now.

Back to waiting, again.

The sheriff sends me one last barbed glance and gets into his car, peeling out of the drive and narrowly avoiding Camille's Honda. Soon, the sirens are nothing but a distant dissonance. I peel my shoulder out from under Camille's hand and stand there, numb. The forest around me is swirling, and the coolness of the evening is quickly turning to heat on my skin. I'm afraid I'll get sick again, so I crouch in the grass, backbone heaving.

It's not Jed, it's not Jed, it's not Jed, I tell myself.

But if it's not Jed, then *who* is it?

Another shadow crosses over me, and I look up at the reverend. He holds out a single hand and when I don't take it, he turns to my mother.

"Come on, Moira," he says, his voice soft, smooth, and bilious. "Let's get you inside. Prayer will do you a world of good."

My vision pitches from side to side—Camille, Roe, the reverend all blurring and rearranging. The anger inside me grows, cascades, and presses against my temples until I'm sure my skull will shatter.

"Prayer isn't going to bring my brother back," I spit. I stick my chin out and narrow my eyes. "Prayer isn't going to find Agatha or help uncover whoever the hell is sloshing in a body bag in the back of Sheriff Lowell's car. Prayer isn't going to do *shit*."

Reverend Byron's lip twitches. His neck turns sharply on an angle, and he gazes down at me from his great height.

Something flashes behind him. A flicker of movement so brief, for a moment, I dismiss it as simply a shiver of sunlight through the trees. But with the flutter of tiny wings, a buzzing black fly lands on the reverend's starched shirt. It clicks beady black eyes open and shut at me, and then over to Roe. For a moment, I think I might be sick.

The black fly opens and closes its wind-whisper wings and takes to the air once more, vanishing into the thick pines. I shake my head, trying to clear my mind, and look over at Roe, who seems just as shell-shocked as I do. The reverend, appearing not to have noticed the insect, leaves my mother's side and closes the space between us before bending down so close I can feel his hot breath on my face.

He smells like bleach, mint-flavored mouthwash, and something else I can't place. Something metallic.

"You might think differently if you tried prayer for yourself, Mila. Maybe you wouldn't be so lost and desperate." He places a heavy hand on my shoulder. "Try searching inside for a heart issue. The Lord will show you your sin."

My toes curl. I bite back bile and the urge to tell him where exactly he can shove my *sin*, but I swallow my words. With a withering look at Roe, the reverend takes Mom by the shoulders and leads her away, up the porch and into the cabin. Heat blooms in my chest, my heart fluttering like an angry bird. Camille tries to get me to stand, but I can't. My bones have turned to lava.

Does the reverend truly think whispering a string of words together is what's going to bring my siblings back to me? I slam my fist onto the ground. Pain ricochets up my arm, my shoulder, billowing out through my lungs. But it isn't just the defeat I feel; it's the ground.

The water beneath the soil is the same sick water filling the bog. It stretches out a thin thread toward me, wrapping around my wrist, settling deep between my very marrow, becoming one with it until my anger matches the emotion curling up from the peat beneath my body.

Roe moves closer, his fingers tangling with mine, and I lock eyes with him. In that moment, we both can feel it: the bog, the anger calling out, reaching for us in desperation.

People always said the bog was different, breaks folks down faster than it should. And now...

"Something is hurting it." The words are like roots on my tongue, sticking to the back of my throat.

Roe blinks slowly and lets out a deep, ragged sigh. Camille crouches beside him, looking between us like we're both going crazy. And who the hell knows, maybe we are.

"What's being hurt?" she asks.

"The bog," I say.

I study the grass beneath my palm. It buzzes with a strange energy, like the steady drone of distant insects. It hovers between my skin and the ground—this electricity—licking greedily toward my fingers. I've lived in the bog for almost my entire life, and I've never felt anything like this before. Heard voices, sure, but *feel* the bog? That's something only Roe can do. I grab Camille's palm and splay her fingers out on the grass. She grunts when I pull her forward.

"Mila, what the hell?"

"Do you feel that?" My voice is edged like stinging nettle.

The skin between her brows wrinkles. She rolls over on her side and steadies herself against the earth.

"What am I supposed to be feeling?" she asks.

I open my mouth to answer and then shut it. Honestly, I don't know how to answer her. It's like the bog is singing in the soil, reaching its damp fingers through the peat and crawling out of the roots of the trees, the flowers, and the grass beneath my body. But it's something even more than that; it's like it has a voice.

A voice that isn't dead.

I finger the hematite necklace still clenched in my palm. The stone is sharp against my skin, centering me and helping me focus.

If the body isn't Jed's but it was holding his necklace, does that mean he's still alive? And is Agatha with him? If the bog really is calling out to me, is it calling out to them too? I roll the hematite through my fingers and lean one ear against the ground.

The sheriff might not believe me. The reverend might not either. And hell, why should they? I've spent my entire life lying to myself and those around me. Lied *to* Roe and made him lie *for* me. I listen to the shushing of the bog's water deep beneath the surface of soil.

The bog and my brother and sister—they might just be the truest things of all.

And I'm going to save them.

9

THE SWARM

When I wake up the following morning, the sun smears across my pillow and licks my eyelids. I roll over, soaking in the fleeting moment when I forget everything that has happened over the last few days. No missing sister, no dead body in the bog, no swarming black flies or voices calling out for me to rescue them from their watery graves. I curl my toes against the cotton sheets and look up through the slanted window at the deep green of the pines kissing the roof.

Just when the wind picks up and flutters the branches, reality sets in. The awful waking-up feeling. Heaviness settles in my chest, and when I try to draw a breath, I can only take in shallow gulps. It feels meaningless, lying here, trying to breathe. I don't even know if my sister's lungs are able to inflate anymore. Or my brother's, for that matter. Am I all that's left of Moira Thomas's wild, fatherless children? Am I the only one who will carry the name forward—the one with the ability to hear the dead things calling out to me from the bog?

As soon as it enters my mind, the dead things are all I can think about. The voices press in from all sides, crushing my skull and making my skin crawl. I want to tell myself to stop thinking about the bog, but it consumes me.

The sheets are deliciously cool to the touch, and I stretch out an arm. The bog is still somewhere far beneath me. Under the floorboards of the cabin, the stone foundation, the surface of peat, and then down deeper, below the bedrock. It shushes and sluices through the core of the earth, skirting around roots and worms and things only sustained by darkness.

It reaches up toward me with damp fingers, moving past all the things in the soil, through the foundation, until it soaks into the logs of the house. It runs up the stairs like a searching tongue and slips in under the door—

My eyes snap open, and I sit up, gasping for air. Each breath shoots pain through my rib cage. When I look down, my sheets are soaked in sweat, and my hair is slicked to my forehead and neck.

A dream, I tell myself. *Just a dream.*

But when I turn and look back up at the window above my head, two beady eyes are peering down at me. The black fly folds its crystalline wings against the glass, poking at the surface with its antennae. I stare at it for a moment, almost daring it to come inside.

Come on. Come get me.

I slide a single finger up, but the insect doesn't move when I tap the glass beneath its wings. It's a strange little bug, all reds and blacks and stained glass wings I've known my whole life. They are no strangers to the boglands around Credence Hollow in the summertime, but why the hell are they...lingering?

None of it is natural: these flies, my missing siblings, the dead body, Roe and I *feeling* the fucking bog. Heat lashes out across my skin, licking up my body like a forest fire. Without thinking, I smash my fist against the glass, startling the black fly. I watch it disappear out of sight, then collapse back onto my pillow.

When we were little, Agatha would crawl up into bed with me, and we'd study the knots in the wood, tell each other they were places where forest spirits had kissed the rough grain. I don't want to lose her. Closing my eyes, I picture the last time I saw her: slinking up the stairs, smelling of cigarettes, her lips swollen from kissing Camille in the driveway. My heart twinges. I curl a fist in the sheets and burrow my face against the sticky pillowcase. Tears slip over the bridge of my nose.

She's all I have left. No more Jed—consumed in some way or another to the bog, and I don't know if I will ever get him back. No more Grandma Ruby. And Mom...I don't want to think of her.

I wipe at the tears with the heel of my hand. No. No crying. Not now. I don't have time.

Roe said the bog is angry. It is hurting.

So, what's hurting it?

Before I can plot some kind of logical answer, my phone buzzes on the nightstand. I flop my arm lazily over to pick it up. The screen glares brightly at me. It's a text from Roe.

> OLIVE IS HAVING ANOTHER
> PARTY TONIGHT.

I swallow hard, my throat like nails. Three little dots jitter across the screen, and I hold my breath for his next text.

> WANNA GO? 10:30

Hell no, I do *not* want to go. The bog is the last place I could possibly want to be right now, but what else is there? If the cops aren't going to find my sister, I guess I'll just have to fucking do it. Before I can stop myself, my thumbs scramble across the keyboard, and I'm agreeing to go to this stupid party.

> YEAH, SURE. I'LL MEET YOU AT
> YOUR PLACE.

I hit *send* and wait for him to respond. When he says nothing, I type again.

> SHOULD WE INVITE CAMILLE?

I chew on the inside of my lip, waiting for his reply. The screen stays still for a moment, and I entertain the idea of taking it back. But maybe this would be good for us. Just the two of us against the world. But then dots bubble across the screen.

> SURE, I'LL TEXT HER TO MEET US.
> SEE YOU THEN.

I shoot back a thumbs-up and drop the phone on my nightstand.

Somewhere deep beneath me, the bog is pushing against its earthy confines, trying to be heard, to be seen. I swallow sharply.

Isn't that all anyone wants?

❦   🪰

The day lags by, and I barely leave my room. Mom stays downstairs, passed out on the sofa. She continues to sleep when I come to the kitchen to make a quick sandwich and microwave a cup of yesterday's coffee. An empty vodka bottle lies tipped over on its side, the last dregs spilling out and bleaching the wooden floorboards while it dries. I tiptoe over to pick it up. A breath escapes Mom's lips and I jolt, but she only turns over on her side and falls back asleep.

She looks like she used to, lying there in the puddle of sunlight streaming in through the high windows. Her cheeks are rosy—probably from the alcohol—and for a second, I picture the way she used to be before we lost Jed.

Even with the reverend always lurking in the shadows, there were good things. Mom humming "Dream a Little Dream of Me" while she did dishes, running her fingers through my bog-matted hair. The summer nights she would take us to the swimming hole across from the creek, or the winter nights she would wrap me up in a wool blanket and take me outside to see the Milky Way. Even without a dad, we were a family, the five of us. There was a love binding us, a sort of strength that came with the knowledge we were together and that was enough. But when Jed left and then Grandma Ruby, our foundation crumbled.

And now, with Agatha missing, what remains but the two leftover, broken bits?

I gently brush hair from Mom's face and find a blanket to cover her. It might be the dead heat of summer, but it feels like the right thing to do. I guess in all my fear, anger, and grief, I forgot no one is taking care of my mother. Sure, the reverend might think he is, but what good are his empty prayers and promises when all Mom has left is the daughter who lies through her teeth about the dead?

"I'll find them, Mom," I whisper. "I'll find them both and bring them home."

As if in some response, Mom rolls over on her back, pulling the blanket up around her chin. I take the vodka bottle to the sink and step out onto the rotted steps of the spongy old porch. The air swims with humidity roiling off the bog through the trees. Mosquitoes skim through the misty beams of light sneaking through the pines, and a dove coos somewhere overhead. I watch the tree line, half expecting a cloud of flies to burst through the leafy undergrowth and consume me, but only undulating shadows linger there.

Maybe I shouldn't have come home. Perhaps I should have stayed in my reeking rental, selling underage kids cheap cigarettes and pretending home didn't exist. At least there I wasn't constantly screwing things up.

Credence Hollow isn't my home anymore, is it? It's just filled with ghosts. Sweaty, pride-drunk spirits who slip from their rusted-out pickup trucks into the warm belly of Sinner's Chapel and come home, preening like peacocks, with Scripture bleeding from their tongues.

This whole place is rancid. A huge leeching organism feeding off itself, sucking the life out of everyone who dares call it home.

It wasn't always like this. At least, that's what Grandma Ruby used to say. Back when she was younger, when the bog didn't act as the all-consuming cesspool to a town crawling with infected souls. It was the mines, she told me, which made the town sick.

The very same mines Roe's grandfather profited from before he started preaching the Good News from behind a pulpit every Sunday. There's profit to be made in winning souls too, I guess. Grandma Ruby used to tell me stories of Cecil Byron, and sometimes, I would ask if they had been in love.

"Define *love*, Mila-May," she would say. "Love is many different things to many different people. For me, it is trust. It is baring one's soul to another and knowing the other person will carry it around like some rich jewel. There cannot be love without trust."

Love without trust.

I roll the words around on my tongue. There is not a single person on this green earth who thinks I am trustworthy. Not even Roe. He said so himself. And I don't blame him. Not after he watched me raise a body from the dead last summer, only to bash its rotten brains in. To skim its skin with my fingers...

But the body in the bag showed me. All it takes is a second touch to send them back.

The boards groan when I sit down on the bottom step and run my fingers through the tall grass. The bog is still beneath me, pressing toward the surface of earth, itching to touch me. I recite the names of those it has taken.

Dani Chartier.

Jedidiah Thomas.

Agatha Thomas.

Owen Shelby.

And there have been plenty of others over the years. Nameless no ones whose bile-bitten bodies have washed up on the peaty shoreline and been briefly mentioned on the nightly news. But usually, all one finds are bones these days, long forgotten. What the bog is given, the bog swallows, and sometimes, the remains are never seen again.

In the glistening heat, a shiver runs up my spine.

This place, Credence Hollow, is sick because the very water coursing beneath it is sick too. Tragedy has touched its soil, again and again and again. Tragedy deeper than the iron mines peppering the landscape like pockmarks. Tragedy eroding away at this town stronger than any lake or river. The bog seeps into the very groundwater that we drink, poisoning us from the inside out.

I glare out to the tree line again. A strange sound slips toward me from the bent birches and thick pines. A kind of buzzing. It rings in my ears, but it doesn't press against my mind, not in the same way the dead do. It only fills my ears, like a steady drone. It comes closer and closer, the buzz making my teeth rattle while it approaches the yard.

A thin line of fear bubbles in my stomach, sweat breaking out on my palms. My eyes narrow against the shadows of the trees.

It breaks from between the trunks—a column of swirling mass.

I stumble backward when a swarm of black flies rushes across the yard. A cry tears from my lips, and I scramble for the screen door. My fingers fumble with the handle. Their drone fills my ears, stuffing my head with cotton. I wrench the door open, stomach boiling, and scuff my knees against the threshold, slamming the door before the buzzing insects.

They pelt the screen, bounce back, and then fly toward me again. My breath halts, and my shoulders shake. I hurry to my feet and slam the wooden door closed, then press my back against it, squeezing my eyes tight while the droning continues.

After a few dragging minutes, the noise subsides. Silence curls around my skin. I turn slowly and peer through the slatted windows of the front door.

A handful of the insects struggle, caught up in the screen, their legs and wings bent and shattered at odd angles. But the swarm is gone. Back to whatever black hole it came from. And I have a creeping suspicion the hole is the bog.

10

THE PARTY

The undergrowth snaps beneath my feet as I march toward Roe's trailer, hot blood pumping in my veins. The sky above molts, purple and blue like an ugly bruise. I ignore the smoke curling up from the small fire behind the trailer and pound on the door with a raised fist. It swings wide when I go in for another punch. Roe stands there in denim cutoff shorts and a flannel.

"Easy there, killer," he says, a coffee mug sloshing in one hand.

Fresh bandages wind around his knuckles—no cracked and dried blood, no dirt caking the exposed adhesive. I push past him into the trailer. It smells distinctly different than it did the day before. The dishes are clean and stacked neatly inside the slanted cupboards to the left of the sink. Only a single coffee mug sits out on the counter—tin with white and green stripes.

"I was going to use that one, but Roe said it was your favorite."

I nearly jump out of my skin at the sound of Camille's voice. She sits with one foot up on the bench seat, her hand resting beside another mug on the tabletop. My lips crack an uneasy smile, and I search the counter for Roe's coffeepot.

"It's over there." He comes away from the door and points at the glass vase resembling an hourglass resting on the stove.

I pour the dark liquid into my mug and lean back against the counter. "Little late for this stuff, don't you think?"

Camille smiles and takes a swig. "Roe has filled me in a bit on what you two think is going on. And damn. Are we sure coffee is strong enough stuff to get us through tonight?"

Heat flushes from the center of my chest, and I down a mouthful of the bitter liquid, knowing full well the caffeine is only going to make my heart race faster. "What did he tell you?"

"That you two think the bog is alive and calling out for help because something is hurting it. Which sounds insane when you say it out loud, but Thomas Bog is weird." She looks down at her mug, grief collecting in the dark circles under her eyes. "Plus, you think it might have something to do with why Agatha is missing."

I shoot Roe a look over the rim of my tin cup. He shrugs and begins lacing up his boots, but I decide to press him anyway. I turn back to Camille.

"Did he mention any bloodthirsty swarms of black flies?"

Camille nearly chokes on her coffee. She looks up, her dark brows knit in a firm line. "I'm sorry?"

I finish off the last of my coffee and run my tongue over my teeth. "I started noticing them yesterday, when the reverend..." A lump forms in the back of my throat, and I try my hardest to swallow it. "When they put the body into the back of the car and I yelled at the reverend."

Camille's brows arch over the rim of her mug. "Yes, I think it's safe to say that we all remember that."

"I watched a fly land on his shoulder right before the bog started—started—"

"Started calling up to us through the dirt?" Roe finishes the sentence and leans forward on his knees.

Camille stands and brings her mug to the sink. She turns on the faucet to rinse it out. No water comes out.

"Don't," Roe shakes his head. "I don't use the water."

Camille stands there, blinking at him. "Is it poisonous or something?" she asks with half a laugh.

Roe mumbles something about how she's not exactly wrong and grabs her mug, adding it to his own beside the sink.

"I just...I don't like using the water from the tank. I get my water from the bog when the bog lets me know it's ready, and then I boil the shit out of it."

Camille crosses her arms over her chest and narrows her eyes. "So, what you're telling me is that you both not only can feel the bog, but you can also hear it too?"

Roe shakes his head. "No, only Mila—"

I shoot him a look. *Don't tell her my touch can raise the dead.* "Only I can feel it all the time. Roe can only feel it sometimes. More like something he can tap into rather than having it"—I drum a finger against my skull—"always inside."

Anxiety ripples across the surface of my skin—I've never told Camille her dead sister's voice calls from the reedy shallows. I give Roe a look that could cut glass and turn back to her.

"We should probably head to the party. The sun is finally starting to set, which means Olive has probably already lit a few bonfires and has also started pouring Jack Daniel's down your brother's throat." I shoot another keep-your-damn-mouth-shut look at Roe and skid my mug across the countertop, where it hits against the other two.

Without looking back at either of them, I head for the door and jump down to the soft turf. A chill already hangs in the air. Beneath my feet, the bog is pulsing, angry. It doesn't like the parties, the crowds of idiots I went to high school with drinking and throwing up into the water. I share a knowing look from Roe. For all the weird shit between us, I don't like the fact he's probably suffering the same way the bog is. Angry. Used. Discarded.

The walk through the woods is a quiet one. The only sound is the deep-toned music pumping from the water's edge. It gets louder when we pass through the trees, and Roe practically vibrates beside me. He's wearing his boots tonight, or I'm pretty sure the bog would have already overpowered him with raking hatred for what is currently taking place on its shores.

The bonfires appear first—three of them—arranged in a rough triangle on the western side of the bog. Half-shadowed faces leer around the flames, red cups and glinting beer cans clenched in fists or slipped between lips. The honey-tinted liquid drips across chins and down throats, while the inhabitants of the swamp grind their supple limbs together in the heat roiling all around them. Music pumps from a large Bluetooth speaker set up on a stump in the center of the undulating throng of bodies.

My stomach swims and churns. I hate these parties. Always have. Agatha, on the other hand, loved them. Cherished the times she could get away with smoking an entire pack of Marlboros she stole from Phil's without Mom or the reverend sniffing around to catch her in the act. Almost like she can read my mind, Camille slips her hand between my fingers. Orange sparks reflect in her clouded eyes.

"I can still feel her, Mila. I can still feel Agatha."

The words slip between my ribs, reach for my heart, and crush it to dust. I squeeze Camille's hand.

"I know. I do too." I swallow, throat barbed. "We'll find her, okay? I promise."

Camille mumbles something, but the music swells, and someone presses red plastic cups into our hands.

"Well, well, well, if it isn't Mila Thomas."

I turn away from Camille. Olive Denton swaggers our way, currently hanging drunkenly off the arm of Credence Hollow's favorite good ol' boy, Simon Byron. My lips tighten around the rim of the cup, and I wince when the whiskey hits the back of my throat, burning its way down.

Simon is the last person I want to deal with right now.

Roe stiffens beside me, and my gaze flicks to him to make sure he's all right. Other than the muscles in his jaw twitching, he appears relatively calm. I'm not entirely convinced, though. *Fucking hell.* What I wouldn't give to punch Simon in his stupid, chiseled face.

"Didn't know you were still alive, Roe." Simon drags Olive sharply against his hip.

She grimaces, then plasters on a smile.

Smooth.

"Figured you wouldn't care either way." Roe's fists tighten at his sides. The bandages pull across his knuckles.

Simon licks his lips like a goddammed coyote. "Oh, I don't. Actually, it's kinda nice not having you around the house. Lots less whining and crying and all that emotional bullshit."

Roe tenses, and my stomach ties itself in knots. Simon is inching close—*too* close—to the anger that makes Roe hit things. And honestly, if we weren't here for a specific reason, I might let him.

"Roe, maybe we should—"

"Quiet, Thomas," Simon snaps without taking his eyes from his brother. "I'm just trying to catch up. Haven't seen much of the little bro since he dropped out of school few years back and moved into Grandpa's old hunting trailer."

"None of that is your business, Si," Roe spits between his teeth.

Anxiety's razor edge slices across my abdomen when Simon's lips melt into a thin line.

"You made it my fucking business the day you abandoned the family and walked out of the house."

"You know that's not how it went down. I walked out of that house because you and Dad gave me no other choice."

They're almost nose-to-nose now, each spitting venom between their teeth.

"Maybe we should all just take a deep breath." Camille steps closer to Roe. Her touch seems to calm him.

"Not your fight, Chartier," Simon growls. His eyes slide to hers. "Where's your little girlfriend anyway?"

I grit my teeth. God, I want to punch him.

"I could ask you the same question," she rasps.

For a second, something softens the look in Simon's eyes. It's there and then gone. But it sticks to my guts like glue. Guilt, maybe?

No one says a thing while the music pulses around us. Olive flicks a lock of dark hair over her shoulder, exposing her thin, sculpted collarbone and her pale, slender neck. I put my eyes back on my cup and finish it off in one swig.

"Following in Mom's footsteps there, Thomas?" Simon's voice cuts through the noise like steel.

I crush the cup, shove it into my pocket, and take Camille's hand, then Roe's.

"Just trying to get through a night where I have to see your ugly face, Byron."

Simon sneers, and Roe squeezes my hand. *Don't test him*, he seems to say.

"Olive, always a pleasure." I tilt a smile and then push forward, dragging Roe and Camille behind me toward the nearest bonfire.

The music pounds in my ears, and already, the heady rush of alcohol is careening toward my brain. Bodies throng around us, and Roe stands tense, his pulse beating a steady drum against my palm. I drop Camille's hand and turn to Roe, stroking my thumb against his hand and trying to only channel calm energy into his shaking heart. A weak smile cracks his face.

"I can tell when you're trying too hard to feel a certain way, Mila."

I shrug and look around for another drink. My gaze snags on Olive and Simon, grinding to the music near Simon's blue Ford. His hand cups Olive's thigh, thumb lifting higher under her blue miniskirt.

How would the congregants of Sinner's Chapel react if they knew their little preacher-to-be isn't as holy and righteous as he lets on?

Camille crosses her arms. "Simon's getting handsy tonight."

Bile slips against my tongue at the thought of Simon Byron and his wandering fingers.

"Mila." Roe's voice cuts across my skin. "Could you let go of my hand?"

I startle, dropping it. "What? Oh, sorry."

Roe wipes his palm on the front of his flannel. "It's fine. I just...would rather not think about what my brother is doing in his, uh, *personal* time. I left that house for a reason."

"You got kicked out."

He shrugs, jamming his hands into his pockets. "I woulda left anyway."

The music booms around us. Someone shoves beer cans into our fists, and Camille throws one back, stopping only to hiccup when the bubbles wash toward her belly.

"So," she says, wiping at her wet mouth. "What's the plan?"

"I think we need to figure out what happened at the last party." I look at the mass of swirling bodies around us. "See if anyone noticed Agatha disappear."

"I should know." A downcast look shadows Camille's face.

"What? No!" I reach for her hand. "This isn't your fault."

Camille's eyes swim with tears. "No? I'm her girlfriend! I'm supposed to keep her safe."

My heart surges in my chest. I know this guilt. It's something I have carried for the last three years, and I refuse to let Camille feel it too. She is too good to be burdened by this pain. I squeeze her fingers. "We all keep each other safe, okay? We're going to figure out what happened to her." I turn to Roe, whose face has twisted up in some kind of unspoken agony. "Roe, you good?"

He doesn't respond for a moment. His eyes remain entranced on the dusky bog beyond us. "What? Oh, yeah. Sorry."

He's lying. It lingers at the corners of his lips, threatening to choke him.

But I don't press. Not yet.

Right now, we should be focusing on Agatha. The bog can wait.

"What about the Boar's Head?" I ask, cracking open the beer in my hand.

I face the far stretch of land crawling along the shoreline of the bog. Past all the trucks, bikes, and ATVs parked and half sunk into the hungry mud, a strange outcropping of rock rises tall into the black night sky.

The Boar's Head is, in fact, not really rock at all, but a bluff of almost solid iron. In the daytime, the red rings wrapping around the rock in thick, spiraling slices glisten like meat against a marbling of fat. Now, in the darkness, all it looks like is a great shadow looming over the party. Some sort of eldritch god we've all come to worship.

"What about it?" Roe's voice is still distant and strange.

"If someone saw something, they're going to talk about it. And everyone loves to empty their shit at the Boar's Head." I take a swig from my can and let the bitter liquid slosh inside my mouth before swallowing. "You know this town. No one can keep anything to themselves. Especially when there's enough beer and weed to go around. Come on."

The other two don't protest, and soon the smell of campfire gives way to the thick, pungent scent of marijuana smoke and alcohol-tinged breath. Camille takes out her phone and switches on the light, casting thin streams of artificial yellow to stain the muddy reeds at our feet.

No one comes to the Boar's Head unless they want a private place to make out or to try something a bit more hardcore than your run-of-the-mill alcohol from Phil's. We stumble around in the thick undergrowth, following our noses to where we'll get the information we need.

I trip over a thick root jutting up from the peaty soil. A curse slips from my tongue, and I brush Roe's hand away when he offers it. We inch along the cold face of the iron bluff and come face-to-face with a puff of lingering smoke.

Perfect.

"Heard Mila Thomas is back in town."

"For what?"

People are talking nearby—two guys, by the sounds of it. I duck behind a spindly brush pine and hold an arm out, flattening Camille and Roe against the rock.

"How should I know? Not like her to go around, asking people's permission to do shit anyway."

That makes me grin. At least I have a good reputation.

Out amid the trees, near the shadows, the bonfires quake and spit in a cold wind rushing from the bog. Camille shivers and switches off her flashlight. Thankfully, not an inch of light from the fires touches the Boar's Head.

No, the rock is as dark as a tomb. And just as cold.

"Wonder if she's heard about her sister yet."

Dillon Johnson. I would recognize that voice anywhere. He used to pester me in biology class sophomore year with questions like, "Hey, Thomas, wanna go have sex behind the school chicken coop?" One day, I finally had enough of it and told him, "Hell yeah, meet me after class." He shut up. Never tried it again.

"Yeah, and I bet she knows what happened to her too. All these Thomas kids, they're all weird, living out here in the bog like the fucking *Creature from the Black Lagoon.*"

Ricky Stine, pothead since eighth grade, father of one since sophomore year, when he had unprotected sex behind said home-ec chicken coop with Vicky Strauss and was probably too high to pull out.

My hand curls into a fist. Camille's fingers brush against me, holding me back from doing anything too drastic.

A fit of coughing comes from the cloud of smoke. "I don't know, dude. You weren't here for Olive's last party, when Owen went missing."

My ears perk up at this, and I lean forward, careful not to snap any of the branches off the spindly pine.

An inhale of smoke and then an exhalation. "Nah, man. I was up in Marquette for work. The mine sent me over for training." Another puff. "What happened?"

Music surges from the party below—low beats and heart-pounding rhythms. My palms film over with sweat, and I inch closer along the rock, breaking away from Camille. Roe doesn't move an inch. I take a deep breath and hold it for a moment, hoping it will calm my racing heart.

"Well, it was pretty foggy that night. The shit was rolling off the bog like smoke. I was sitting near one of the fires with Sydney Parker, talking about some shit with the Blueberry Festival, and all of a sudden, I hear

Simon Byron freaking out behind us. So I look over, and he's got Owen's shirt, like, clenched in his fist. And he's shaking him, screaming something about 'Don't you dare touch my fucking girlfriend, you fucking piece of shit, or I'll kill you. I'll fucking kill you.'

"Then Olive tries to jump between them, to stop Simon, and he, like, pushes her off and she falls down." Dillon pauses to take another puff on his blunt. "At this point, everyone is kinda like, 'Shit, what do we do?' You know? Well, Olive just gets up, brushes the dirt off, and grabs a bottle of whatever the hell off the gate of Simon's pickup. And holds it high into the air and is like, 'Let's fucking party!' And everyone forgets about it."

There's a long pause, and I remind myself to keep breathing, nudge my heart to maintain a steady rhythm in my chest.

"But what happened to Owen and Agatha? Like, did you see where they went?"

I whisper a silent *thank you* to whoever gave Ricky Stine enough brains to ask that question.

Dillon lets out another exhale. "Owen, I have no idea. But I did watch Simon walking away from the party a few hours later, and then Agatha, I don't know, followed him or some shit. And the air smelled weird, dude. Like, you know how the meat cooler smells at Phil's? Yeah, something like that, but if you left it outside for too long, unplugged."

I grimace, and my stomach roils. Camille shakes behind me, and when I turn back, moonlight reflects in the tears streaming down her cheeks. I wrap my fingers around hers. She's freezing.

"That's sick, bro," Ricky wheezes. "Do you, like, remember anything else?"

Through the pine branches, a glint of orange coals brighten and drop, crushed under the heel of a boot.

"Nah, man. Mac Walters brought some shrooms, and I got super-high after that. Went home with Sydney."

A pause, a rustle of a paper bag. I'm just about to lead Roe and Camille back to the party when Dillon coughs, a horrible rattling sound.

"Actually, wait. I do remember something."

I freeze, skin rushing with adrenaline.

"Flies, dude. I remember there were flies. Everywhere."

11

THE THING OF TEETH

A branch of pine switchblades across my cheek as I throw myself through the dead-stand trunks and grab Dillon Johnson by the throat.

"What do you mean, flies?" The words leave my mouth like drips of poison, lashing across Dillon's face.

He cowers in the darkness, swinging his arms wildly.

"Whoa, what the hell. Who is it?" His voice hinges somewhere between panic and anger.

Roe is between us fast as fire, but I'm quicker. I push him aside and smash Dillon back against a tree.

"It's Mila Thomas, you fucking idiot. Where is my sister?"

I grow more accustomed to the blackness. Dillon simpers, his eyes pooling above his cheeks like oily puddles.

"Shit, Mila. Let him go," Ricky says from a cloud of smoke somewhere behind me.

"You should probably get out of here, Ricky," Roe growls, "if you want to keep your balls attached to your body."

Ricky whimpers. Branches snap behind us as he flees. I tighten my grip around Dillon's thick neck.

"I asked you where my sister is, asshole."

"I don't know, I swear! After Simon left, she just followed him, okay?" His eyes dart behind me like a frightened deer. "C'mon, Camille. You were there. Tell her. Tell her I didn't do anything to her sister!"

Camille, sniffing and wiping at her cheeks, shakes her head. "I didn't see. I went to grab a beer from the cooler, and when I turned back, she was gone. Just gone...I don't—I can't—"

She falls against Roe. My fingers tighten around Dillon's throat, shaking him by the collar.

"You said you saw flies. Like, a swarm of them?"

He shrugs his shoulders, still trying to flatten himself against the tree trunk. "Yeah, I guess. They kinda just started coming from the bog. Huge clouds of them. The party had to shut down. It was a real drag."

My lip curls in a snarl, stomach filling with disgust. I push myself away and wipe a hand on my thigh. "Yeah, that's the real drag, you dick. The flies. Not the fact that my sister and Owen are *missing*."

Dillon stays pressed against the tree. His eyes dart to wherever-the-hell Ricky disappeared to. The music pumps against the Boar's Head, and my head rings. My fingers fidget at my sides. A chill licks up my spine, curling around my neck, and icy tendrils of something press gently against the soft flesh of my brain.

No. Not now. Not here. Not in front of all these people.

A hand presses my shoulder, steady and strong. Roe pulls me aside and steps in front of Dillon. His phone is out of his pocket, flashlight on, and the shadows streaking across his face make him look like some avenging angel.

"Look, Dillon," he says. "I know you're not a bad guy—"

"That's debatable," I interject, rubbing at the soft skin of my temples.

"Well, no matter what anyone's opinion is of you," Roe continues, his words pointed and sharp, "we know you aren't a murderer. We just want to know if you noticed anything else that night. Anything at all. About Olive or Owen or Agatha or—" His voice chokes, and his Adam's apple bobs in his throat. "Or my brother."

In the light from Roe's phone, Dillon's watery eyes jet between me, Camille, and the dark woods of the Boar's Head behind us. He looks wild, like an animal caught in the headlights of an oncoming vehicle.

A jolt of electric fear rushes through my mind, and I jerk my head to the side. The voice strings through my tissue, swimming deeper into my consciousness. If I don't block it now, the dead thing will have me on my knees before I can stop it. Camille brushes my shoulder with her hand, but I shrug it off.

"I'm fine."

But I'm not—I'm *really* not—because the spirit is worming its way deeper, and time is running out. Spots fizz through my vision.

"Just tell us where you saw Simon go," Roe demands.

Dillon babbles something, his voice thick, eyes rimmed red.

I clench my jaw, trying to thread together some kind of defense against the voice, but it unravels. Every wall I've ever built crumbles, and when it crashes against me, my knees sink to the rocky turf. I barely feel the scraped skin and the bruises already forming. Blood has burst from capillaries, like wine splashed against snow.

I curl in on myself, shaking. The voice penetrates every part of me: every pulse, every nerve, every cell. Roe and Camille are somewhere above me, and in the cold light of the phone, they move. Thick blurs against a black sky. The music from the party pounds a steady rhythm against my skin, but I can barely feel it.

Can barely feel anything.

And then the voice slips into my mind like spider silk, cold and clear and thin as water. It seeps in, pressing against my brain like leaky pipes, its rancid water blooming against carpet. When the words finally do come, they stream together, but it is not human. Not even a dead human.

It is the bog. Its lips are wet against my ear, curdled and choked with weeds. It floods my tongue with the taste of metallic earth, muddy water, and bones. So *many* bones.

He is coming, it whispers.

He is coming now.

A scream tears from my lips. The sound rakes up my throat and across my tongue like fire. Roe's hands scramble with my shoulders and pull me against him. He siphons the pain into his own veins, his own sinew. I want to break free of him, to save him from the agony coursing through my muscles.

Jed.

Camille starts screaming. She faces toward the starless sky, mouth wide, red, and open.

Swarms of black flies descend. They come from every direction, seething up from the Boar's Head glowing like fresh meat in the light from Roe's phone. Their wings beat furiously. The buzzing is so loud, I clamp my hands around my ears and bury my face in the earth. Bracken and brush scrape at my cheeks, but I don't care. I just press my skin deeper, hoping it will rid my senses of the swirling, dark mass above me.

Somewhere, Dillon cries, stumbles over a rock, and smashes his face into a tree protruding out of the Boar's Head like a broken arm. His cries turn to shrill shrieks, and he scrambles through the undergrowth. Warm, sticky blood drips down his jaw. Between the sticks and stone digging into my flesh, I watch the flies swarm toward him. Their sound fills the air and sets my teeth on edge. Fog clouds my mind, and panic shoots through me. But I don't move.

I *can't* move.

Camille whimpers as the insects drone, their sound leeching into the very ground.

I search for Roe. My fingers graze his hand, and we lock together. His phone landed with the light shining up, and when I dare a glance toward the sky, all I can see are the swarms of flies, like tendrils of smoke curling into the ever-beating darkness of the night.

He is coming. He is coming now.

The voice slices through my mind, causing fresh jolts of pain to fracture my skull. The buzzing continues. It becomes so loud and constant, my brain turns the sound into words.

Look around, the insects drone. *Look around.*

But I don't know how. Where do I look? Who is coming? What does the bog want?

Something crashes through the undergrowth on the far side of the Boar's Head, and Roe whimpers. I squeeze his hand tighter, wishing there was a way to take his pain. To siphon it into my own veins like he can, to make it so we can both share the fear. The cold, bright dread crawling up our throats and slicking like oil over our tongues.

Look around. Look around.

Camille's hair brushes my cheek, and I reach for her, dragging her behind me. I inch closer to Roe until the heat of him presses against my lips. His skin is tense, his muscles hardening against the noise and the fear bleeding from the bog.

"Roe, we have to get out of here," I whisper.

"We can't. Something's coming." His voice cracks, breaks, shatters into a hundred thousand pieces. The undergrowth beneath us shivers and shakes. "It's already here."

Cold sweat breaks out along my hairline. I want to pull Roe in close, drag Camille to her feet and flee. Run until our legs are scraped and bloody and the four tin walls of Roe's trailer close like a cocoon around us. But it is too late.

The flies drone louder—*Look around, look around*—and so I do.

I turn away from Roe and toward the shaft of blinking light from the phone settling among the grass. Beside me, Camille's outline is curled against the rock, her arms wrapped over her head, face shielded. The scent of blood tangs the air with iron. Dillon is slumped over a fallen tree, dark streaks running down the pallor of his face.

My skull cracks again with the voice, and Roe whimpers, his fingers weakening in mine.

He is here.

My heart seizes. I stay as still as I possibly can, focusing on the swarm above us. But then, the insects shift. They fly higher until they are nothing but a whisper. And close by, branches begin to crack. Underbrush shakes and the ground at my cheek vibrates. The dread claws up my chest, reaching fingers like a stranglehold around my neck, squeezing the bones until they snap.

A thick smell fills the air—pungent and overripe, like fish rotting in shallow mud. I gag and roll my cheek to the cool ground. The nausea moves through me in waves.

He is here.

The voice slips through my mind and vanishes somewhere into the night. But I am not alone. Slowly, I push myself up off the ground. My ears ring with the absence of the swarm. The music beats from the bog, but around the Boar's Head, the air is quiet. *Too* quiet.

I fold back on my knees and scan the brush around us. My gaze snags on a quiver of movement behind Dillon—a single, small shift of shadow. My mind translates it to nothing at first. No danger, no fear. But when Roe's hand tightens around mine and I glance at him, there are tears in his eyes.

I scramble in the grass for his phone, but I am too slow. Something breaks from the undergrowth. Dillon screams, and the noise is followed by a crunch of bone, a tear of skin and tendon. His cries are cut short, and all I can do is stare.

A creature—made from what, I have no idea—bends over Dillon's body, back against the spine of trees, and drinks from his bloody rib cage. Dillon concaves, lifted into the air by invisible strings while the monster ripples. The air around it wavers like a mirage, and the pale muscles of its body tighten. It drinks from Dillon until there is nothing left of my old classmate but a ragged corpse.

The creature's breathing is slow and deep—a steady pulse, a heartbeat.

Cold fear runs through my veins, freezing me to the grass. Roe shakes beside me. I try not to move, to barely breathe. And then the light of the phone gutters, and the creature's head spins on its axis.

Two white holes carve deep into a pale face without features. Humanoid, but devoid of anything that makes one human. A lipless mouth, nothing more than a black line, slits the skin from jaw to jaw. The thing reeks of rotting viscera.

It sniffs at the air, and my skin crawls. My heart pounds against my rib cage, telling me to run. But I can't. The bog has reached up with roots and keeps me in place.

I stare at the creature, exposed, and watch while it smiles. The lipless line rips, shreds of skin popping when jagged teeth are laid bare. It's a funny, lopsided smile. Like...

Like Jed's.

I open my mouth to scream, but it's not my voice that fills the space. It's not my face that rips through the trees and vibrates against the rock at our backs. The monster turns its head as another body explodes from the bog. A blur of white and black and blond hair crashes through the trunks of aspen, and the creature shrieks. Without thinking, I plummet toward the ground, pull Roe and Camille into me, and shrug against the bluff.

The music from the party thrums, but all I can focus on is the monster undulating in the light from Roe's phone, fighting whatever has come up from the bog—a mess of white, slimed limbs against those covered in ripped fishnet and flannel.

Roe is still shaking, and I lift his hand to mine; it's as cold as ice. I twist around for Camille, but her eyes are fixated on the melee in front of us, the swirl of white and black and empty eyes, a lipless face. The creature—like a human so sick with worms and parasites, it has become one itself—shrieks again, and a smell like wet iron fills the small clearing. It yelps and rolls away, edging back against the trees. And that's when the other body stands to its feet, a bloody knife swinging in its fist.

"This isn't over, motherfucker."

The voice breaks me in two.

Without paying heed to the danger creeping back into the bog, I scramble and race toward the figure in the clearing. I grab a lithe arm and spin the body around to face me. Blond hair, hazel eyes, tattered sleeve slipping from one shoulder, a smear of blood...my stomach sways, and my head spins, but I grip the wrist in my hand harder.

"Agatha," I say breathlessly. "Oh my god, Agatha."

They have found each other—the bog's infantry. The two who will march into battle among the cattails and reeds. The two whose blood pumps with the same that created the curse so many years ago. Which burdened the bog with the worms now prowling its shallows, leaving blood trails to swirl in the gray-green water of its depths.

The creature slinks away into the shadows, nursing wounds the avenger left on its body. It slips against stone and sinks into cool water and the bog wants nothing more than to purge the worm from its muck. Over the years, the monsters have brought nothing but shame to the bog, nothing but sickness. A poison now consumes the entire town, turning the bog acidic and hungry.

The bodies on the shores, dancing in the glow of the firelight don't know, but they feel it, the pain oozing through the sand. So they pour more liquor to numb the sin. They dance harder and faster and longer, hardly noticing the girl they called Olive sitting all alone now, rubbing saltwater tears from her eyes. The loneliness she has felt her entire life sinks deeper into her blood.

But she is not the bog's problem, not now.

The bog settles into itself, forming and shushing its body into a gentle embrace. Tonight, it can sleep and find some semblance of peace. It has laid the groundwork; it will be ready for the next battle.

The general is approaching.

12

THE AVENGER

My blood runs thick with an overwhelming urge to punch something. Doesn't have to be a face, but that's what I ultimately prefer. A soft, fleshy space to sink my fist into while the fear boils hot inside me.

Cops swarm the house. Their boots scuffle the creaky stairs. They come around the corner, not watching where they're going, and almost knock into the potted plant barely holding onto life. Mom paces in the hall, one hand fisting an unmarked bottle, the other pulling at her hair.

Agatha sits on her bed, hands fidgeting at her sides. Her fingers run over the red and creams of her patchwork quilt. I watch from the edge of the door, waiting for my sister to open her mouth and say something—*anything, dammit*. But she just sits there, staring across the room like a damn scarecrow.

This isn't Agatha. It can't be. Something about her eyes. At first, I decided it must be remnants of the trauma. Since she was little, Agatha has had hazel eyes. Like Mom's. They were like that in the bog, like she had a moment of recognition.

But now, with her head cocked sideways, blond hair falling in greasy strings about her neck, my sister's eyes are black like midnight oil. Like the flies that swarmed away at her coming.

I swallow the lump in my throat.

"She's fine, right?" Mom whispers over my shoulder. Her breath is like the inside of the town bar. "She'll be all right?"

I turn to face her and take in her sunken cheeks, the putrid tinge of her eyes. She is exhausted and hungover, and she smells like she needs a bath. I lay a hand on her arm, squeeze it, and smile.

"Hey, Mom." I rub little circles over the sleeve of her sweater. "Why don't you go relax. Maybe run a hot bath. I got this, okay? Everything's gonna be fine. I can handle it."

From the corner of my eye, I watch a woman with red, kinky hair, in a blue smock coat that smells like bleach, lean over Agatha and pick weeds from her hair with a pair of glinting tweezers.

Mom puts a cold hand on my cheek, and it takes everything inside me not to recoil. Her skin feels like the underbelly of a snake. "You're a good girl, Mila-May. I'm sorry for what I said earlier. Thank you for always being here to take care of us."

My mouth floods with a sour taste. Like bad wine. Or vinegar. But I force a smile on my face.

"Of course, Mom. You just go rest, and I'll make sure Agatha gets cleaned up and squared away."

Mom nods and takes another swig from her bottle. She angles toward the stairs and disappears. I let loose a deep breath and turn back to the room.

The sheriff sits on a stool at the edge of the bed, nursing a cup of steaming coffee. He looks as though he hasn't slept in days. Which, between Owen missing, the body in the bog, and now Agatha, he probably hasn't. Not that he's doing much about any of those things either. But hey, keeping up appearances is tough, right?

I hope his coffee tastes like dog shit.

Sheriff Lowell leans forward, rubs the center of his forehead with a thumb and forefinger, and sighs.

"Agatha, do you remember anything from tonight? Your sister here says she found you on the bog's western shore. Just...alone."

He looks to me for confirmation, and I nod. *Alone* is better than, "Oh, I found her fighting a monster made of wriggling white flesh and claws and teeth, who killed Dillon by snapping him in half like a gingerbread cookie."

I made Roe and Camille agree on the story: We found Agatha half-conscious in the shallows and revived her enough to walk her home and call the police. Dillon's body was left for them to find.

I did not touch him. Whatever happens when I do, I couldn't. Not then.

The cops brought him back to the morgue and called his death an animal attack. Not the work of some hellish monster that shouldn't even exist.

But then, hey, I hear voices of the dead. Humanoid worm monsters with headlights for eyes isn't that far of a stretch for me.

Agatha doesn't respond to the sheriff's questions. She just sits there, staring blankly. My throat sharpens when I swallow and shift my weight. Agatha hasn't said a thing since the bog. Not a hello, not an "Oh my gosh, Mila, you found me." Nothing. She stayed silent and angry while we practically drug her from the swamp.

Roe left as soon as he was able, shaking and white, looking like he would be sick at any second. He won't respond to any of my texts.

I pull my phone from my back pocket and check again. Nothing. Instead, there's a text from Camille.

I look from my sister to the sheriff and duck out onto the landing. He doesn't need to be sniffing around in places he has no business being. If he seemed half as interested in Jed as he does now with Agatha, maybe he wouldn't have been so goddamn useless. I blow a curl from my face and unlock the phone.

Camille's text stares at me.

HOW IS SHE?

I reply with two simple words.

NOT GREAT.

Camille is quick to respond.

I'M COMING OVER.

NO, DON'T. NOT YET. IT'S LATE. I'LL
LET YOU KNOW WHEN SHE'S READY.
SHERIFF IS STILL HERE.

I drop the phone in my pocket and slip into the room. Sheriff Lowell is now guzzling down his coffee and sighing loud enough to grab my attention.

"Mila, maybe you could get your sister to talk to me?" He puts the mug down on the floor between his feet and takes the hat off his head, wiping the thick line of sweat beading at his hairline.

I look at Agatha. The woman with the tweezers is pulling wooden splinters from my sister's left cheekbone, and Agatha is not even wincing. I want to scream at them both to stop, to get the hell out. It's like I'm juggling too many things: Agatha, Jed, Roe not answering, Camille texting, and Mom.

I heave a sigh. The least I can do is try...again. I cross the room and bend down beside the bed. One hand rests on my sister's knee, where her pale skin shows through ripped black fishnets.

"Aggy, it's me. It's Mila. Can you look at me?"

Mud clings to Agatha's hair, clumped and caked along the blond roots. Blood and dirt smudge her skin, and her black silk dress is torn and stained. Her dark eyes stare ahead numbly. I lean in closer, and the woman with the tweezers takes a step back.

"Aggy, I need you to tell me what you were doing out in the bog." I lift a palm to turn my sister's face toward me, but Agatha is unmovable, her jaw rigid.

Up close, her eyes are as deep and dark as the night sky. No separation between the iris, pupil, and what should be the surrounding milky white.

My teeth tremble against my lip line.

Part of me doesn't want to know what is making her this way. She's like a puppet controlled by invisible strings, and it terrifies me. Images of last night play over and over in my mind, rocking me back on my heels. Roe crying beside me, Camille curled against the rock, Dillon...I close my eyes to shake the cobwebs, to remove the blood and gore from my mind. But all I see are the creaking hinges of the monster's jaw when its mouth ripped open and its bloody teeth glinted in the moonlight. Fear tightens my throat while the memory replays. The sure feeling of death thickens the air.

And then there was Agatha, spilling from the shallows, hands raised against the monster's hide, screaming, hair streaming white like some avenging angel. I took the knife from her fingers when she collapsed and buried it in the muck of the shallows, hoping the bog would lick its watery tongue around the blade and swallow it whole so the police would never find it.

Agatha's fists clench. Her nails scrape along the rips in her tights, where bruises and scrapes form along the pale skin.

"Agatha." My voice is a whisper, barely a breath.

I brush hair from my sister's face. When the blue-smocked woman tries to protest, the sheriff hushes her. I inch closer to Agatha, planting palms on both her knees.

The skin on her jaw twitches, and her eyes dart sideways to the door before coming back to me. There's a flicker of something in my belly. I want to claim it as hope or faith my sister will open her mouth and spill all the bog's secrets. But this isn't true.

The feeling carving out space along the pink flesh of my belly is *fear*. Fear Agatha will only stay silent. Fear she will open her mouth and talk about monsters, shredded bodies, and a bog that speaks.

Fear she won't be my sister anymore.

"Mila." Agatha's dry lips split, and tears pool in her eyes.

My sternum cracks with emotion. It spills thick, rolling off my skin in waves. I collapse against my sister's knee, my shoulders shaking. The name—*my* name—alone is enough to break me. I peel hair from Agatha's face and wipe her tears.

"Yes, it's me, Aggy. It's me."

Agatha crumples forward, and I scramble to sit beside her, to let her curl against my body like the perfect fit of a shattered necklace. Two halves, still broken, our sides chipped enough that we feel the pain when the impact happens. But I press closer, because what else is there? We are sharp-edged girls, our spikes fitting together. The two of us fall into one another, all saltwater tears and gripping fingers.

After a moment, the sheriff clears his throat and drags his chair forward. The legs scrape against the wooden floorboards. Agatha lifts her face from my shoulder, still shaking. But as soon as she sees the sheriff, her eyes go blank, her body rigid. She turns toward the window and stares unblinkingly at the first rays of lemony dawn drifting in from the other side of the glass.

God, when was the last time I slept? I bite back a yawn.

The sheriff sighs and gestures to the woman with the tweezers. She goes back to picking twigs and clumps of dried mud off Agatha's dress.

"Agatha, would you mind telling me what you were doing out in Thomas Bog?" The sheriff's voice sounds heavy and thick, as if he has swallowed a mouthful of stinging bees.

Silence rings out through the bedroom. The only sounds are the call of early morning birds and the drone of insects in the cedars. A shiver runs through my bones when I recall the flies, all buzzing and swarming and filling my teeth with vibrations. And then Dillon and the tenor of ripping flesh—

I blink away the memory. How we just left him there in the swamp to rot.

When Agatha doesn't speak, the sheriff gets to his feet and walks to the door. He leans against the wooden frame. I want him to leave—give up—but he turns back around and fixes us with a look both exhausted and angry.

"Look, girls. I have your brother back in my morgue, your mother is inconsolable, and I need to somehow help her piece it together so she can move on and heal." He wipes a hand down his face. "Don't you want to move on too? Put this all behind you?"

Agatha turns to me then. The grip she holds on my hand turns to a vise.

"He's wrong," she whispers, her voice rushed. "He's wrong about everything."

I search my sister's face for some kind of truth, trying desperately to hold back tears. "What's he wrong about, Aggy? You can tell me."

She opens her mouth to speak, but Sheriff Lowell closes the space between us and kneels in front of the bed. "What am I wrong about, Agatha?"

As soon as his voice enters the air again, Agatha's face goes blank, like she's nothing more than canvas waiting to be painted. I lift my hand to her chin and draw her gaze back to me. When our eyes meet, life returns to Agatha's face.

"Get out." The words slip from my tongue before I can stop them.

"Excuse me?" The floorboards creak behind me when the sheriff takes a step back.

My eyes flash up to him, taking in his weak chin and his watery gaze. "I said, get the hell out of my house. She's not going to talk to you."

I expect a fight, but his shoulders only slump. He is just as exhausted as the rest of us.

"Fine," he says. "Fine. I don't care who the hell she talks to as long as she *talks.*"

I turn back to my sister and lift a hand to her cheek. She flinches.

"Agatha, tell me what the sheriff is wrong about."

Her lips crack with a smile. The dirt and blood smearing her face are like some kind of mask. I grind my teeth when Agatha begins to hum, swaying back and forth. The notes are familiar, but I can't place them. Maybe an old hymn? I look pointedly up at the sheriff—*get the* fuck *out*—but he only sighs.

"I don't have time for this. Victoria, make sure you get everything off her. Dirt, weeds, even her clothes. Everything needs to go to evidence so we can figure out what the hell happened out there." The sheriff shoots a glare straight through my bones. "If she does end up saying anything useful, call me. Otherwise, just take care of your mother, okay? None of this is easy for her."

I want to tell him to shove it. Remind him there is no one to take care of *me* right now. He is an idiot who doesn't know who is currently laid out on a slab at the county morgue, but it sure as hell isn't Jed. But I don't. I just wrap my arm tighter around my sister's shoulder and squeeze.

My mother might be inconsolable, my brother might still be missing, but my sister is here, and she's safe. When she is ready, she is going to tell me everything.

By late afternoon, I know for certain the girl sitting upstairs in the white nightgown, freshly bathed and scrubbed, isn't my sister. She might look like Agatha, even sounds like her, but it's not her. Not really. Or at least, there are pieces missing. Bits of the real Agatha replaced by something else. Something darker. Which still smells of bog water and the iron tang of blood, even after a long shower.

I sit on the countertop in the kitchen, nursing yet another mug of boiled coffee. Sleep feels impossible.

Mom slumps in one of the chairs out on the porch, wrapped in her blue cardigan, gazing blankly out at the trees. I told her all she needed to know. That Agatha is fine. Or fine enough. So, she's back to crying over the swill-smell of the body Sheriff Lowell loaded into the back of his truck, even though I've reminded her numerous times it isn't Jed.

How could it be, when the single eye roving in the skull was the wrong hue? The body upstairs *might* be my sister, but the body swathed in black nylon and weeds was *not* my brother. Not in looks, flesh and blood, or anything that would make that case of skin Jed Thomas.

I take a swig from my mug and press my tongue to the roof of my mouth when the bitter liquid washes down my throat. So, if that body isn't Jed's, whose is it? Could it have been like the body Roe and I stumbled across last summer? Just a drifter, someone passing through? A person who won't be missed? A stranger the bog's acidic tongue corroded before anyone could claim the face as someone they knew?

The last thing I want to do is remember the details, but I have to. What other way is there? Grandma Ruby used to say the only way across the bog is through it. There is no second or safe option. We stick to the paths, and we make our way through. I finish off what is left of the lukewarm coffee and concentrate on the remaining dregs.

Eyes like mud in rotting sockets. Eyes that, at first, hold no familiarity for me. Eyes that are not cornflower blue, so how can they be Jed's? I sink deeper into my own memory, sifting through images and blurs of recollection, like flipping through a collection of photographs at an art gallery. Brown eyes like soft sand. Brown like the first peek of spring earth after a hard winter. Brown like bog water. Brown like...

My mind stops in its tracks. An ache breaks out in a band above my brow. The radio announcer's voice echoes in my mind, tinny, like he's speaking through a can.

"Police in Leo County are still searching for local missing person, Owen Shelby, last seen the evening of June fifteenth in the vicinity surrounding Thomas Bog..."

Owen Shelby, who walked into the bog and hasn't been seen since.

Owen Shelby, who helped me with algebra homework sophomore year of high school, when all I wanted to do was rip my own hair out. Owen Shelby, who smelled like freshly laundered clothes and lavender soap. Owen Shelby, who leaned over my desk one day, so close I could see his eyes.

His *brown* eyes.

The realization hits me like a punch to the gut. I've been so distracted with finding Agatha, this is the first time I can sit and think about this, and goddamn, I *know* this guy.

Why are the police complete idiots?

I'm slipping down off the counter and spinning around to vomit into the sink before I can stop myself. Nothing much comes up, just a thin line of brown sick. Before I know it, I'm crouching on the braided rug, my hands still clinging to the edge of the counter above me. My rib cage expands and contracts. Bones and muscle shifts while my lungs gasp desperately for some semblance of air.

I snap the band on my wrist.

One, two, three, four, five.

The body swaddled in black nylon was Owen Shelby. The body currently laid out on a slab in the county morgue, a cardstock ticket tied around the big toe with my brother's name written on it, *is* Owen Shelby. My viscera swims. All my insides undulate, and I try to gain focus on what my memory has just discovered.

The body I raised and returned to peace.

Surely, the sheriff knows by now Jed's eye color is not brown. He must know the brown eyes and disfigured flesh don't belong to the man who has been missing for three years, but rather the one who has been missing for only a handful of days. So, why hasn't he called? Why hasn't he looked at the facts and admitted his mistake?

I let my hands drop to my knees and turn on the rug, pressing my back against the cupboard. My heart starts, heat flushing my skin.

Agatha stands in the archway behind me, eyes staring blankly forward. Her white nightgown slips from one shoulder. Her head is cocked to the side, and there is a frozen sort of smile on her face.

My blood pumps harder. I reach for the countertop to pull myself up onto shaking legs. A lump gathers on the back of my tongue, threatening to choke me if I don't swallow it down or cut it out with words. I grip the counter hard, committing to memory the way the metal smooths out against the granite. My teeth bite at the flesh outside of my lip.

"Agatha. What are...what are you doing out of bed?"

Her wholly black eyes blink open and shut.

"Didn't the, uh...didn't the nurse tell you to rest until tomorrow?"

My voice wavers, and it's like she can sense my weakness. Her neck cracks to an upright position, and the smile on her face widens.

"There is no time to rest."

The words spill from her lips like water, like snow melting down a hill. I swallow, sense the dry flesh of my throat, and grope for my now-empty mug. My fingers meet the handle, and I spin around to fill it with water.

When I turn back, Agatha's face is mere millimeters from mine. My heart thrills, sending heat scattering across my limbs.

"Water?" I say, holding the mug up to her.

She regards it with deep skepticism. Her eyes barely blink, and her nose wrinkles. She sniffs at the contents of the cup.

"That is not water," she finally says. "Not true water. That is stolen from us, pressed through pipes until all life has been sucked away." Her neck snaps back up, eyes cold and dark. "I am the living water."

Fear crawls along my skin like freshly hatched spiders. The hairs on my arms stand on end. I set the cup back on the countertop and gently take Agatha's shoulders, leading her back through the living room and ushering her toward the stairs. When we reach the bottom step, Agatha stops. She turns to look at our mother crumpled on the porch.

"She knows the story." It is a statement more than anything else. She repeats it, each time stronger, harder.

Something akin to fear whispers across my skin, and I feel lost, stuck here between my sister and the woman who birthed us both. I gather Agatha's wet hair in my fist and twist it around, forming a knot at the nape of her neck.

"I think you need to rest, Aggy." I turn her back toward the stairs. "Just for a bit. Just for—"

Just for me to figure out what the hell is going on.

Much to my surprise, she goes, feet slapping damp on the stairs. I watch her make her ascent until she turns at the top and disappears around the corner. Chest heavy, I lean against the wall, trying to count my breaths, attempting to make sense of it all.

Mom sits in her chair, staring out at the trees, her shoulders still. There are no tears left to cry. Nothing left for the woman who has lost it all—all but the daughter she stopped loving so very long ago.

I follow our trail back toward the kitchen, and something wet leeches against my bare toes: droplets of water laced with muddy weeds. And they aren't the only ones. Every few inches, watery sludge slimes the floor. I grab a towel from the kitchen and sop up the mess, thinking it must have come in on the sheriff's boots.

But then I remember the sound of Agatha's feet hitting the stairs.

Didn't she dry off after her shower?

Nothing makes sense. My brain beats against the inside of my skull with confusion. I am lost. Afraid and utterly alone. I curl into myself there, on the floor. Fresh tears sprout like seedlings from the hollows of my eyes. There is something happening here that is so much larger than I am. It is within my grasp, if only I knew how to reach up and take it.

A deep aching for my brother fills me. For someone to share the burdens with. If he were here, he would know what to do, what to say. I bite my tongue until I taste blood.

"How am I supposed to do this without you, Jed?" My breath is hot against my knee. I turn in on myself—heart, lungs, and guts swirling together inside until I'm like a storm at sea.

It was always supposed to be the three of us: Jed, Agatha, and me. A merry band of misfits. Us against the world. Now, one is missing, one is broken, and the third sits upstairs on her bed, dripping nothing but hidden truths and bog water.

She knows the story.

The words filter through my mind like water through a sieve.

She knows the story.

Mom has been no help since the day Jed slipped into the swamp and never showed his face again. I turn my gaze out to the porch, studying her still frame slumped in the chair. She is bitter and broken, but then again, so am I. We have both lost the same things, both grieved the same souls.

I wipe the tears from my eyes and get to my feet, ignoring the trail of bog water leading up the stairs. Mom doesn't acknowledge me when I slip out onto the porch, not at first. The heat assaults my skin when I settle into the chair opposite her, curling my aching legs underneath me.

I don't know how to ask the question teasing my tongue. It's like I've always been too afraid to ask. Like, if I know the truth, it will only make me feel more cursed. But I let it out—blunt and cold and unpolished.

"Can you hear the voices too?"

The noise of the woods around us fills in the awkward space. Crows in the treetops, blue jays in the maples. The wind shushes down, making the cedars creak and the potted flowers swing from iron curls. She doesn't answer me at first, and for a moment, I worry she'll only get upset. Or worse, stay silent.

But then she slowly turns to face me. Exhaustion pools in dark puddles beneath her filmy eyes.

"No, but your Grandma Ruby could."

Her words jar me. Not the answer itself, but the fact Mom is offering it so willingly. So, I push further.

"Is there...is there a reason you couldn't?"

She returns her focus out to the trees, pulling her sleeves down around her yellowing fingers.

"I never almost died. That's what it takes, you know? A near-death experience. Something to push you through all the static to the other side."

I nod, remembering Grandma Ruby's words.

Mom shifts in her chair. "Do you remember the last time I went into the bog, Mila?" she asks, her voice soft.

I sigh and gather my thoughts. It's a strange question and not one I have ever sought the answer for. But now that I think about it, I don't remember a single time I watched my mother walk into the cedar downs of Thomas Bog.

I shake my head.

"That's because I don't go there anymore." Mom's voice is hitched and twisted. "I watched what that place did to your grandma. I watched what it did to all my friends. I watched what it did to the countless faces that went missing in its waters, never to be seen again. And I know what it did to me."

She turns back to me, her eyes red, face hollowed out like a skull. It takes the breath from my lungs.

"And then after I watched it devour everyone around me, I stood idly by as it took everything else I loved. It swallowed my son, and it killed my mother, and then it took my daughter, only to spit her back out again." Her voice cracks at the mention of my sister, and I fight the overwhelming urge to run to her, to wrap her up and tell her everything is going to be all right. Because how can it?

How can life be all right after so much bad has happened?

I chew on the fleshy lining of my mouth, not stopping even when iron floods my tongue.

"Then why did you let us all go in there?" I bite back each accusatory word as I say it. "Why did you let us go when you knew it would only hurt us?" I pound on my skull, fresh tears pricking my eyes. "I hear them all the time, Mom. All the fucking time. And I don't know how to stop them because Grandma Ruby is gone and I have no one left to ask. No one left—"

I shatter then. Breaking into a hundred thousand pieces and scattering to the wind.

This is not the trip home I wanted. I planned on staying for only a few nights. Just enough time to say goodbye to Agatha before she went off to college. I planned on getting drunk and avoiding Roe, riding my bike with Camille and Agatha to the swimming hole. Leaping off rocks and crashing into the cold water, feeling my heart leap to the reaches of my throat. I planned on forgetting about the body in the bog, about my missing brother, that I belonged to a place so poisoned. Planned on keeping the voices at bay, like I have been doing for the last thirteen years.

I have failed in every single one.

Mom doesn't console me. Just stares. "I tried to keep you from it. I tried to protect you and make all the right calls, but you were too wild. Born broken."

My cheeks go red with anger, and the only thing finally getting me to stop crying is the sound of an engine in the driveway. When I turn toward the house, a single face stares back at me through the glass, and it's smiling.

"I wondered if I'd find you two out here." The reverend's grin widens when he notices the tears running down my cheeks. "Will you be at service tomorrow? It would be good for the community to see Agatha returned to us, safe and sound."

I say nothing, just look down. A strange feeling prickles on the back of my neck, as if something is watching me from the tree line. Thick glops of dark mud stain the reverend's boots.

"Out for a walk, Reverend?" I ask, my voice thick and milky with saliva.

He blinks at me and cocks his head at a strange angle. And I notice how very large his eyes are behind his glasses. Like they're being magnified, studied under a microscope while his body is pinned to a slide.

"Just out doing a bit of community service. Cleaning up the trash, so to speak."

My tongue curls around the edges of my teeth, but I say nothing because the skin on my neck has turned to ice. Slowly, my gaze drifts back over my shoulder. I'm half terrified the monster from the bog will be there and half hoping it is. Half hoping Agatha will come crashing from the second-story window and rescue me again because I realize now that I too need saving.

But only three sets of tiny eyes blink back at me from their places in the air.

The flies are beginning to swarm.

13

WATER OF LIFE

I force myself to stay awake well past midnight. Agatha is in Jed's room across the hall. The reverend thought it best we sleep apart, and like everything else that man says, Mom went along with it. She bends to him, cowers like a weeping willow, and it makes me wonder what he has on her. Surely something. She might be a spineless drunk, but at the end of the day, she is a Thomas, and that means *something*.

Something I'm still trying to figure out.

I push up on my knees and peer out the window, at the lawn swathed in moonlight. Being a Thomas means being connected to the bog, whether we like it or not. We can't get away, no matter how far we go. The bog is always with us, like being born here means it leaves a stain. A kind of birthmark we can't wash off. It turns us, one way or another.

I'm a curse, Mila.

My nose starts to tingle, and I fall back against my pillow, squeezing my eyes shut. I don't have time to cry. Not now when there's so much left unanswered.

Something hard pings off the glass of the window, and I freeze.

My heart flips into my throat, and my eyes snap open in the breathless dark. What the hell? And then I picture it—the monster—all coiled white muscle, the way it sucked life from Dillon's chest, seemed almost to grow. I curl against the wall.

Go away, go away, go away.

The sound comes again. A gentle *thwack*.

A monster wouldn't be that quiet. Something like what I saw in the bog would rip the roof and walls to shreds just to get to me. I slowly roll onto my back and stare up at the wooden knot-faces in the ceiling.

"Don't let me die tonight," I whisper to them.

Without giving myself time to think, I scramble up onto my knees and peer down at the moonlit lawn.

It's empty.

Lightning bugs glitter at the edge of the woods, and a bat swoops from somewhere overhead, devouring mosquitoes in a single snap. The yard is still, given over to a nocturnal state. And then something flashes in the corner of my eye.

A dark blur just behind the pine tree, which used to host a tire swing.

My insides heat with fear.

The blur grows. An arm, a head, the shadowy build of—

A pine cone bounces off the glass, and I flick back the lock, throwing the whole window open.

"Roe?" I whisper-hiss.

He steps fully out from behind the tree, backlit by pearlescent moonlight. The wind tongues a cowlick through his hair, and he reaches to shove it back. His ragged shirt tugs upward, revealing that slice of abdomen. My stomach throbs, and my palms moisten with sweat.

"What the fuck are you doing down there?" I choke.

The air feels like last summer. Before we pulled the body from the bog and I made Roe promise not to tell a single soul what I could do. Made him bottle it all up and let it consume him from the inside out.

"Can I come in?"

I should say no, tell him to walk back through the woods to his trailer. That we'll talk tomorrow. But I don't. Because now we've both seen things. Things we can't ever shake. And if I owe Roe anything, it's the chance to speak it out loud so he stops feeling the fear the bog is feeding him. I will do anything just to tear a little corner off his darkness.

"Hold on." I duck down off the bed, lift the lace skirt, and peer into the black beneath my mattress.

It's still there—the knotted rope I smuggled up here when we were ten. When the beatings started and it was easier for him to spend the nights here, curled up in a pile of quilts on the floor. My fingers brush away dust bunnies, and I pull the rope out into the thin light. Acting on muscle memory alone, I secure one end to my bedpost and fling the rest of it out the window, where it barely brushes the tips of the dew-damp grass. It stretches taut when Roe grabs hold and starts the climb.

His eyes peek over the top of the windowsill, and my stomach drops. What are we doing? We aren't these kids anymore. The two of us are broken, bloody things. Hungry.

But Roe Byron is in my room and I'm only wearing one of Jed's oversized T-shirts, and there's nothing I can do about it. He catches sight of it. The corner of his lips lifts just slightly, and the air between us seems to shrink.

"What are you doing here, Roe?" I ask before he can say anything. "You've been ignoring my texts all day."

He reaches up to brush sweat from his forehead. "Sorry. I've just been... processing. But I came to check in on you. Make sure everything with Agatha was...okay."

I cross my arms over my chest. "Nothing about Agatha is okay right now."

"Sure, makes sense." Roe gnaws on his lip and sits down on my bed. The mattress creaks.

I'm reeling back to last summer, when I snuck him up here. We kissed and laughed, and Agatha and Camille caught us.

All before the body.

And now, the monster.

"Will you at least come sit by me?" Roe pats the bed beside him, smatters of white bandages on his fingers.

God, yes. The tension building between us these last few days is damn near ready to spark. And yet, I can't. I don't want to hurt him. To *keep* hurting him. But he's so soft sitting here, and I owe him this—the space to try to forgive me. I take a breath and sit down beside him, our shoulders brushing.

"Why are you here?"

A breeze kicks in through the still-open window, rustling his hair. "Because I think I owe you an apology too."

It's not what I was expecting, and I blink stupidly in the following silence. "What?"

He shrugs. "Look, after last summer...well, things could have been different. I could have tried to talk to you about everything, even after you'd left. But I just didn't. I bottled it up and kept what I was feeling from the one person who could have understood." He wraps his fingers through mine, his eyes like pools. "You."

"Me?" I choke and shake my head. "Roe, no. I was wrong. We should have told someone, and now it's too late, and things are spinning out of control. I mean, look at my sister." Tears collect like storm clouds in my eyes. "What the fuck is wrong with her?"

Roe wraps his arms around me and pulls me against his chest. For a moment, my bones go rigid. When was the last time someone comforted *me?*

But I melt into him, and even though he's feeling every bit of anger, fear, worry, and guilt I do, I let him take it. He's warm and soft, and I breathe in the rich scent of him. Coffee grounds, weed, woodsmoke. For half a second, I let myself wonder if he tastes of those things too.

"I don't know what's going on with Agatha," he whispers in my hair. "But we're going to figure it out."

Tears drip down the edge of my nose. I didn't come back home for this. But it's happening anyway, and I don't want to stop it.

I push away and look up at him. "I wanted to avoid you on this trip. It felt like, after everything, I didn't deserve you—your friendship, or anything really."

His face splits with a gentle grin, and he squeezes my shoulders. "That's the thing about me. I'm like a bad cold; you can't shake me, even if you tried."

I laugh and Roe lifts the hem of his shirt to wipe my tears, revealing rigid muscles. My breath catches.

"I'm sorry too." I try to distract myself from the heat once more boiling in my belly. "For everything."

He squeezes me again. "I know."

It's not an "I forgive you," but it's something. It's another step closer. We sit there in silence a while longer and let the night breeze kiss the napes of our necks. A tree frog trills somewhere in the pines, and part of me wishes we could stay this way forever.

The moonlight catches the rugged bandages around his knuckles. I slip his fingers into mine, and when I look up, his eyes are shining bright.

"I think the bog might be possessing Agatha." My words break the silence like a wrecking ball.

Roe's grip on me loosens. His eyes are wide and wild, breath hot. "What?"

Gosh, I shouldn't be doing this. I should just shut up and let Roe hold me until the sun tips like honey against our backs. But I can't.

I pull away. "I know it sounds stupid and impossible. But what you said about the bog the other day, it makes sense. It's like the water has a mind of its own, like it's hurting and hungry, and it's making her do things. Talk a certain way, act a certain way. Maybe that's why it acts so strange, you know? Not like other bogs. Eats people faster." I shake my head. "I don't know, you probably think I'm an idiot."

Roe grabs my hand again. "No, I don't. I'd never think that. And I don't think you're wrong either. I feel something. Here." He beats a finger against his chest. "Something wrong. It's why I boil all my water. It's like the bog is poisoning us because it's so angry and sick."

I picture Dillon, bent over, his chest caved in and bloody. *Maybe because it has a fucking monster murdering people*, I want to say. But I don't.

"Maybe that's what Agatha is, then. A manifestation of its anger."

Roe's head swivels to the empty bed on the opposite side of the room. "Where is she, by the way? Shouldn't she be in bed?"

"Your dad said she'd sleep better in a separate room."

Roe tenses. "And you trusted him?"

"Mom did."

He drops my hand and gets to his feet.

"Roe, what is it? What's wrong?"

I follow. His hand is already on the door, pushing it open. He walks out into the hall, and the floorboards creak beneath his feet. His shadow looms before the door to Jed's room. He lifts his fingers, then hesitates. A string attaches to my gut and pulls me beside him. I intertwine our hands again. He's vibrating, eyes as bright as lightning bugs.

"Roe, tell me what is going on."

"I feel it. The bog." His chin jerks down, and our gazes lock. "It's here."

I don't think. A sound emerges from my throat—part woman, part animal. I thrust the door open with a palm and freeze in the shadowed frame.

Agatha sits in a puddle of moonlight, and though I can't see them, I swear her eyes are trained on me. My heartbeat races, and my hand scrambles to my throat.

"Aggy?" My voice is a thin sliver of fear. "Aggy?"

She doesn't respond, not at first. Her chest rises and falls in an even pattern. Breath in, breath out. She must still be sleeping...

But then her mouth opens. And opens and opens and opens.

Bog water leaks from between her teeth and drips down the front of her pajamas. Her body jerks at the navel, and she leans forward, crawling on all fours to the edge of the bed. Roe's hand is on my back, warm, steady, and I am anything but. A tight, hot lump chokes my throat. My breath turns to wheezing, and my lungs deflate.

"Aggy?"

Her head cracks violently to the side. Bog water spills over the footboard, splashing down onto the floor.

"It's in them, Mila-May," she says, her voice a singsong of buzzing, vibrating notes. "It's in all of them. He'll take them all."

And then she rushes me, fingers cold and scrambling at my collarbone, my mouth.

Roe's hand clasps down over my lips, and the scream there turns to ash. I stagger away. Roe wraps around me and drags me from the room, shutting the door on the thing that was once my sister. He pulls me back into my bedroom and shuts and locks the door. I stumble to the bed, fisting the cotton sheets and grounding myself to reality, the here and now.

"What the fuck was that?" I breathe.

Silence. Nothing but bugs out in the yard. Energy crashes through my chest. Roe's hands come to my shoulders.

"The bog, Mila. That was the bog."

And I know the thing can't hear me, but I whisper anyway. "Leave her. Leave my sister alone."

Roe rubs circles on my back. "'But whoever drinks the water I give them will never thirst. Indeed, the water I give them will become in them a spring of water welling up to eternal life.'"

I sit up, eyes bright. "What?"

"It's from the Bible. John 4:14. Dad used to quote it all the time. Listen, I should go. Let you get some sleep." He stands up and leaves me wishing his hand was back on my skin, comforting, taking the pain. Before I can stop him, he's tossing the rope out the window and swinging his legs down. "I'll talk to you tomorrow, okay?"

This change in him has me breathless. I should push. Ask him what it is he's not telling me and why he's suddenly quoting Scripture. Why he's quoting his father. But then a memory fishhooks in my belly. The flies buzzing around the reverend.

Look around, look around.

Like they're trying to warn me. But of what?

I want to ask Roe, but instead, I let him go.

"Okay," I whisper.

He takes the first step down the rope.

"Just keep me in the loop?"

He nods, failing at a smile. "Of course, absolutely."

When I'm about to turn away from the window, he calls my name. I lean out. He's a few feet down, dangling over the lawn like a Christmas ornament.

"Mila?"

"Yeah?"

"Don't drink the water."

14

THE STORM

I sit on the hard, wooden pew, my legs going numb and my heart beating a thick staccato against my rib cage. The reverend's voice pricks my skin—a needle slipping into the soft flesh beneath my fingernail.

I look around at the congregation and pick out a handful of faces who might be wearing pressed slacks and puffed sleeves, but I know for damn sure have rot seeping from their perfect, flawless skin. Mom's resentful eye turns on me, and I shift my hands beneath my thighs, hoping the pressure will be enough to keep them from fluttering around like a pair of birds.

Or maybe, like a pair of flies.

I shiver at the thought. The buzzing echoes when I close my eyes and when I wake up. And Dillon's screams. I hear that even when I'm awake.

The reverend stands at the wooden pulpit, droning on about forgiveness and mercy and the righteous power of a soul. My gaze moves from the cross nailed on the far wall to my sister beside me. She sits rigid against the back of the pew, dressed in fishnets and white cotton. Moisture clings to her exposed skin, and I whisper a silent prayer it's just sweat and not bog water. When Mom tried to fight her outfit choice, Agatha took Mom by the throat and pushed her up against the doorframe until her eyes bulged like a frog.

My Agatha would never do that.

She might have been opinionated. Agatha might not have given two shits about what Mom approved and disapproved of, but she wasn't violent.

She must feel me staring because her neck snaps sideways, and she catches my gaze. Three scratches are etched into my collarbone from when she reached out to me last night, whispering words that made no sense.

It's in them.

She smiles crookedly, and I look away.

Anywhere but into the eyes of whatever is possessing my sister. The bog, I'm sure of it. All of its anger. She is its soldier against that thing crawling in its waters.

I scan the crowd of faces for Roe, more out of habit than anything else. He hasn't stepped foot in a church since the day his dad kicked him out of the house. My gaze snags on Simon sitting in the front row, next to Olive and her parents. He appears as cool as a cucumber, hair swept sideways, collar pressed, tie knotted expertly around his thick neck. I stare hot daggers at the back of his head, wishing that, for just a second, looks could actually kill.

The reverend preaches, his sermon falling on fallow ground. The rest of Credence Hollow turns their bulletins into fans to combat the wet heat clogging the sanctuary. I fight the urge to tip my head back against the pew and fall asleep.

"And now comes time for our most holy of traditions."

The change in the reverend's voice has me blinking my eyelids and sitting up straighter.

Deacon Denton walks up the aisle and lifts a purple cloth off the altar, revealing a silver tray filled with bread and another with little plastic cups.

Communion.

The reverend's shiny black shoes shush in the carpet when he steps down from the pulpit and raises each tray in his hands.

"Communion is a time we come together, to praise Him who gave us eternal life. By the sacrifice of His soul, we are set free from the sins of our own." He passes the tray of bread to Deacon Denton and keeps the one pocked with little cups.

The organ kicks in with "Springs of Living Water," and both men start down the center aisle, passing out the bread and cups to each congregant. When they reach our aisle, Mom takes what she is given and skips Agatha, passing the trays to me.

"Her heart is not in the right place for this right now," Mom whispers.

The metal is cold in my hands, and when I look down, my tongue dries out in fear.

When I was little, the cups were filled with red grape juice. Couldn't have the good people of Credence Hollow drinking alcohol. But these cups don't contain anything resembling the blood of Christ.

They're filled with bog water.

The reverend watches me. My throat tightens.

Don't drink the water, Roe said. Is this what he meant?

I take a cup and a chunk of bread before passing it along the pew. The reverend nods. Crumbs of algae settle at the bottom of my water. My stomach sours. Mom is bent over her own cup, lips muttering a prayer I can't hear.

I steal a glance at Agatha from the corner of my eye. She's curled over, shoulders swaying back and forth. And she's whispering something I can't make out. I trace the scratches on my collarbone with a fingernail.

It's in them.

My stomach lurches then, a sharp punch hitting my ribs before settling cold and hard against my pelvis. The people of Credence Hollow aren't just walking above the raging waters of the bog; they are *becoming* it.

Welcoming it into their bodies. Weak and willing flesh.

When, at last, everyone is clutching a cup of the stuff, the reverend rises to his place behind the pulpit and lifts his own share of the communion.

"Do this for everlasting life," he cries. "And in the name of sacrifice!"

"In the name of sacrifice!" the congregation echoes, splashing the water against their tongues.

Mom smacks her lips, licking the last drop from her chin. She crumples the cup in a fist. My stomach swills. I wait for someone to speak up, to question the reverend. But the sanctuary is silent. The only sound is of people tipping their cups back for that final, unholy taste.

Below me, the bog churns. I feel it. Angry and sick. I lean down and dump my cup onto the floorboards.

Let the bog claim it before it takes us all.

By the time we are all standing and singing the final hymn, the scent of the bog in my nose is like salt. Out of habit, I reach for Agatha's hand when we slowly begin to filter from the pews and out the front door. Her skin is cold—too cold. But I squeeze tighter because, even if she's not my sister, I need some semblance of love to get me through the rest of the day. To help me find a way for this to all make sense.

I tighten my fingers in hers. Even though she might not be my Agatha right now, she *feels* like her, and that is enough to keep me steady. To hope there is a way to get her back from the bog for good.

We empty out the large front doors. I sidestep to avoid shaking hands with the reverend, but he reaches a sweaty palm out and stops me. The sun glints off his round glasses.

He had no eyes.

Dani's words sift through my mind, but I push them away. I don't need dead things on top of whatever the hell is going on with Agatha.

"It's good to see you in church again, Mila," he says.

I bite my tongue because I want to say something hateful. But I don't. I only try to steer Agatha away from a reaching group of older women intent on making sure she is okay. Instead, I force a tight-lipped smile and move down the steps toward the parking lot.

The reverend sneaks his meaty fingers around the bare flesh of my arm. For a moment, no words pass between us. He just stands there, staring at me, as if the rest of his congregation has vanished into thin air. And then his lips part.

"I heard you were down at the bog party a few nights back," he says, his voice low, only for me to hear.

Says the man feeding his congregation bog water. "I don't think that's really any of your business, Reverend." My hands remain firmly on Agatha's shoulders.

The reverend's smile widens. "I believe the condition of all my parishioners' souls is my business, wouldn't you agree?"

I try to move away again, but his greedy hands hold me in a sort of gravity. His eyes pour into mine, the sun's reflection nearly blinding me. I blink. A moment passes, two, then Mom calls my name. The reverend's smile peels wider, and he blinks. A cloud moves in front of the sun, and I see his eyes for what they are—nothing but muddy puddles set above sallow, jagged cheeks.

"Have a good rest of your day, Reverend." I bite back the anger threatening to overtake me and guide Agatha down the steps.

"You have a good day too, Mila. Hope to see you at the Sunday School picnic." He winks, and a familiar jag of ugly, dark anger cuts through my chest.

I'm about to say, "Over my dead body," when Mom pipes up next to me.

"Already signed these two up to volunteer for setup."

He doesn't take his eyes off me. Just nods. "Good, good. Have a great day, Thomas girls."

I fight the urge to flip him the bird and just say nothing until I get Agatha into the car beside Mom, who one hundred percent should *not* be driving, judging from the bitter, sharp smell boiling off her in waves. I slam the passenger-seat door and move to get into the back, when it hits me.

Heat sears me from temple to temple, skewering me to the spot. I have to shield my eyes from the beating sun.

This is not the same as the voices. Different even from the sensation of the bog beneath my feet, which I can feel even now, running like poison beneath the town. This is more like a warning, like sirens blazing inside my skull. A kind of energy ripping up from the bog to consume me.

The drone of black flies floods my ears, but I see none. I squeeze my eyes shut tight, trying to ward off the sound and the heat blazing through my skull. My fingers fumble with the door handle, and I slump into the back seat, barely able to buckle myself in before Mom peels from the church parking lot.

If she notices the agony I'm in, she doesn't say anything. Agatha ignores me too, swaying gently from side to side in the front seat and humming a song I don't recognize. It isn't until we're pulling into the drive that the feeling retreats from my head. I blink bleary eyes, noticing the orange Honda parked beneath the cedars on the far side of the house.

Camille.

She's leaning against the porch railing, legs crossed in front of her. I get out of the car immediately, helping Agatha as I go. When she does finally notice Camille, a flicker of recognition crosses her face.

"Agatha!" Camille blasts from the porch and collides into my sister, her slender arms wrapping around Agatha's neck.

Agatha remains unmoving for a moment, like the shock of it all rings hard against her body. But then her arms slowly wrap around Camille's waist. Hope thrills through me. Maybe whatever it is possessing my sister's body will not be strong enough to stand against the love pouring between them.

But when Camille pulls back, the hope inside me gutters. Agatha's eyes still bead black, and when I look at the car, my gaze snags on the puddle of brown water and algae pooling on the front seat. Her wet boots have been discarded in the grass.

I've been mopping up everywhere Agatha walks. Even this morning, when I woke up, Agatha was sitting up in Jed's bed again, staring straight ahead at the wall. Her sheets and blankets were soaked and stained with muddy water. It makes no sense, and if Mom has noticed it, she hasn't said anything.

Camille, who looks like she's about to cry, brushes a damp thatch of hair from Agatha's face.

"Aggy?" Her voice is small and soft. "It's me. It's Camille."

Agatha doesn't respond. Her neck cracks sideways, and she smiles. Camille takes a step back, eyes frantic.

"What's—what's wrong with her?" she asks.

Mom bumbles from the driver's-side door and makes for the porch. "She's fine. Mila said she was fine."

She disappears into the cabin before I share a concerned look with Camille.

I rush to grab Agatha by the shoulders. "Let's just get her inside for now."

When we reach the front porch, my sister stops, her skin and bones immovable. She turns to the tree line, and the smile stretches to the sides of her face until I'm worried her lips will snap.

"He is coming," she says, her voice vibrating through the air. "Can't you feel it?"

I ignore her—or at least, I try to. Camille's gaze darts between us and the cedars, sweat beetling on her skin.

"What is she talking about?"

I have my suspicions—*I'm a monster, Mila.*

We pull Agatha toward the house. She remains unshakable, like her feet have rooted to the porch. The skirt of her dress sways. She just keeps repeating the same thing over and over.

"He is coming, he is coming, he is coming." It's barely a whisper, like wings on wind.

"Agatha, we need to get you inside," I say.

But she is too strong. She pulls away from me and walks down the steps toward the tree line.

I rush forward, Camille on my heels, and reach for Agatha's hand. Her fingers slip through mine, leaving a wet residue on my skin. I stumble over my own feet when I try to get in front of her. She moves as if stuck in a trance, each step fluid and slow, her eyes trained on the trees in front of us. Her lips continue mumbling the same three words.

I look around for Mom, but she's stumbling out onto the porch with a bottle in her hand. Who knows if she's clumsy from the alcohol or the bog water communion.

"Camille," I call. The wind picks up around us. "You need to help me get her back into the house."

Camille's eyes are filled with panic. "Who is he, Mila? Who is she talking about?"

"Jed, okay?" Rage courses through my veins. And fear.

Camille's mouth drops open, and she blinks.

There. I've said it. Said what I've been terrified of for the last twenty-four hours.

That *thing* in the bog is my brother. He knew what he was becoming, so he left. And he is the one who murdered Owen, Dillon, and God knows who else.

I'm a curse, Mila. There's something stuck inside me. Something I can't just pull out. And I'm scared one day it's gonna hurt somebody.

"That's impossible," Camille says, the wind whipping at her curls.

I grab Agatha's arm, her skin slippery and cold. "There's a whole lot of impossible shit going on, but right now, we need to get my sister into the house before she goes back to the fucking bog!"

Camille blinks again, processing. And then she grabs Agatha's other arm.

We're pulling my sister away from the swamp calling out to her with everything it has. She stretches forward, like smoke after an extinguished candle flame. Camille is sobbing, her voice echoing through my ears. My chest cracks with helplessness. Because who is left to help anymore? Who is left to save us?

Maybe I am all that is left.

And maybe I need to save myself.

I look back toward the yard. My truck is angled out against the pines. The keys are in it, scattered on the dash where I left them. But if I touch them, if I force them into the ignition with my shaking, wet fingers and peel out of the drive, I will leave and never look back.

But I could save myself.

Camille's cries turn to words, my sister's name spilling from her mouth over and over. Saliva drips down her chin. The wind kicks up, whipping hair across my eyes. Above us, the sky darkens, and rain spills from the clouds. The cold nearly takes my breath away.

Agatha's dress is plastered to her skin, writhing down her body in snowy sheaths. She moves deeper into the forest, pine needles sticking to the soles of her feet. Her hand brushes a knot in the side of a cedar tree, and my stomach jolts. The memories replay like old movie film.

Agatha, her pale hair around her face like a halo, baby-fat cheeks full of life. Agatha, who only ever loved. Agatha, curled up beside me, whispering prayers to the spirits in the trees to keep us safe from the bog monsters.

Except now, she *is* one of those bog monsters—or at least, she's fighting one. And there are no spirits in the trees. Not really. They're in the water, and I'm the only one who can hear them. Who can maybe even talk back, instruct, ask for help.

The rain lashes against my face, bitter and cold, drips down my spine, my throat, the arch of my brows. I cannot let her do this alone. Fight the thing with teeth and claws all by herself.

She is my *sister*.

The bog can *feel* them coming. Their feet brush its soil. It reaches out to its infantry, to the two women who march toward its waters. One hungry for revenge because the bog made her so. The other for justice, though she doesn't know it yet. Doesn't have all the pieces.

The bog can sense the monster too. It creeps alongside the western front—bloody claws, searching eyes, and a chest empty and devoid of a soul. For that was how the curse was formed, how it was made. To make those men ravenous for the souls they lacked. To grow closer to gods with each one taken.

Forever.

It started with the first girl, the one they called Ruby, who sat on the banks of the bog and told the water stories. And when the tales came back to her—when the voices in the depths spoke their magic into her ears—she knew she had found a special place. Ruby wanted to share the secret of the magic she had found there in the depthless waters.

So, she told the one who made her feel special.

The boy who grew lavender and rosemary in his mother's garden and braided crowns for Ruby to wear in her blood-red hair. The boy whose father beat him and then spoke the Good Word to anyone who would listen. The boy who, when Ruby showed him the magic swimming in the bog, decided to take it for himself. Decided to build a town around it and siphon away the bog's life, leaving only the dregs behind to leech into the very town he'd built. He became obsessed, stealing the very thing the girl treasured, the thing she had peeled her heart back to show him. The boy stole it and fell in love with its power.

So, the girl cursed him.

She took the bog into her hands and wove a spell making the boy who had broken her heart into a monster, one who would live ever soulless. Forever intent on taking the life from things, stealing the spirit to leave behind a poisoned shell. And she made the bog sick. Ravenous. An acid-washed thing licking away flesh and revealing bone quicker than it should.

She didn't know her curse would be felt by generations. That her draw to the boy with lavender-stained palms would plague her daughters and granddaughters, tying them together in an inescapable knot.

But the bog knew. And the bog wept.

But now the bog rejoices.

It cannot let them go. Not now, when they are all so close.

15

THE CHILDREN OF THE BOG

When we break through the trees, the smell hits me first—upturned earth and rotting meat. The same smell that permeated the church. I gag on my own breath, my fingers raking down my arms, trying to center myself. Agatha's feet squelch in the mud, and she presses forward to the shoreline. The water laps greedily against her skin.

Camille shakes beside me and watches my sister enter the bog.

"What's wrong with her?" Camille's eyes are panic-stricken, and there's nothing I can do about it.

She is only ever love, Camille Chartier. The girl who lost her sister to the bog and is now about to forfeit the one her heart beats for to the murky water. I take Camille's hand in mine. Squeeze it gently.

"I don't know how, but it's going to be okay."

But I can't be more wrong. Nothing here is okay, not in this place.

Agatha moves deeper into the marsh, her body held in a kind of trance. Her feet stick to the paths, leaping lithely from the clumps of cattails shivering under our weight. I follow, keeping Camille close at hand. She will not meet her sister's fate.

Dani.

The words swirl out of the water and punch me in the gut. Wind rushes from my lungs, spreading vapor into the air.

He had no eyes.

No eyes. Only pools of white light. I can't breathe, quaking on the weak turf. The roots beneath me tremble in the water. No eyes. The thing that killed Dani. The thing that killed Dillon...

And then more words. Jed's words.

I'm a curse, Mila.

The fear turns sour in my stomach, lurching up my throat and spreading across my tongue. I swallow it and fight against the thoughts threatening to undo me. To say it out loud is one thing, but to believe it deep down in my bones. Stare out at the putrid water. There's no denying it anymore. I've spoken the words to Camille. The truth. The necklace once clenched in Owen's fist is now tucked beneath my pillow. The lopsided smile of the creature before Agatha attacked. My knees buckle beneath me, and the wet ground seeps in through my dress.

That thing, the pale and fleshy monster with no eyes. The worm.

It's Jed.

Something shatters within me. Deeper than flesh and bone. And when I open my eyes to the rain pelting down, darkness rushes in. I can't describe it; I can only taste it, and it tastes of soil. Of ancient water and weeds that have grown for centuries. It licks along my teeth and squirms down my throat, taking root in my stomach. And that's when the pain breaks in fissures along my skull, so fast and hot I might crack open like an egg and bleed out into the sand on the shoreline.

A hundred thousand voices come rushing in. All dead, all calling one name.

One that isn't mine.

Ruby, Ruby, Ruby.

My mouth snicks open, wanting to let out a scream, but all it emits is a rush of hot air. A breath that doesn't even feel like my own. Camille is beside me, her fingers on my shoulders, on my jaw, pressing me to look at her.

"Mila." Her eyes are filled with horror. She looks between me and my sister swaying in the shallows. She is afraid. Confused. "What is going on?"

My gaze snags on Agatha, knee-deep in the water. She moves gently back and forth, the hem of her dress billowing out around her. I half expect to see a sword in her hand—Lady of the Lake. Lady of the Bog.

But she is so much more than that, and when she turns around to face us, when my eyes meet the black pools that have taken up residence in my sister's face, I know *it* is so much more than that.

She *is* the bog.

And yet, so am I.

"Give her back to me!" I scream to the water.

It licks through my veins like someone has shot me up with saline. Angry, coursing through me like a river after the spring melt. Voices swell inside me, all calling me by my grandmother's name. I get to my feet, cattails shaking, and walk the path until I reach my sister, leaving Camille standing alone on the shore.

Agatha is sinking deeper into the water. Her dress like clouds about her body. Her eyes closed, fingers outstretched.

"Can you feel him, Mila?" she asks, voice so soft I can barely hear it, not when a hundred thousand dead things are screaming in my ears.

But yes, I feel him. Or *it*. The thing creeping through the shallows. The monster without eyes.

Jed.

I'm a curse, Mila.

Saliva collects at the base of my throat. Thick and wet. He must have known what he was turning into and left to protect us. My stomach swishes.

"We're going to kill him." Agatha's words are pointed and sharp, and for a moment, the bog's hold on me breaks.

I turn and look at my sister. Gray-green algae has started sprouting at her hairline. Bog mud gathers in the hollow of her throat, net-like webs connecting her fingers.

"We can't kill him," I say. "He's our brother."

An explosion of water breaks behind us.

I spin, skin hot with the voices screaming in my mind.

A shape bursts from the bog, dripping in sludge and smelling of dead things. And when a shadow passes over the sun trying to bleed through the rain, I think it is merely a cloud. But it isn't. It drones, vibrating the very roots of my jaw.

Thousands of wind-whisper wings buzz down with the drops, alighting on cattail and rock, on sandbar and broken tree. They fill the air, their noise juddering through my ears. I spot Camille on a clump of cattails not far from the bank. She crouches among the weeds, eyes frantically watching the pale figure lumbering through the water.

It spots her, its empty eyes roving over her. Its featureless face begins to peel apart formless lips and spread its teeth toward her viscera.

But it isn't the monster that scares me. It's the way the water has already started to soak up the spit of land Camille stands on.

She's going to drown.

Without thinking, I leap across, legs flailing beneath me. The monster whips around, lips sewn back together in a gory grin. But I don't have time to be afraid. Flies take to the wind, and the rain dances on the surface of the swamp, swarming up around the creature's eyes. It bats at them. A shriek tears from the rip in its face.

"Camille!" I shout above the noise. "You need to move!"

She's a doe caught on the train tracks. Her legs buckle when she goes to jump, and the earth gives out beneath her. I lunge, trying to stick to the path Grandma Ruby taught me, trying to save everyone and everything. Whatever kind of magic is swimming through the bog, I need it now. My hair catches in my mouth when I turn toward Agatha.

"We need to help Camille!" I scream over the worm's roars.

My stomach rushes up into my throat. Fear is palpable in the air around me. It's so close now, my nose fills up with the scent of rotting flesh and decaying weeds.

But Agatha doesn't move. She just keeps sinking into the water. It teases her neck, and her hair blossoms with cattails.

A glimmer of movement alerts me to the southern tip of the bog. Roe is breaking through the trees at full speed, and he's not alone. Simon is with him, eyes wild when he takes in the creature flailing in the water.

What are they doing here?

Camille screams, and the wind is whipping. It doesn't matter what they're doing here. None of us are safe.

"Camille! Help Camille!" I shout, pointing to where she struggles.

The marsh is sucking at her waist, tangling her legs in roots. They are closer to her than I am. The flies fill the air all around us, turning my brain to oatmeal.

Look around, they say. *Look around.*

My foot plunges through a clump of earth, and the water slurps at my ankle. It is cold, like thawing ground. Something twists around my skin, and when I look down, the bog swims with green light—pulsing, dancing, swirling all around me. A scream ignites from my lips, fear hot in my belly.

Roe shouts for Camille. Simon gasps in the shallows, watching the monster in the bog.

"Agatha!" My throat is raw from calling her name, but when I turn to look at her, she's gone.

No, no, no.

Give her back. *Please.*

I wrench my foot from the dead thing's grasp. Its voice brushes the nape of my neck, but I push it out and build my walls. The flies dive around me, pinging off my skin like fleshy, buzzing bullets.

Look around, look around, they drone.

The bog is a torrent of movement.

Roe crouches across the water from Camille, a hand outstretched. The worm bears down on us all. Tears pour along Roe's face, and something like relief floods against the terror in my chest when he hugs Camille to him. I search the bog for my sister, but my gaze snags on something else.

Back near the old cabin, a flicker of movement between the reeds.

My skin crawls. Now is not the time for town lore and tricks. But I swear, there is something there, hiding amid downed, dead pines and murky waters. I squint my eyes, intent on finding whatever it is.

Another flicker of movement, blue and off-white.

A scream rips from the bog, sending my heart teetering toward a quick death. I spin, catching my foot in the water, and scramble back onto my portion of peaty earth. Camille and Roe drip wet on the shoreline, blood soaking down the white T-shirt plastered to his chest. Simon stands behind them, his face swimming yellow and sick. I almost feel sorry for him.

But the scream is not coming from them.

In the middle of the bog, churning like a hurricane, stands the monster. It rears its ugly, bald head, nothing more than a pallid swirling mass, long arms like whips. Its very flesh seems to be made from bloat and death. Only its eyes beat with brightness, scanning the bog like the beacon of a lighthouse. My stomach swills with nausea.

It's staring at something hovering above the surface of the water, and I almost choke on my cry when I realize what that something is.

Agatha floats a foot above the bog, her chest protruding forward, arms arched toward the clouds. Flies buzz, swarming like wisps of smoke against the white of her dress. The scream rips from her mouth. It twists and curves around the monster like a net, and still, she keeps crying. It pierces my ears like nails on a chalkboard. Breaks across my skin, threatening to undo me. I try to race forward, but a hand grasps my arm.

When I look back, Roe stands behind me. Blood smears his cheek. Whose, I don't know. But the metallic smell of it chokes my throat.

"It's going to kill her." My whole body is numb, frozen with this stupid fear, and there's nothing I can do.

My sister hovers there in the air. Her cry grows wider, louder, flinging its net over the bog. The water ripples with it, silencing the rain and the buzzing flies. The monster buckles at its wiry knees. Joints in its wrists snap when it splashes into the bog.

And then Agatha begins to speak. It isn't her voice, but the collected words of the damned dead.

"We are the children of the bog. We are those who have been slain by your hand and the blood-slicked hands that have come before you. Your time is almost at an end."

The sound reverberates through the trees around us, making the water quiver and the bones in my face grind. The monster sinks deeper into water, lips sealing in a grim line. Roe's fingers tighten on my skin, drawing me back away from my sister.

"Let go of me!" I shout, scrambling forward. The reeds rip at my feet.

The worm slips below the surface of the water, but something tells me the creature is not gone. Not for good. Agatha's body drops to the bog with a splash, and I leap forward, tearing from Roe's grasp. The bog sucks at my heels, but I don't care. All I want to do is get to my sister. Tears pour heavy down the swell of my cheeks. The clouds break above us, and the sun slips out. The flies angle toward the sky, their message turning to vague echoes on the wind.

My fingers grasp Agatha's shoulders. The water bubbles up around her face and kisses my knees. Her skin is winter white, and the algae and cattails have disappeared. I brush a curl of yellow hair from her cheek and pull her body up onto the clump of land barely keeping me afloat. She looks like a porcelain doll in the thin light streaming from the clouds. I press a palm against her face. She's ice-cold.

"Agatha." Her name is thick on my tongue. "Agatha, please don't be dead."

Her body is heavy and limp in my arms, waterlogged by the marsh. I pull her closer, an inverted, unholy replica of the Pietà. Mary cradling the dead body of Jesus to her breast. All I want is for Agatha to open her eyes and nestle in against me. But she is cold, so very cold.

A cry rips from my throat, primeval and from somewhere so deep I don't recognize it. It crashes out across the landscape, splintering through the trees. Tears spill hot down my cheeks and drip against my sister's skin. I cannot do this without her.

Camille cries from the shore and collapses in the sand with no one to comfort her. Roe is still where I left him, kneeling on the peat. The pain on his face matches the one splintering through me. Simon is gone. Where, I don't care. I don't want him here anyway. My fingers peel the wet hair from Agatha's face and brush the moisture from her pale brow.

"Aggy." My voice croaks. "Aggy, I need you to be alive."

Her face stays perfectly still, eyes closed, lips curved up as though she is smiling. Whatever semblance of a heart I have left shatters inside my chest. I curl around her, rocking back and forth. The sobs break from my lips.

"Mila?" The voice beneath me is so soft, I barely believe it's true.

I pull back from my sister. Her eyes flutter open, returned to their familiar stone gray. My chest heaves, and I hold her tight, crying. This time from the sheer relief overcoming my body. Agatha moves against me and struggles to sit up, her feet still dangling in the water.

"Where is he?" she asks, her eyes scanning the bog.

"I—I don't know." I'm half terrified to tell her I think he's dead. All I can think about is Jed and how he used to tell me he was cursed. How there was something inside him he was afraid of getting out. Of hurting someone. "He's not dead, is he?"

More relief fills my bones when she shakes her head. Jed isn't dead. Not yet.

"No, it's not that easy. But it's out of me. The bog. For now. It let me go now that we're all together."

I draw in a sharp breath, not yet ready to believe. Not sure *what* to believe. "And you...are you okay? Are you *you* again?"

She laughs, water sputtering from her mouth. "Yeah, I'm me. The scream...I think it woke me up. Pulled the two sides of me apart."

The water surges around us, and my palms tingle. "What happened?"

Her eyes go blank for a moment, and she stares up at the clouds. "I don't remember much. Just that in one second, I was having fun at the party, and the next, I was so angry I could kill something." She lifts a hand and flips it over. "It's still there, the anger, just...separate. Like I can tap into it when I need to, but I can also just be...me."

I swallow. None of it makes sense. The monster, the communion water, the way the bog's anger still swims in my sister's veins. But she's here and she's alive, and she sounds like herself. I am willing to let that be enough.

Water splashes up behind us. Camille is pushing me away, and I let her. She wraps Agatha to her chest and cries into her mussed, blond hair.

"Oh my God, oh my God, Aggy. I thought you were dead." She sobs, cradling my sister. "Don't you ever pull that shit again, do you hear me? Never again."

A smile lights on Agatha's face, and she lifts a hand to wipe moisture from Camille's cheek. "I just like keeping you on your toes."

"Shut up," Camille says breathlessly, then smothers Agatha's lips with her own.

I turn away to let them have their moment. Roe crosses toward me through the water. Alone.

"Where's Simon?"

Roe's brow wrinkles, and he looks behind him. "I don't know."

I want to ask him a million questions. Why the fuck is your dad feeding the town bog water? Why did you show up here with your asshole brother? But Agatha's voice fills the space between us instead.

"Did you ask her for the story?"

I blink down at her. "Mom? Mom's useless."

Agatha pulls away from Camille. She scrambles up on her knees and clamps her hands around my shoulders, staring me so dead in the eye that it shakes me to my core.

"Not Mom, Mila."

A flicker of movement in the reeds again captures my attention, and my eyes drift over her shoulder. She shakes me.

"Mila, look at me!"

The force of her voice steals me back, and when I look at her face, I notice the gravity of whatever the hell is going on.

"Then who? Who knows the story? What story are you even talking about?"

Agatha's fingers sink into my shoulders. "The story about how that thing came to exist. About how the bog has been trying to fight it off for ages, and it's finally found us. The bog children. I told you to ask her the story."

Frustration curls on my tongue. "Who?"

"Grandma Ruby."

16

THE CONFESSIONAL

The next morning, Agatha and I meet Camille at the church. The field has already been set up with wooden tables and chairs, some boasting white tablecloths held down by empty glass vases. A dozen women wearing ill-fitting skirts and slacks bark orders at each other, smiling in one moment, sneering behind one another's backs in the other. I fold my arms across my chest, surveying the field of battle.

"Remind me why we're here again?" I ask, my mind still trained on the monster in the bog.

"Because," Agatha begins, her voice as sweet and good as I remember it. "If anyone knows any secrets in this town and they're guaranteed to gossip about it, it's church ladies. Plus"—she slams a white sheet of paper into my chest—"Mom signed us up. Remember?"

I grab the paper from her, thankful she has stopped leaking bog water and is back to her normal self.

"Volunteers needed to help set up for the annual Blueberry Festival and Church Picnic. Lunch will be provided." My stomach rumbles. "What time is it?"

Camille pulls the phone from her pocket. "Nine-thirty a.m."

I yawn and stretch my arms behind my back. "Holy fuck, I just want to go back to bed. You'd think after almost being eaten by a human worm monster two nights this week, we'd have earned some sleep-in time."

Agatha breaks from our line and turns around to face me. Something in her eyes still swims with the black of the bog. "Look, if we're going to figure out who the hell—or *what* the hell—that thing is down there, then we're going to need to listen. We have a few hours to snoop around and see if—I don't know—anyone's husband didn't come home after church yesterday. Or their son came home with his eardrums blown out or whatever. There's got to be something. Just"—she gives me a gentle shove and slings one arm around Camille's shoulder—"play nice."

I fight the urge to tell her I already know who it is—it's Jed—but my phone buzzes. My eyes scan the screen, where a text from Denise waits.

HOW'S THE FAMILY SITUATION?

Something warm and sticky clogs my throat. God, what am I supposed to type? Oh great, just rescued my sister from a bog monster that might be my missing brother. No big deal. Instead, I just type out a jumble of words and shove my phone back in my pocket.

STILL GONNA NEED A FEW MORE
DAYS. LOTS OF SHIT.

Lots of shit is right. Because I find myself standing in front of a table where a woman sits, legs crossed in tan slacks, a golf sweater tied around her bony shoulders. Phyllis Denton, Olive's mother, smiles up at us when we approach. Phyllis is what I would describe as an oatmeal person: beige, boring clothes; beige, boring makeup; and a beige, boring personality. She has taught Sunday school for as long as I can remember, and two years ago, Agatha texted me to say there was a rumor going around that she was sleeping with the reverend.

Honestly, I wouldn't be surprised. The reverend seems to take pleasure in fucking with everyone's lives.

I wonder if Mrs. Denton drank the bog water on Sunday. And how long they've all been drinking it.

"We're checking in to volunteer for the morning," Camille says in a cheerful voice.

I want to know who she's paying for that kind of energy. Because, hell, I want some too. I flick a speck of dirt from beneath one fingernail.

Mrs. Denton's smile pulls at her already-too-tight skin. "Oh, Agatha, we were so worried about you. And with the rest of your life ahead of you.

College and all that." She makes a pointed look in my direction. At least one of us Thomas kids isn't a complete failure. "Well, I just prayed every day that the Lord would bring you home to us."

My stomach sours. "The fuck you did," I whisper beneath my breath.

Her eyes snap to me. "What was that, Mila?"

"Uhm, nothing."

"Of course," she says, her smile sweet and toxic. She looks down at the clipboard she's holding. "I think we've decided to have Agatha and Camille help Susan over there with setting up the stage." She points to where a short white woman stands on a wooden platform, fixing garlands of faux greenery to poles. "However—" she stops and looks between the two of them.

My neck and arms prickle, ready for her to say something uncalled for and probably super homophobic.

"Maybe we shouldn't put the two of you together now that you're— you're—"

"Dating?" Agatha interjects, eyes sparking.

The skin on Mrs. Denton's neck bobs with a tight swallow. "I just, well, I can't say that I agree—"

"Oh, shove it, Phyllis," I snap. "Welcome to the real world. Girls kiss now, and they don't give a fuck about what your judgy little opinion is."

Beside me, Camille stifles a laugh with a fist.

"Mila." Mrs. Denton gives a syrupy smile. "Pleasure to have you back in town. You'll be helping Simon rake the leaves away from the church and bag them up in trash bags."

Right then and there, I want to slap that look off her vanilla face and make her eat it. But instead, I match her sticky smile and reach for a pair of oversized gardening gloves lying on the table.

"Great, that's *exactly* how I was planning on spending my morning, Mrs. Denton."

Agatha jabs me sharp in the ribs. "What she means to say is, she can't wait to shovel leaves with Simon, Mrs. Denton."

I glare through my smile at my sister. "Yes, of course. That's what I meant." I thread the words through my teeth. Shovel leaves *down his throat*.

Mrs. Denton, who is looking back at her clipboard, completely ignoring all of us, mutters something like, "Yes, yes, have fun," before waving us off with a perfectly manicured claw.

Agatha grabs my elbow when we turn away.

"Just listen, okay?" she spits in my ear. "He was there. Maybe ask Simon what he knows. And where the hell he disappeared off to."

I had almost forgotten Simon showed up with Roe yesterday. My stomach turns somersaults when I look over to the shaded side of the church and see him raking up damp leaves.

"He didn't stick around very long," I reply.

"He stuck around long enough to watch Agatha float up into the air and scream at a bog monster until its head nearly exploded," Camille interjects.

Fair point.

I continue to glare down Simon while he shovels the leaves into a black trash bag. "My head is going to explode if I have to spend the morning with Simon motherfucking Byron."

Agatha rolls her eyes and slips her arm through Camille's, leading her away toward the stage. "Just, if you're going to kill him, try and do it off church property, okay?"

I scrunch my nose up and flip her my middle finger. The absolute last thing I want to do is help Simon rake up dead leaves. The trees across the road creak with wind, bringing a scent of bog water and damp grass with them.

I need to be out *there*.

Looking for whatever killed Owen Shelby. Even if that means I'll find Jed with blood on his hands. The need to locate my brother and keep him safe from the monster bubbles inside me like hot tar.

That might mean keeping him safe from himself.

I'm a curse, Mila.

What will I do if I find him twisted and blanched white, his mouth full of teeth? What will it be like to stare into the face of a monster and know the eyes are Jed's? Will I kill him? Sink my hands into his soft tissue and squeeze until he remembers his humanity? But then it might be too late, and the gaping wound in my chest that has bled for the last three years might finally be my undoing.

I close my eyes for a moment. Even if it means ending the brother I lost so many years ago. The voices of the dead still ramble about in my mind.

Ruby, Ruby, Ruby.

Agatha said our grandmother knew the story. But how am I supposed to ask her? Her body is nothing more than a skeleton rotting in the cemetery behind the chapel. I sigh and turn back to face the shaded trench alongside the front of the church. The paint is peeling, the white chipping off and revealing a sandy brown. Black mold breaks out in splotches beneath the eaves, and thelia moss creeps along the wooden siding. I look down at the garden gloves in my hand.

Well, I guess if anyone knows anything about the seedy underbelly of this town, it's the guy who thrives off it. He's heading into his third year of seminary school in the fall and has probably already taken the "How to Suck the Life Out of People and Call It Ministry 101" class. I slap the gloves on and plow across the field toward the church.

"Guess I'm supposed to help you with the dirty work," I say, coming up behind him.

The shadow of the church sends a chill across my skin. I untie the green flannel from my waist and sling it over my shoulders. Simon looks up at me from where he's crouched in the grass, raking up more dead, wet leaves with his hands. He mutters something about just his fucking luck and stands up.

"The extra rakes are over there." He points to a small woodshed leaning up against the wall of the church. "You can start raking the leaves up from that point, and we'll meet in the middle."

I am tempted to say something like, "You'd like that, wouldn't you," but I don't. Instead, I keep my mouth shut and do as I'm told. Better not to stir up the proverbial waters.

We work for a better part of the morning, neither speaking while we remove wet leaves from the sopping ground and deposit them into the garbage. I lift a handful of sweating foliage to the open mouth of a black bag. My gloved finger skims the dark plastic, and suddenly, I'm back, staring down the gaping maw of a body bag. Owen Shelby's single brown eye roves up at me through his half-decayed skull. I fall back, the wind knocked out of me. The shock of memory rushes from my lungs. Dillon's voice plays out in my mind.

He's got Owen's shirt, like, clenched in his fist...screaming...I'll kill you.

My skin flushes hot, even in the shade streaming off the church.

"You good, frog-face? See a spider or something?"

Simon towers over me, his big, greedy hand outstretched, eyes leering down. I want to scream, but I push his hand away and scramble up on my own.

"Did you kill Owen?"

The question is loose on my tongue, and I want to take it back just as quickly as I say it. Smooth move, laying it all out there in the open.

Simon's face goes blank, eyes blinking. He withdraws his hand.

"Oh, you've got to be kidding me." He shovels sweaty hair from his face. "No, I did not kill Owen, all right?" He runs a palm over his eyes. "What makes you think he's dead anyway?"

Simon stares daggers at me, and I almost swear tears pool in his eyes. He throws the rake down on the ground beside me, hard, and I flinch.

Stupid, stupid, stupid. I should never have asked.

"Honestly, fuck you," he says.

Guilt grinds in my stomach, and I am half tempted to apologize, but his back is already turned to me. I put my head down and rake at the dead plant matter collecting like hair in a shower drain. Plants that shouldn't even be here. Sedge grass and cattails grow in the bog, not at the foothills of Sinner's Chapel. My brain hurts from trying to make sense of it all.

I look across the field to where Agatha and Camille are stringing lights up on the stage. They're laughing—a brush of skin there, a moment-long glance there.

I want that.

The safety that comes from knowing someone else has your back. That someone will hold you up, no matter what life throws at you. I lean forward onto my knees and hang my head toward the grass. My phone buzzes. I pull it from my pocket, and the screen lights up.

It's Roe.

HEARD YOU'RE AT THE CHURCH.
EVERYTHING GOING ALRIGHT? I CAN
COME OVER IF YOU NEED.

My heart flutters for a moment. Agatha—she must have told him. The last place he needs to be is here, on the ground where his father preaches the Good Word and, after, used to go home and beat his son.

I unlock my phone.

> YEAH. MIGHT HAVE JUST ACCUSED
> YOUR BROTHER OF MURDER.
> NO BIG DEAL.

I pick at my lip, awaiting a response.

> OF OLIVE'S SELF-ESTEEM, MAYBE.
> ARE YOU SURE YOU DON'T NEED ME
> TO COME OVER?

I look around the field. Everything seems to be under control. Mrs. Denton is currently sipping lemonade from a plastic cup and peering over her cat-eye sunglasses at where one of the more handsome deacons is helping Olive plant petunias in the raised beds at the front of the church. Good Lord.

> NO, EVERYTHING IS NORMAL. MRS.
> DENTON SEEMS TO STILL FORGET
> SHE IS MARRIED.

> YEAH, I KNOW. I CAN SEE HER. I'M
> ALREADY HERE, TURN AROUND.

I almost drop my phone when I spin in the grass. Roe is coming up the hill on the far side of the field.

Absolutely not. This is the last place he should be.

I hurry to meet him. He grins when I reach him, and the sunlight reflects in his eyes. Holy hell, I suddenly want to kiss him.

"I've always wanted you to run across a field and meet me in the middle," he teases.

Heat spreads in my belly, so I punch him in the arm.

"Mature response," he quips.

"Look, we were almost mauled to death by a worm creature with headlights for eyes the last two nights. The last thing on your mind should be me. Plus, you still haven't forgiven me for last summer, right?"

I ask it as a joke, my classic avoidance tactic, and thread my arm through his. He breaks away from me and turns to stare directly into my eyes.

"Are you kidding me? Mila..." Roe takes my hands in his. The calluses are rough and oddly familiar. "Forget last summer. I mean, even after all that, you're always on my mind. Especially since everything that's been happening. I don't...I don't want to—"

"Your dad is feeding people bog water." Another avoidance.

Roe blinks.

I take a deep breath. "During communion, at church, your dad has switched out the grape juice for bog water."

Roe sighs and shovels a hand through his hair. "I know."

"You *know*? Why is he doing it? Is that why Simon was with you the other night? Why you told me not to drink it? You're trying to figure it out?"

He nods, and his face puckers like he has bitten into a sour grape.

"And?"

"Look, I'm still trying to piece everything together, but—"

"Oh, Roe!" Mrs. Denton's voice cuts through the field.

She waves us over and leans across the table when we reach her. I want to press Roe, ask him what he means, brush my skin against his again, if only for a moment. If only to push him away again because I get too scared. But Mrs. Denton is already doling out battle strategies.

"Roe, dear, it's so lovely to see you back at church."

I wince. *Well, that's the absolute last thing he needs to be hearing right now.*

Roe smiles politely. "It's nice to see you too, Mrs. Denton. What can I help with?"

She moves to pat him on the cheek, but he dodges, swatting at a fly that has conveniently landed on his shoulder.

I stiffen. Black flies. Again.

"Well, if you wouldn't mind, I need a few more tables and chairs brought up from the basement. I'm sure you remember where they are." She turns her face to me. "Mila, can you help?"

I nod.

"Good," she says, smiling that syrupy smile. "Seems as though you've already scared one brother off. Try not to frighten the other."

My lips peel apart, but Roe grabs my hand.

"Pretty sure there's no chance of that happening, Mrs. Denton. We'll be right back."

He tugs me forward, but not before I shoot a look back at Mrs. Denton that could melt the northern ice caps.

The inside of the church smells like dust, musty coats, and an underlying scent of something wet. A massive air conditioner rumbles over the top of the stairs, chilling the whole place like the interior of a tomb. Roe tugs me toward the basement steps, but I stop him.

"What is it?" he asks.

I lift a finger to my lips and nod toward the steps leading into the sanctuary. "I hear voices."

He looks at me, doubtful. "So what? Dad's probably up there with someone. Let's just get the stuff for Mrs. Denton and get back outside." He shivers. "This place makes my skin crawl."

The voices spill out from underneath the wooden doors at the top of the staircase. I can't make out what they're saying, but judging from the hushed tones, I have a feeling this is going to be the exact kind of information Agatha dragged us here for in the first place.

I pull Roe up the carpeted steps. "Just a few seconds, okay? Let's just hear what they're talking about."

His shoulders sag, and he rolls his eyes, but he doesn't take his hand from mine. We creak up the stairs, feet soft on the carpet. I gently place one hand against the door, whisper a silent prayer it won't make any noise, and slowly press it open.

The sanctuary is empty. Just rows of pews, a few lined with green velvet. Like it was on Sunday, but without the entire congregation sucking down bog water. There's a door opposite leading down into the kitchen and one to our right that leads to the reverend's office. But my eyes train on the dark polished wood of the confessional box.

It looms from the floor on the far side of the sanctuary. Green velvet curtains are drawn across both doors, and one set of shoes occupy each side of the screened wall. Black, polished loafers—the reverend, no doubt. And mud-caked leather work boots.

Simon.

I turn to face Roe, one finger pressed hard against my lips. My heart thumps in my chest, and I widen my eyes.

Don't say a word.

Roe's hand sweats in mine, but he nods and follows behind. We slowly weave our way through the back pews. Simon's voice slips out hushed and hurried. I motion to one of the benches and bend my knees, softly rolling under the seat. Roe follows suit. I hold my breath and listen to the voices spilling from the confessional.

"He's still out there, Dad. You and I both know it." It's Simon, fear thick in his voice.

"And so what if he is? He can't hurt us. You just need to keep your head down and do the good work." The reverend's words come out short and stunted, like a sawn-off limb.

I've never heard him talk this way to Simon before. Roe, sure. But his golden child?

I look at Roe over my shoulder. The moist rot of the bog leeches up through the sanctuary floorboards.

Are you listening? I mouth.

He nods.

"Does he know what he is?" Simon asks. "Is that why he's out there?"

My ears prick at this, and I study Roe's reaction.

The monster, he mouths.

I shudder and stare at the pew bottom above me.

Of course. *Of course* that's what they're talking about. Simon was with us last night. He saw the monster and knows it's out there.

"Him knowing or not knowing is none of our concern," the reverend scolds. "But you do need to be more careful with your choices, Si. Do not become a disappointment like Roe. A wayward soul is a wayward soul, and you need to learn wisdom in the hunt. I have already lost one son; I will not lose my second to his own foolish decisions and my third to his own ignorance."

My heart thrills. When I look over at Roe, pain and confusion beat in his eyes.

Three sons?

But the reverend only has two sons, not three. Unless... My stomach turns to knots inside me. Unless the truth is something uglier. He might preach faithfulness from the safety of his pulpit, but out there, in the world, he's a false prophet. Who knows how many women he's bent to his will and called it God's.

Simon grumbles, followed by a smack of palm against wood. Roe jolts on the floor, and I reach over, weaving my fingers into his. I'll pass along my own fear, but I'm hoping I can steady him too. He smiles—or at least, he tries to.

"It's not fair, Dad!" Simon hisses. "We know everything. We hold all the cards. You don't need him if you have me. We could squish this whole town with the truth if we wanted to, but instead, what? We have to go on pretending? Why is it taking so damn long?"

"*For what will it profit a man if he gains the whole world and forfeits his soul?* Simon." The reverend's voice is calm and steadying, almost nurturing. He has used the same voice before with my mother. "We must bide our time. It will all work as the Lord wills. We gain nothing by telling the truth of the bog before our moment has come. You must stay the course if we are to earn everlasting life."

Silence settles in the sanctuary, and my heartbeat drums against its walls. I don't dare move a muscle.

And that's when I see it, crawling toward me across the underbelly of the pew.

A single black fly.

I wrench my hand from Roe's and scramble further up on the carpet. It's coming closer, beady black eyes blinking at me, antennae rubbing together. Cold fingers of fear spread up my chest and grip my throat, choking me. The insect closes in. My skin flushes hot, and Roe's hand curls around my shoulder. I turn toward his wild, green eyes.

"What?" His voice is hushed, but not hushed enough.

Scuffling echoes from the confessional, a sound of metal scraping metal. The velvet curtains are tossed aside. The floor shakes beneath me, and I'm frozen, unable to move. I can't breathe, just like the other night in the bog. As though I'm being stared down by those wide, empty eyes, with nowhere to go.

In a flash, Roe's hand is covering my mouth, and we're rolling toward the back of the church, under and over each other, until I gently hit the wall of the sanctuary. My nose presses against Roe's neck, and I notice the salty sweat clinging to his skin. His arms wrap tight around my head and waist, holding me so close I think I might burst. Our chests beat against each other, breaths heavy while we try to quiet them.

God, he smells good.

"Si? What is it?" It's the reverend's voice. His shoes still stand inside the wooden box.

"Thought I heard something."

Simon's boots leave dry clumps of dirt and weeds on the floorboards of the church. He walks over to the pews Roe and I were lying beneath only moments before. His fingers curl beneath the wood, probing, searching, each appendage outstretched. And then he smacks the wood. I jump in Roe's arms.

"What is it?" The reverend's shiny shoes come to meet his son from another row of benches.

Simon peels his hand off and straightens. "Just another fucking fly. I'm gonna go back outside and finish raking the leaves. But then I'm out. I can't stand being around that Thomas freak for one more second."

He follows the same path Roe and I took in, leaving a trail of mud and greenery behind him. After a moment, the reverend heaves a sigh and walks around the pews to the far corner of the church. The door to his office opens, then shuts. Roe and I stay interlocked for what feels like an eternity, and when we finally do separate, both of us are drenched with sweat.

We stand quietly to our feet and inch toward the doors leading out of the sanctuary. My foot slips into something soft and cold, and muck squelches up on the sides of my sneakers. I bend down and drag a finger through the stuff. It's not just mud.

Bog weeds and dry pine needles stick out like grave markers.

Without thinking, I grab Roe's hand and yank him behind me, running down the steps to the basement of the church. His wrist is tight in my hand. I spin around and press him up against the cool concrete wall, fixing him with my eyes.

"Roe Byron, what the fuck is going on?"

17

THE PUNCH

"I don't know, okay?" Roe holds his palms up to me and shrinks against the wall. "My dad used to talk of a way to everlasting life. He would make me drink the bog water. Said it was like medicine, healing for my soul. It's why I told you to not drink anything you don't boil. The bog is the whole town, Mila. You know how people talk about how it's sick. That it didn't used to be this way."

I let go of his wrist and sag beside him. "I know. But Simon's boots are covered in mud. They were obviously talking about the monster, and oh, surprise! You might have another brother."

Roe groans and unwraps one of the bandages on his knuckles. It falls away in white strips, revealing the broken and bloody skin beneath.

"Roe!" I reach over and grab his hand.

Each knuckle on his left hand is bandaged, brown blood dried to the skin where it leaked out. I hold it up, inspecting each finger.

"When did you do this?"

He winces when my finger brushes his broken skin. "The other night after I left your house. After I...thought too much about everything."

His voice trails off, and I match his eyes with my own. There's so much pain there, welling up inside him, and I'm afraid the dam is near breaking.

The doors to the church bang open, and footsteps echo on the floor above.

"Shit, that's gotta be Mrs. Denton. Help me grab the end of this table." I drop Roe's bloody bandage to the floor and flip over the end of a white folding table.

"Roe, Mila, are you down here?" Mrs. Denton's heels click on the concrete stairs, and then the door swings open, revealing the woman herself.

I smile sweetly over the end of the table Roe and I lift together. "Sorry, we had trouble finding where everything was down here."

Mrs. Denton, who doesn't look mildly convinced, clicks her beige manicured nails against the back of her clipboard. "Grab a few chairs while you're at it. And then come back outside. Can't have the two of you down here, getting up to heaven knows what."

This would be a real nice time to just punch the woman in the throat.

"Sure, Mrs. Denton. We can grab a few chairs. Wouldn't want you ruining that manicure." The words shave off my tongue.

For a moment, she doesn't say anything, but her hands tighten around the edges of her clipboard. "Right. Well, just see you do it quickly."

Once she's gone, Roe lets out a rumbling laugh.

It surprises me at first. I haven't heard him laugh like this since we were kids, and it awakens something in me. Something warm and soft, like how it felt when he snuck into my room and wrapped his arms around me. I've been missing it for a very long time.

There in the cold, dim light of the church basement, I study him. His stormy eyes, his dirty dishwater hair, the cutoff jeans he's wearing, and the blue bandanna tied around his neck. There are wrinkles around his eyes I haven't noticed before—smile lines that have been missing for so long. And I have the sudden urge inside me to never let those lines disappear again.

"What are you laughing at?" I ask, pushing him forward. We angle the table through the door.

He stops on the first stair and looks at me as if everything else around us is melting into itself. "You. I fucking love you, Mila Thomas." Roe blinks, and my mouth drops open.

We're both laughing because, for the first time since last summer, it feels right between us.

Healed.

By the time we're all standing around the table outside, shoving cold-cut deli sandwiches into our mouths and washing them down with pops bought from Phil's—we refuse to drink the church's lemonade—Roe's words are sinking into my bones.

But so are the reverend's.

I have already lost one son; I will not lose my second to his own foolish decisions and my third to his own ignorance.

I pick a piece of spinach from my teeth and down the rest of my drink. If the reverend does have three sons, who is the third? He has always been friendly with his parishioners. And of course, we've all heard the rumors. The reality of him sneaking into the cabin at night when he thought all of us kids were asleep. But another son? I take a bite of my sandwich and chew until it turns to mush in my mouth.

"So, did you hear anything juicy?"

Agatha is at my elbow, her nose and cheeks pink from the sun. Camille stands beside her, fitting an iced sugar cookie in the shape of a cross in her mouth. She licks a crumb from the corner of her lips. I look around the field. Everyone is piled around the table, save for Simon, who is talking with Olive nearer to the church.

"Yeah, but we should probably discuss it somewhere else."

Agatha's eyes widen. "Oh shit, it must be *spicy*."

I shove the last of my sandwich into my mouth and grab Roe. "Define *spicy*."

The four of us check out with Mrs. Denton and head toward our bikes lying in the tall grass beside the road. Agatha offers hers to Roe and climbs onto the back of Camille's. My feet are on the pedals, when we hear the shouting.

"You always do this, Simon! You always just leave!"

Olive stands in front of the church, tears streaming down her face, mud on her blouse. Simon stalks across the dusty drive, headed for his truck. He looks angry, fists clenched tight at his sides. His boots are still caked in bog mud, and my stomach boils.

What the hell does he know?

And where is he going?

Olive runs toward him and grabs his wrist. "Simon—"

He spins around, voice low and dangerous. "You're making a scene, Ol."

Simon rips from her grasp, only to tighten his own fingers around her skin, turning it white as snow. He's going to leave bruises, just like the ones she is trying to hide on her throat with that stupid scarf.

No one in the field is paying any attention. Typical. Everyone turns a blind eye when it's Simon Fucking Byron. Heaven forbid the next leader of Sinner's Chapel is an abusive asshole.

I drop my bike to the dust.

"Mila, no," Roe says, but I ignore him.

I'm sick of Simon Byron following in his daddy's footsteps and acting like he owns the women in this town. In four steps, I'm across the parking lot, and my hand slips into Olive's.

"Take your hands off her, Simon."

His nose wrinkles like I'm a bad scent, and God, it makes me want to punch him so bad. My fingers itch for it.

"This isn't your fight, Thomas." His eyes don't even leave Olive's face.

"It shouldn't even be a fight at all, you idiot."

That moves his gaze to me, and I immediately regret it. I want to pluck out his eyes and squish them under my sneakers. The air between us tightens, and I move Olive behind me. Her breath blows on my neck, hot and fast. I keep her hand in my own. Her fingers are shaking.

"What did you call me?" Simon asks, moving his face inches from mine. His breath smells of cheap beer and deli meat.

I gag, forcing myself to swallow the bile rising in my throat. "I called you a fucking idiot."

My fingers squeeze tighter around Olive's, for my own sake now more than hers.

"Mila—" She reaches up and grabs my shoulder.

"No." Simon takes another step forward, backing me up into Olive. "I want to hear her say it one more *fucking* time."

It's a tease, a threat. A *come on, say it and find out* ultimatum. And right now, the blood pumping in my veins is so hot, I might burn up from the inside out. I drop Olive's hands and press my palms against Simon's sweaty chest.

"You're an idiot. You're an idiot and a bully, and you know what—I should hate you. I really should. But I don't." The words spill from my tongue like fire, hot and quickening. "I *pity* you. Want to know why? Because in order for someone to act as cruel and heartless as you, they would

have to hate themselves enough that they don't care what anyone truly thinks of them. They would have to hate themselves so much that they don't believe that they are worthy of love, and that is just sad. You are *sad*, Simon Byron."

My words hit their mark. The sting of them sears across his skin. The corners of his lips narrow, angling down until his mouth seems to almost disappear from his face.

And then they break open, revealing his white teeth. "And your brother is dead."

I don't know what comes over me, but in a matter of moments, my fist sinks into the taut skin of Simon's face. Blood drips all over the dirt at our feet. Shouting comes from the field. Mrs. Denton gasps, and a few of the women rush over to Simon, who is crouched, holding his nose in his hands. Red oozes between his fingers.

The world around me spins as if I'm falling in slow motion. Olive stands, unmoving in the dirt. Her eyes dart between me and her boyfriend on the ground. One of the women whispers something about my temper, about being raised without a father, and I turn away. If I stay a moment longer, it won't just be Simon splayed out in the church parking lot.

Roe says nothing when I hop on my bike, but the look in his eyes tells me I've gone too far this time. I don't care. The impact of Simon's jaw on my knuckles lingers on my skin, and it feels good. It feels *right*.

And he's lying. Jed isn't dead. He is still out there. And I have a feeling Simon Byron knows it too.

When we get back to the cabin, Mom's car is gone. The four of us drop our bikes on the lawn and hurry into the house. We take the stairs to the loft two at a time, and soon, we're all spread out on the beds, telling each other what we heard.

Agatha and Camille have a whole lot of nothing. Mrs. Denton has been drinking again, but we all know that, and the reverend hopes Simon will propose to Olive as soon as he graduates from seminary school next year.

I gag at this. "Must be fun, having your entire future arranged. Does Olive have any say in it?"

"We'll see now that you've gone and ruined half of Simon's jaw." Camille pops a grape between her lips and smiles.

Roe, who hasn't opened his mouth since we locked the cabin door behind us, sighs and tightens the bandage on one of his knuckles.

"You really shouldn't have done that," he says.

I sigh and lean against him, my head on his chest. "I know, but it felt good."

"I'm not kidding, Mila." He pushes up off the bed. "You don't get it."

Heat flushes in my chest. "Oh. I'm sorry I don't punch dents in trailer walls instead of taking it out on the people who actually deserve it."

Roe's eyes flash. He takes a step closer to the bed. "You *don't understand,* Mila—"

I fly off the bed, my chest heaving. "Yeah? So, then help me understand, Roe. Tell me why I shouldn't have punched your brother."

We are standing barely inches from each other. His breath is hot on the skin of my throat, and I want to wrap my body around his, like it was beneath the church pews, sinking into each other until we are as close as we can possibly be. My eyes drift down to his lips, his jaw, the vein pulsing on his neck.

"Holy shit, you guys seriously need to make out a little and get it over with." Agatha grins.

The tension in the air swims thick around us, and I fight the sudden urge to punch my sister. I shoot a glare her way.

That's when I notice it—the water leaking from the corner of her lips. It dribbles down her skin from where her lopsided smile angles strangely on her face.

Shit.

"Guys, it's back." I drop down in front of my sister, my hands on her knees. Her skin is damp and cold. Algae grows along her hairline.

Camille yelps, leaping off the bed and swatting at the wet patch bleeding across her thigh. Roe scrambles behind me. Agatha's eyes go black, and her head cocks to one side. She studies me in the afternoon light.

"Agatha," I say tentatively. "What's going on?"

"He is coming," she says. The muddy water puddles in her lap.

I leap into action before I can think through anything else. "Roe, lock the door and windows."

He does as I say, and I throw Camille a bathrobe tie from my dresser. "Help me secure her to the bed."

Camille looks at me, dumbstruck. "Are you kidding? I'm not tying her up."

My heart beats in my throat. The sweat beads on my skin, and my sister begins to sway back and forth, echoing the same three words.

"The last time she fought that thing, it almost killed her. And from what I can tell, she can't exactly control it. I don't know about you, but I'm not willing to toe the line of almost losing my sister again, okay?"

Camille's throat bobs and she nods. Agatha barely struggles while we loop the bathrobe cords around her wrists, securing her to the wooden bedposts. Roe is pressed against the angled window, his breath steaming up the glass.

"See anything?" I ask.

"Just a shit ton of flies."

He pulls away, and I understand why the room darkened. The entire window is sheathed in buzzing, black bodies. They wriggle and squirm, their drone dull through the glass. But still, I can hear the words.

Look around, look around.

Downstairs, the front door snaps open, the weak lock giving way, and someone stumbles into the kitchen. The blood quickens in my veins, and I want to be sick.

"Mom."

But then the screaming starts, thick and wet. I grab Roe by the collar.

"You're coming with me. Camille, stay with Agatha."

Camille nods. Roe and I run out onto the landing and down the stairs. The screams turn muffled, like they're bubbling underwater. I stop Roe on the last step, my hand firm on his chest.

"Whoever it is, whatever is happening, don't touch them, okay?"

He nods. I curl my hands into fists before slipping around the corner to the kitchen.

Roe gasps behind me. I stop, and the metallic stink of blood fills my nostrils.

Olive Denton lies on the floor in a pool of what can only be blood and bog water. Her chest is caved in, limbs scratched and torn to shreds. Her eyes are wide, mouth open, quivering.

Any other thoughts leave my mind—only Olive. My feet slap in her warm blood. Her screams are silenced now, but her eyes follow me.

I reach for her torn flesh, only to pull back when I notice it. Her heart, still beating—albeit, slowly—exposed between shredded skin and jagged bone. Her feet are bare, and her lipstick is smeared, like she's been freshly kissed.

"Who did this to you?"

"Olive..." Roe's voice cracks.

I scan the kitchen for anything to staunch the blood flow, but nothing will help her slowing heart. Though I want to run, scream, and tear apart whoever did this, I steel myself and wrap my fingers through hers.

She will not be alone in her final moments. Even if I can bring her back, I can't heal the gaping wound in her chest.

Olive takes a breath. Blood gurgles between her lips. "He's so close, Mila. He only needs a few more before he'll live forever." She spasms and chokes, and I squeeze her hand tighter. "Your brother...I saw Jed."

18

THE CEMETERY

Red and blue lights flash in the gathering dark. Sheriff Lowell and his deputies load Olive's body into the back of his car. Her dark hair sticks out from between the body bag's zipper like unkempt thorns. Roe stands at my back, spine straight, fingers flexing.

Victoria, the red-haired woman from the morgue, picks at my cuticles with a pair of tweezers. She already washed my hands twice but can't seem to get the stain of Olive's blood out of my nail beds.

It just sits there.

A memory.

Olive's caved-in chest, her heart like a deflated red balloon. *I saw Jed.*

My eyes fill with tears, but I blink them away. I don't have time for crying. Agatha said Grandma Ruby knows the story. Maybe she will tell me if Jed is the monster who ripped Olive to shreds. She has to.

Victoria adds another bloodstained cotton ball to an evidence bag and straightens. "You're free to go."

"Not so fast." Sheriff Lowell jogs across the lawn, his flashlight bobbing and catching mosquitoes in its beam. He stops in front of me and stares. "Give me one good reason I shouldn't bring you down to the station, Mila."

Roe steps in front of me, but I nudge him away.

"I already told you what happened. Agatha is sick. I was helping her into bed when the front door blew open and Olive tumbled in, just like you saw her," I say tightly. "Maybe you can do your job for once and figure out what happened to her. People keep dying on your watch, Sheriff."

He frowns and wipes sweat off his brow. "I *am* doing my job, Mila. And I'm starting to notice a pattern. See, people keep dying around *you*."

The vitriol in his voice stings my skin. Before I can come up with a reply, he's gone. Turned on his heel and strutting back to his car. The deputies load in behind him, Victoria with all her bags and metallic tools in tow.

Roe's fingers curl into mine. "Don't listen to him, Mila. He's an asshole."

A pause. A beat of silence while I gather my unruly thoughts. "He's not wrong, though. Dani, Jed, Grandma Ruby, Dillon, now Olive. They're all connected to me." I hold my hands up in the moonlight. They're shaking. "Maybe Mom is right. Maybe I *am* the broken thing."

Roe's arms come around me before I can stop him. I breathe in his woodsy smell, and the soft fabric of his flannel soaks up any tears slipping through the cracks.

"You're not broken, Mila," he whispers into my hair. "You're the farthest thing from broken I've ever known."

I can't bear to look at him, so I grit my teeth and pull away. Too close. Later. We can have this moment later. For now...

"We need to go talk to my grandma. Agatha said she knew the story. She'll know if Jed...if he's the killer."

Roe's eyes go glassy, distant. I shouldn't have pulled away so fast. Without a word, he jumps off the porch and mounts Agatha's bike, nodding for me to follow. The wind sifts softly through the trees, rustling the leaves and needles.

"Do you have a plan?" I ask. "You're acting as if you have a plan."

He sighs. "Remember the day we felt the bog, when Sheriff Lowell was loading that body—"

"Owen," I interrupt. "It's Owen in that bag."

The spark hits Roe's eyes while he stares out at the trees. "Okay, well, we'll dissect that truth bomb later. Right now, focus on that feeling you got, when you felt the bog deep below the earth."

I don't have to bring the memory to mind. The bog runs somewhere beneath me, rushing over rocks and roots, shushing its way through the underside of the town, and infiltrating our water system.

"Okay, so what does this have to do with anything?" I ask.

Roe brushes his nose with a thumb. "Ever since we were kids, you've heard the voices, right? All the dead things in the bog?"

I cross my arms over my chest and stare at him hard in the moonlight. "I hear the people who've died in the bog and *stayed there*, Roe. Grandma Ruby is buried in the church cemetery. They fished her from the water and stuck her in the ground behind the church."

Roe's eyes break from the tree line and match mine. "The bog is everywhere, Mila. Don't you get it? The bog is under this house and under my trailer. And it's under the church cemetery."

His words hit me like a wave of ice water. Tremors run the length of my legs. Roe is right. Here, the bog touches everything. I leap off the porch and mount my bicycle.

We are going to go talk to my grandmother.

The cemetery is silent. Even in the night, a thin fog wraps around the grave markers like the tails of black cats. Roe and I pedal silently around the side of the church, careful to avoid the light streaming from the reverend's office window. We drop our bikes at the spiked iron gate and slip in among the angel monuments undulating with shadow and dew-slick moss.

Grandma Ruby lies in the family plot at the back of the graveyard, tucked under a willowy birch tree and two wild rosebushes. No men beside her. Just like my mom, the men came and went, leaving only the children behind.

It has never bothered me before that Jed and I never knew our fathers. Just that they were different. Agatha's dad, Niall, only stuck around for a few years, but even he left. When it all got to be too hard. They were all just men passing through, not ready to stick around and settle down. But now the thought niggles at my brain, like a splinter caught beneath a fingernail.

The ground squishes and sponges beneath my weight. A shiver runs the length of my spine. Behind me, Roe breathes heavily, and almost instinctively, I reach out and slip my fingers between his. We creep along the worn paths. The only witnesses to our journey are the crickets in the unkempt grass, chirping with ferocity.

The path ends, and we mount a small mound of grass crowned by a plain, dark shape. I pull my phone out and turn the light toward the headstone. My chest clenches. I drop to my knees and run a finger through the words inscribed on the cold granite.

RUBY THOMAS
BORN DECEMBER 14TH, 1944
DIED JUNE 29TH, 2022
"ALL THAT LIVE MUST DIE,
PASSING THROUGH NATURE TO ETERNITY."

A hot sob crawls up the back of my throat and spills from my lips, wrapping ashen fingers about my neck. Roe's hand curls around the back of my shoulder. I pull away and turn to look at him. A jolt runs through my body.

It's him, trying to take my pain, to feel it too so I'm not alone.

"You can't." The words are broken on my tongue.

He blinks in the strange, shadowed light, and his fingers still grasp toward me. "Mila, look. I know you think your pain is too much for me to handle, and maybe it is, but I don't care. Not anymore. Let me help you. Let me understand."

I don't know what to say, not at first anyway. All I can do is stare at the boy I'm pretty sure I've loved since the day we met. And I think that's when he started to love me too. His fingers skiff the curve of my shoulder, warm and calloused and wholly familiar. I want to kiss him, right here and now. Sink my lips against his until all we feel is one another in the softening moonlight, until all there is to do is understand. But I can't. Not now.

I need to hear *the story*.

With Roe's hand steadying me, I turn back to Grandma Ruby's grave and stretch my fingers toward the stone. A part of me whispers that I won't be able to do it. Won't be able to open whatever portal there is drifting along the in-between places. Places like the bog. But I still have Roe's skin against mine, solid and warm, and it centers me.

The air susurrates with night peepers in the cemetery pond, owls somewhere high, hiding in the thickets of willow and oak, and cars driving by, their tires crackling on gravel. I close my eyes and focus on one thing—*the* single thing.

Grandma Ruby.

I picture her soft wrinkles and downy white hair. The way her arms used to wrap me up, pulling me in so close I could smell her coconut and tea tree soap. Even now, it drifts beneath my nose on the cool wind coming from the aspens beyond the road. It overwhelms me and brushes against my skin until I am nine years old again, sitting on the front porch of the family cabin while Grandma Ruby braids my hair and sings me old Irish folk songs.

Over in Killarney, many years ago
My mother sang a song to me in tones so soft and low
Just a simple little ditty in her good old Irish way
And I'd give the world if I could hear that song of hers today

The lyrics whisper from the soil at my knees, mingling with the steady drone of the insects and the gentle coo of birds. My body is light and heavy all at once, like I'm floating on my back in the water, face tilted toward the darkening sky. I breathe deeply and push the words out through my fingers toward the ground.

Grandma Ruby, can you hear me?

Silence rings loudly in my ears, stretches out, through and all around. The crackle of the wind in the trees grows stronger as the night waxes darker. Roe's fingers tighten on my shoulder. I almost break away, turn around to tell him no. He does not need to feel this pain too.

And that's when it happens.

Not the usual crack of pain against my brow, the familiar weight of bone-weary death, like a hand on the back of my neck, or the pressure turning my very brain to dust and ash. Just a gentle slip of wind, like a kiss of gossamer on my skin and fingers running through my hair.

I am here, Mila-May.

My breath catches in my chest. There are a hundred thousand things I want to say, words I should have shared so many more times and never had the chance to. I sift through them all, weighing them for importance and trying to pick out the right one. But they are legion; they overwhelm me, threatening to drag me under and drown me.

Roe's hand presses firmly against my skin.

"Just ask her the question." His words brush gently against my ear. "She already knows all the rest."

I swallow and lick my dry lips, trying to form all the thoughts, all the breaths and moments and visions, into a single string of words.

Agatha told me to ask you the story. She said you would know. Who is the third son?

There is silence again, almost deafening this time. It stretches long and hazy, like a strip of fog across a field. The wetness of the bog leeches through the soil and kisses my bare knees. I sink deeper into it, letting the water give me what it has taken. The scent of coconut and tea tree grows stronger, swirling in great swathes about my face.

Mila. My grandmother's voice is an echo of breath on my ear. *Look around.*

I press my fingertips against my skull. A thin line of pain breaks out along my brow. When I open my eyes, my vision blurs.

There is a girl who knows the magic running through the bog's depths. Can sing to its waters and soothe its murky soul. She emerges from the tree line, a young wisp of a thing with fire-orange hair spilling over white shoulders like molten gold. Her feet beat bare against the soil while she dances under the worrying moon, and the bog reaches up through roots to whisper its secrets to her. It loves her, loves the way she makes it feel alive. Fresh and whole.

The girl hears the voices of all those who have found their way to the bog, like coins lost between cushions. They call her name—Ruby, Ruby, Ruby—as though she is their king, and she revels in them. She rejoices that she is no longer alone.

Back home, in the cabin that teeters toward the water, she is only alone. There is no one to want her, not anymore. Here, among the cattails and clumps of wavering earth, she is beloved. And the bog feels joy at the brush of her dancing feet.

And so, every day, Ruby comes to the water. She washes in the waves—a baptism, she calls it. And the bog calls her its own. She grows in the magic, learns the paths through the marshes while she stretches toward womanhood. The more time she spends in the bog, the more she becomes at one with the mud beneath her toes, the weeds clinging to her dress, the water filling her lungs each time she breathes.

She learns the voices of those caught in the bog's in-between, listens to their stories and leans into the magic they offer. The ability to truly understand, the command she learns to have over the very water itself—telling it where to go and how to spread light and love and everything good that echoes from her soul.

The bog falls in love with the girl, with Ruby, and the bog grows jealous.

I snap forward, almost hitting my head on the gravestone. Roe's fingers press into my collarbone, pulling me back.

"Mila?" His voice is swift, edged with concern. "What's wrong?"

My chest heaves, heart clenching like a hot fist. I shake my head. "It's not finished. There's more to see." My words are hurried, desperate. I shut my eyes tight again.

Show me more.

And then I'm gasping for breath, face turned toward the heavens. All I can see is dust.

The girl has always come alone to the waters, to slip her ankles beneath the waves and hear the stories of those who swim with bones beneath the depths. But the bog felt a different cadence to the steps that day, a second pair of feet coming through the cedars. And when the girl broke from the heady scent of sap and damp bark, the bog saw she had brought another with her. A boy whose eyes sparkled green like envy.

He made Ruby laugh in ways the bog did not like, ways she used to laugh with only the water. The boy made her smile and dance harder, shaking the roots below, tangling them into knots. They came out, day after day, spilling from Ruby's cabin with rose-petal kisses still flush on their lips. And the bog began to weep. The water quickened beneath the earth while it wept, emptying its pain, its emotion, into the town, until some of the folk began to notice how strange they felt when they walked across the earth. How they were able to lay hands on their fellow townsfolk and feel what it was they were feeling. Because the bog now swam through them all. What it felt, they felt, and some even learned how to feel it in others.

But the girl, Ruby, ignored the bog's anger. Her heart only belonged to the boy, whose heart seemed to beat for her and her alone. But the bog knew differently. It had seen the greed in the boy's eyes the first time Ruby showed him the magic. She bent the water, showed him how she could tell the waves where to go, how to walk the paths through the bog so they wouldn't slip and go down to join the rest of the dead things. How she could raise the dead with merely a touch and send them onto peace with another. And the boy's hunger grew inside him, changing from a lust for Ruby into a lust for the bog. A lust for the magic running through its waters, the power over souls that turned Ruby from girl to witch to king. He grew bitter. Hungry for the power. And the bog knew its time had come.

Roe grips me with both hands while my lungs strain for air. My heart flips in my chest, pressing flush with my skin and cracking back against my ribs. But there is more.

My grandmother's voice reaches up from the boggy waters below.

Look around, she says. *Look around.*

And so, I do.

The boy belonged to the most powerful family in the town. A family whose men could open their mouths and have the whole world on their knees. And so, when the boy knew Ruby wasn't looking, he tried to bend the bog. He reached deep into the waters, like Ruby had shown him, and tried to force the water where he wanted it to go. He tried to control it, just like he had been controlled—a puppet with a master hungry for power.

And the bog was helpless. It let him sink his greedy fingers into the depths and suck up the magic into his veins. The boy tried to raise the dead and give them rest, only if he so chose. The boy became a god. And it broke Ruby's heart. Broke her to know that the boy she loved, the boy she had shared her secret with, only wanted to use it for his own selfish gain. But the bog did not know how she would exact her revenge.

The bog didn't know she would bend deep over the water on the night of a full moon, while the boy clung to the shallows. The bog didn't know that a broken heart could be as powerful as her, powerful enough to strip back the flesh of a human and reveal what was truly underneath.

It started as merely a shush of water, a gentle trickle pouring from her fingers and lips. But as the waves deepened and the boy shrieked, he began to change. It started in his toes, the mud curling up to wrap in sludge around his body. The bog cocooned him, covering his mouth and his nose, but not his eyes. Those turned to puddles of light, huge empty spaces glinting out into the darkness. He tore into the water, desperate to wash away the muck crawling across his skin, and when the bog fell away, it left behind the very thing the boy had always been.

A worm.

White and sinuous and wriggling in the moonlight. And when he tried to open his mouth to plead with the girl who had loved him, who had shown him the magic, his pale flesh ripped in a jagged tear, and his teeth gnashed at the moon. His arms were too long for his body, dragging behind him through the muck and the mire while his pale feet sunk deeper and deeper.

"You did this to yourself, Cecil," the girl cried, hands curling in the churning

bog. "I loved you. I showed you the most important thing to me. And in turn, you have shown me that nothing beats in that empty chest. No soul. Only greed."

The water whipped around them, deepening its roots into the ground, into the very town around them. It churned beneath the curved claws of the monster in the shallows. It took on the feelings of the girl. The bitterness. The acid that clung in her throat.

"I curse you now to walk soulless on the earth for all generations to come. But only in those who are like you—who take advantage, who crave power."

The boy screamed. Pieces of flesh hung from where his skin had torn. And the girl thought her curse was right and just, but she didn't know the extent of what she had done.

For to be soulless is to yearn for that which you do not have. And the boy's desire to be godlike only grew.

Cecil learned to crave the souls he could no longer keep inside his own viscera. The more he consumed, the more he became like a god. Powerful, almost immortal. And the curse was passed along. He taught his son to hunt, to stalk the town, looking for souls at night who no one would miss. Cecil soon fell into his father's work, but at night, his flesh would rip and tear, and he would become the worm creature and leave the bones of those whose souls he'd taken to rot in the bog.

The bog grew sick. Quicker, it ate away at flesh. No longer a haven for those who had passed, but a prison. It corroded sinew and muscle until all it had left to spit back were the bones of those who had died in its depths. And there were so many. So many dead things in the water.

The bog pleaded with Ruby to undo the curse, but her own bitterness, her own pride, kept her from freeing the boy she had once loved. And when she fell pregnant by another boy she'd brought into the bog, she knew she hadn't just cursed Cecil's line.

She'd cursed her own.

The magic she used came with a price. A responsibility and duty no one should bear.

To protect the town from the very thing she had created.

So, she moved away from the bog, abandoning the old cabin in the shallows. She grew terrified when her daughter gave birth in the shallows to the son. Terrified when her daughter's daughter began to hear the voices. She knew that the curse would soon show itself, and she would be too weak to fight it.

So, she let the bog take her. And the bog was willing.

19

THE CHASE

Roe catches me when I fall away from the gravestone. My chest heaves and crashes, and I gasp for air like a fish caught in the sand. My lungs burn, and my skin crawls. It is as though I've been swallowed by the bog and spat back out like poison. When I look down, my clothes are soaked in water.

"What the hell just happened?" Roe's voice is urgent, tangible across my damp skin.

I clear my eyes of bog water and blink up at him. The sky beyond is as black as pitch, not a single star in sight. Water bubbles in my throat, and I spin, sitting up to cough it out onto the grass. I wipe away weeds from my lips and lean back against Roe.

"I don't know," I say. Because it's the truth.

How am I currently sitting in the cemetery, drenched, when Roe remains dry? Why does the ground at Grandma Ruby's grave smell like peat and rotting cattail roots? What is it I just saw?

I do know this: The bog is angry, and it wants war.

It hits me, the feeling as though I'm being dragged beneath the water. Tears spill hot on my cheeks, and my fingers claw into Roe's arms. I observe my grandma through fresh eyes—the realization of everything finally settling into my very marrow. All I can do is cling to Roe while the grief pours over me in fresh waves.

Grandma Ruby dancing in the moonlight, plunging her hands into the waters, talking with those who find themselves caught in the in-between of the bog. My grandma with blood on her hands after she birthed my mother, alone, in the shallows of the bog.

Mom giving birth to a...son.

No. I push the thought away. Jed is mine. *My* brother.

I heave, holding back whatever is left in my stomach so it doesn't come out in thin lines on the grass. Roe's fingers pull at my face, but I can't turn to look at him, not now.

Why have the women in my family always been alone? A line of witch-king women who birthed babes in the shallows and have known nothing but loneliness? Because we are meant to be protectors. To take care of those who have died in the bog. The worms leave the bones in the water, and we help the souls find rest.

But Mom refused.

And the bog is too full.

My chest aches with the need to be loved and understood, more than it ever has before.

I picture Agatha and Camille, the love between them almost something you can see, swimming in the air around them.

And I think of Jed, who left when he felt he would only hurt those he cared about.

The ache bleeds down into my belly and makes me sick. Roe's grip on me tightens. He pulls me deeper against him, until the smell of midnight sky is replaced by that of woodsmoke and coffee grounds.

Roe holds me, there at the foothills of my grandmother's grave, and all I want to do is fall into him. For him to help me feel a little less lonely in this fucked-up world. To experience what Agatha has with Camille—a safe place. And when I think about it, Roe has always been that for me.

Even when I couldn't see it, he has always been there to steady me, to reach out and understand the dull throb that so often threatens to undo me. Forgiving so easily, loving so selflessly. Even when everyone breaks him apart, like chaff in the wind, he holds himself together for *me*.

Roe's fingers comb through my hair, and all I want is him. And I think he feels it too. His hand comes beneath my chin and pulls me to look up at him, there in the moonlight.

"I don't know what happened just now, Mila." His voice is thick and slow. "But I'm here."

I sit up, not bothering to wipe the tears still streaking down my face. "You always have been, haven't you?' My voice is barely a whisper. "I'm so sorry."

His nose wrinkles. "For what?"

I punch him gently on the shoulder. "For being an ass."

"Oh, shut up," he says, his words low and gravelly. "You've always been an ass."

And then his hands are in my hair, on my waist, pulling me down against him there in the dew-damp grass. My legs tremble when his lips brush against mine, tasting like day-old coffee and sweat. He gasps, the slightest flutter of breath against my cheek, and I laugh, unable to help myself.

And then he laughs, and our teeth clack together, our tongues, wet and honey-sweetened there in the white moonlight that burns against our open skin. My hands dip beneath the edges of his shirt, and his skin rises hot to meet mine. I forget all about everyone else I've ever kissed. There's just this. There's only ever been this—me and Roe.

His lips burn against my throat, turning from the lightest of cigarette coals to blazes of white fire. I forget all about the worm in the bog, the images of Grandma Ruby bent over the water and spitting words of righteous fury, the empty spaces carving away inside of me since the day I first heard the dead voices. I forget everything but Roe—his hands skimming my thighs, his warmth beating against mine, the groan he presses against the tender skin of my ear.

I forget everything but this feeling of no longer being alone. And I let it sustain me when Roe lays me back against the grass, and the ground rises to meet us.

I don't feel the damp while he moves over me, collecting my hair in his palms, studying the way it curls with sweat against my forehead. He grins, wicked and teasing, and a warm ache presses against my thighs. I slip my fingers under the edge of his shirt. His skin is cool to the touch, but he's still not close enough. He leans in, brushes his cheek against mine, and my lips part in invitation.

God, I want him.

"Mila." My name is communion wine on his tongue. Not bog water. Not some fucked-up version of holiness. But the real thing. Truth and beauty. And it makes my legs tremble with need.

He pulls away then, finger tracing my jawline, my throat, curling around the highest button on my flannel. My breath hitches.

"Roe," I manage, allowing my fingers to explore the taut muscles of his torso.

He presses a finger to my lips. "Do you want this?"

For a moment, I think I might cry. Everything tastes too sweet. Like if I take a bigger bite, it will disappear, just food in a dream. But my God, yes. This is what I want. It's what I've always wanted. I lock my gaze into his, study the way the moonlight dances in the darkness of his eyes, and nod.

A groan escapes his lips. He's hard, I can feel it. Roe dips his nose to the hollow of my throat, breath hot. His fingers trail down, down, down.

"I've waited years for this, Mila. For you." He slides his tongue up my neck to my jaw. "To be held by another person and it doesn't hurt." Kisses sprinkled on my cheek. "It doesn't take my breath away like it does when I've touched others. Your pain, Mila. It's the same as my pain." His lips brush the edge of mine, and my hips roll, hungry.

Always so damn hungry.

"Then let's feel it," I say. "Together."

Roe laughs, deep and throaty. Our lips crash into one another, ravenous, tongues threading through teeth. He tugs at the buttons of my shirt while I loosen the belt of his pants. I slide my hands to meet him, and I forget everything else. His lips skim down my neck, my sternum, my breasts.

He pulls the sides of my shirt away, and God, I feel so *good*. So fucking good I forget everything else. That everyone around me seems to die. That I'm a liar, and there's a curse on those I love.

Right now, everything is Roe. His touch, his skin against mine, the kiss he presses to my ear. He groans my name and gets harder with each stroke of my hand. His own fingers move lower, sluice beneath my waistband.

"You make me feel everything," he murmurs against my throat, drawing me higher. "And it doesn't hurt."

His fingers move to the grass, and then his head is between my thighs. The sky is growing lighter, more filled with stars. I reach my hands to tangle in his sandy hair, and my core clenches, becoming so tight I might burst and break into a thousand shards of light.

"Please." The words leave me in a gasp. "Roe, please."

He breaks away, fingers trailing down, down. "Do you want me, Mila?" he asks.

And I groan. "Yes."

We become a tangled thing, pants tugged off and discarded. Reaching fingers and tongues. And when I finally come apart, when I don't know where my pain ends and Roe's begins, I lose myself to this knowing. To the realization I no longer have to carry this pain alone.

Time passes, and I blink myself back to reality. Roe is curled up next to me while a steady orange glow lights the eastern break of sky. I could stare at him here forever, I think. Bottle this moment up and keep it at the center of my soul, where we both can feel it for eternity. His arm slips around my waist, lips inching toward my ear.

"We should probably go."

I smile in the cold air and tuck deeper beside him. His flannel rubs soft against my cheek. He smiles, hair like a milky halo in the dimming moonlight.

And then I hear them, from somewhere behind us, the steady drone of whisper-wind wings. The breath catches in my throat, and I scramble up, searching the dawn for hordes of black flies.

"Hey," Roe says breathlessly, catching my wrist with his fingers. "What's wrong?"

I narrow my eyes, but it's too dark. "Can't you hear them? Flies."

I try to hurry to my feet, but the anxiety clenching in my chest keeps me rooted to the spot. Roe stands and stretches out a hand. My legs shake beneath me when he pulls me back through the cemetery, to where our bikes were stashed in the grass. I mount myself up on the slender, white seat, but already, it's too late. The drone has turned into a hellscape.

They come from everywhere, buzzing against my brain and sending my teeth rattling in my skull. My shoulders hunch up around my ears, and I freeze, tongue sticking to my soft palate like old gum. They swallow us, churning like wisps of shadow.

"Pedal!" Roe shouts. "Now!"

It takes everything I have to lift my toe to the lip of my pedal and push with all my strength. I can't see anything, even in the dim haze of morning. The flies block out what little sun is peeking over the horizon. They blind me, swarming around my eyes and nose, threatening to fly into my throat if I so much as take a breath. I follow the sound of Roe's tires digging into the dirt and wave a hand in front of my face to clear the cloud of insects. But they only grow, thicken their fat bodies in the air, becoming an impenetrable wall.

Look around, look around, they say.

The words slip in my ears and down my throat like honey, sticking in my chest and making my heart stop mid-beat.

Those words. Her voice.

Grandma Ruby.

I skid to a halt somewhere on the road toward home. Where I can't tell. The cloud of bugs is too thick.

"Roe!" My voice does little above the drone, but somewhere up ahead of me, his tires skid.

Look around, look around.

The noise swallows me and drills into my ears. What I want to do is scream until my vocal cords spill out across my tongue like bloody coils. This is my grandmother's voice. She has been calling to me since the day I arrived home.

And I am finally ready to answer.

I spread my arms wide. The flies zing across my skin like little, beady-eyed bullets.

"I am here!" I call above the din. "I am ready."

In response, a deafening roar seizes the wind, choking out my voice and the buzz of the flies. Roe is somewhere behind me, screaming, and the taste of him lingers on my tongue. The howl sounds again, and for the first time in perhaps my entire life, I am not afraid.

I *am* ready.

When the flies clear, the gaping hulk of him comes across the edge of the trees, cutting through the thin light of early morning like a sharp knife. He drips in ropey phlegm. The two slits above his nose carve out beams of white-hot sight.

Cold fissures break along my skull, and when the voice comes through my mind, I do not fight. I simply allow it in.

He has no eyes, Mila.

Dani. Of course. A girl whose soul could have embraced the whole world. Whose soul was taken from her by a monster, twisted and bent and made in the image of a boy who wanted too much power. A boy my grandmother loved.

A smile hints at the corners of my lips, like a finger to draw away the blood after a bite. I hold my ground while the monster approaches. It brings itself to full height and towers before me, dripping with mud like newspaper ink stains. And when its lips shred, when it peels its mouth apart and shows its teeth, my own smile widens.

"Hello, Cecil."

The monster, stretching tall before me, looming against the treetops, claws slick with bog water, stops dead in its tracks. The glowing orbs that rove in its thin skull fixate on me, and something pierces my belly. It isn't fear or the cold ache one gets before they die.

It is rage.

The bog courses deep beneath my feet. The tremor of its waters is trapped in the air on my face and awakens an energy in me. Something pulses in the chest of a red-haired girl, whose heart was broken and shredded to pieces by the boy who only wanted her for what she could offer.

I take a step toward the monster. Roe calls my name, but I ignore him. My eyes stay trained on the thing in front of me.

"I know everything about you." The words cut deep across my tongue. "I know what you've done, what you continue to do. I know about Dani and Owen. I know about all the people you've killed over the years." It isn't until the moisture runs down my wrists that I realize my fingernails are cutting my palms. But when I look down, it isn't blood licking along my skin; it's water—muddy and dark and filled with weeds.

I have claimed the bog, and it, me.

My eyes snap back to the creature standing in front of me. Its outline turns concrete when the sun spills over the trees and silhouettes the thing in fire.

"Do you know who I am, Cecil?" I ask, voice low. "I'm the girl who's lost everything."

I expect it to charge. To roar and scoop me up into its tightening fists and squeeze until my insides have turned to strawberry jam. But it doesn't. Its lips peel further back, cutting deep across its blank face. I am almost sure it will sever its own head.

And then a sound emits, not a roar, but that of hail hitting open water. Of rocks being thrown down a cliff.

It's laughing at me.

My heart pounds in my chest—too fast, too wild. A curve etches its way along my brow, along the tilt of my smile, burning away at my skin until the bog water lingering there has turned to ash. Roe yelps behind me. His fingers press against my wrist, slipping on the moisture leaking from the wounds in my palms.

"Mila, we have to go." His voice is rushed at my ear, and even though I know he's right, the bog spilling through my veins wants to stay, wants to *fight*.

I turn and run for my bike, leaping onto the seat, pedaling with everything I have away from the monster, with its gravelly laughter and reaching white hands. The road clouds with red dust behind us. It isn't until we've ditched our bikes on the side of Roe's trailer and clambered up into the bed on the far end, wrapping ourselves in the blankets and trying to regain a steady rhythm to our breaths, does the feeling in my chest give way. The water on my wrists begins to dry, and I no longer taste mud in my mouth.

Mud, like the underside of a grave. I shiver in the sheets that smell like Roe, but when I try to curl beside him, he pushes me away. His eyes are wide, stretched with fear, with worry. When his skin comes into contact with mine, he jolts and pulls back.

My skin sweats. I scramble up. "Roe, what is it?"

Roe's teeth catch on his bottom lip. The skin there flushes red-hot. "Why—why did you call it by that name?"

"What? Cecil?"

Roe nods. A splotch of blood dribbles down his chin. There is silence for a moment, ringing out against the tin walls encasing us like a tomb. And then his mouth opens, and the words spill out. Each one burns like fire on my skin, with a truth I think I've known and been denying for days now.

"That was my grandfather's name."

I nod. My throat fills with sharp edges, thumbtacks being pressed against my tongue. I have known this. Since Grandma Ruby's voice whispered his name: Cecil Byron. Roe's grandfather. Who disappeared into the bog and was never seen again. Everyone just assumed he drowned. Taken by the bog and eaten, just like Grandma Ruby's curse consumes everything that goes in there.

But he didn't die. He only festered.

I cup Roe's cheek in my palm. The rough bristles of his unshaven jaw prick my skin. His eyes are wide, body coiled like a spring ready to pop. I brush my thumb over his lips, draw them down in the center, and fight to press a kiss there.

"I know, Roe. I know."

D eep in the bog, two feet are pressing against the shallows. The mud soaks through the old cabin's floorboards, leeching in like blood beneath fabric. The cabin is a crooked place, all wrong angles and sloping, rough-hewn floors. Remnants of its bygone days collect dust and trailing spiderwebs like ornaments, like jewels on some thick, primitive crown. The cabin creaks and groans.

A gentle wind stirs up from the shallows, brushing against its pine logs and crumbling mortar.

The two feet stay planted in the mud, crouching in the low reeds to the east of the cabin, eyes watching through the shifting, papery stalks. They have always been watching, waiting for the time they knew would be right. And the bog knows the time is fast approaching.

Tonight, tonight, tonight, it whispers up through the two feet, the sturdy legs, the heart of the young man who kneels in the shallows, the water licking around his ankles.

The bog is almost giddy, lapping against the blood-soaked shoreline, reaching out deep beneath the ground, toward the town that will now be set free. Free from pain, free from the shackles that have bound it for so long.

Tonight, tonight, tonight, the bog beats again, prepping the young man in the shallows, the general the bog enlisted so many years ago.

And the young man smiles.

Because tonight, he gets to go home.

20

THE PLAN

Cecil is Roe's grandfather.

Cecil *Byron*, the preacher's son who married a girl from some other town and disappeared at the ripe old age of seventy-five. People just decided he wandered into the bog too late one night and lost his footing. Got swallowed up, like the rest of the things venturing into those waters, weak and willing, and left the church and a mining fortune to his son.

His only son, Titus Byron, who birthed two more sons with his own wife.

No, three sons.

My mom, giving birth in the shallows, bog water mixing with blood. To a son.

I draw my knees up to my chest. The truth of everything carves hot blades across my skin. In my mind's eye, I watch the things Grandma Ruby showed me—Cecil in the bog, changing from boy to man to monster in the shallows, screaming when her magic revealed his soul.

"*I curse you now,*" she said, "*to walk soulless on the earth for all generations to come. But only in those who are like you—who take advantage, who crave power.*"

My heartbeat quakes in my chest, and I force myself to look at the boy in front of me.

"Did you know?" The words feel stupid on my tongue, numb and oblong. "About the monsters? About what...what was in the Byron blood? Did you know?"

Roe's brow quirks, and his teeth set on edge. For a moment, I think he's going to play dumb, but then he runs a hand down his face and sighs. That coiled energy leaves him like steam from an engine.

"Only pieces," he relents. "Only fragments of things that never made sense. I came real close to figuring it out the day Dad told me to pack my bags and never come back, but even then, I wasn't totally sure. I just knew something about him was...off." His Adam's apple bobs sharp in his throat. "He used to speak of us having a destiny, like we were gods or something. A way we could reach eternal life by helping others find rest."

I swallow bits of barbed wire and refocus my eyes on Roe. "Not rest. Torment. That's what these...things, worms, whatever, it's what they do." I picture Grandma Ruby's vision—Cecil turning into a thing of pale flesh and teeth and groping fingers. "They devour other people's souls for power, Roe. They think it will help them live forever."

He shovels a hand through his hair. "But Grandpa Cecil, he's dead. He died. So that thing out there, it can't be him."

My stomach curdles. "What if he didn't die? What if the bog holds him in a kind of stasis? Those souls in the water can't find peace unless I raise and help them. I didn't get it at first. Last summer, when I touched that body and then bashed its skull in, I thought it was wrong. That it was the monster. But it only needed my help." There are tears in my eyes now, and this time, I don't blink them back. I stare at Roe, who has gone hazy through the saltwater.

"That thing isn't my grandpa, Mila." He gnaws the swollen flesh of his lower lip. "It's my dad."

The breath whooshes from my lungs like a punctured tire. First, relief. If it's the reverend, then it can't be Jed. But Olive's words still haunt me.

And ice water threads my veins. A generational curse. I twist the sheets in my fist until my knuckles go white.

"Are you...can you turn into—"

He shakes his head, and for a moment, I wonder if he'll be upset with me, wounded I would believe him—I picture Dillion's body, sliced like butcher meat—capable of such things.

"No, I can't. That's why everything went down between my dad and me, I think. He realized I wasn't like...*him*." He looks up at me, tears welling in his eyes. "I didn't know what he meant. I thought he just wanted me to follow him into ministry. I get it now, what he meant. But until today, I had no idea about the truth. Why I was a disappointment."

In the end, that's what breaks me. Not the sins of those who came before us or the loss of Jed, or even the way I watched bog water pour from my sister's mouth when she recognized the monster who has been walking among us for years, pretending to save souls while he sucks the life from them. No, it's the fact that the boy I've loved since before I could form words on my tongue, the boy who held me like no one has ever held me before, believes *he* is the disappointment.

I pull him into me, so close his pulse beats against my own, and we stay there like that. For how long, I don't know. But in that space, we exist together. The liar and the empath. The girl who hears voices and the boy who feels them. Just two kids who are paying for the sins of those who came before.

I don't want to think about it—the truth about the reverend—but it's there, peeling back my skin and flushing me with fear. When I close my eyes, I picture him, the man who has preached from behind a pulpit my whole life.

But only in those who are like you—who take advantage, who crave power, Grandma Ruby said.

I pick the words apart with my teeth. She might have cursed Cecil. Hell, she might have cursed his whole damn line. But these words stick out to me. *Who take advantage, who crave power.*

Titus Byron craves power. I've seen it in his eyes a million times. Watched while he loomed over Mom like a phantom, used Scripture like Band-Aids over bullet wounds, and helped her tip the bottle closer to her lips. He might not be stealing her soul, he might not be ripping her open with a mouthful of white teeth, but he is draining her life all the same. Just as he's done to so many others. He killed Dani. He killed Owen and Dillon. And maybe—I swallow hot bile—maybe Jed too.

I pull away and cup Roe's face once more with my palm. Wipe a tear with my thumb.

"We need to stop your dad."

Silence permeates the air around us, already thick with humidity leeching in through the trailer's cracks. He winces.

"Yeah. I know we do. I just don't know how."

Truth is, I don't either. I've already thought about fifty different ways—lure the reverend into the bog and let Agatha finish him off, for one—but look how far that got us last time. Agatha almost died.

"What about today?" Even the sound of my own words make me flinch.

Roe turns to look at me. "Today?"

The thought comes so fast it scares me, but I don't hold back. There's no point now. "Today, at the festival. We could lure him into the church during the crowning ceremony and then..." I can't believe I'm about to say this.

"And then what?"

I almost laugh, but it's too serious, so I bite my cheek instead. Iron floods my mouth. "We burn it all down."

Roe raises his eyebrows. "Mila, are you *insane?* We can't burn down the church."

"Why not?" That place is nothing but an opening to hell anyway. A place of lies and deceit and cruelty. Preaching the salvation of souls and sucking this town dry.

There's a strange look on Roe's face when our eyes meet again, a crack in that soft anger, something shifting beneath skin and bone and blood.

"Mila, he's my dad."

Fuck. That thought hadn't even crossed my mind. He's only a beast—a terrible father, an abuser, a literal monster hiding among the sheep, a worm feasting on all the bones he's bared. My tongue suddenly feels dry, sandpaper against dead skin. I reach across the sheets and fold my fingers over his.

"Shit, I'm sorry, Roe. I didn't—"

He waves a hand. "No, God, no. It's fine. You're right. We have to stop him. Your plan sounds like the way to go. I just...I don't want to kill him."

"Of course you don't." The words feel funny when they leave my mouth.

Even though I know the loss of a family member, I can't see Titus Byron as anything but the thing with teeth and claws from the bog. He has always been a monster to me.

"What about the bog water?" I ask. "You told me not to drink it, and the next day, your dad was giving it to everyone instead of normal communion juice."

His brow wrinkles. "Maybe it's easier for him to take souls who are in contact with the water. That's where they've always been killed in the past, isn't it?"

I nod, not liking where he's going with this.

"And maybe he figured that if he brought the water to them and had enough of them drinking it—"

"He could take all their souls at once." My knees jitter at the realization. God, no. I grab Roe's arm. "We have to stop him. Grandma Ruby… she didn't just curse them to *need* the souls of the dead. I think she accidentally made them near-gods. I think the more souls they get, the more powerful they become. Almost immortal."

Roe shovels a hand through his hair. "*For all have fallen short…*"

My brow wrinkles. "What?"

"Just another thing Dad used to say. It's from the Bible. It means no one is perfect. But I remember he used to say the rest of the verse weird. Like, it didn't match the words I was reading."

Trepidation fizzles in my bones. "What did he say?"

"*For all have fallen short to bring one to glory. For all have fallen short so one may be raised eternal.*"

I might not have extensive knowledge of religious texts, but even I know what Roe is saying is wrong. The corner of my lip twitches into a snarl. "He knew exactly what he was doing. Taking life so he could avoid death."

Silence hangs heavy, the truth weighing on our bones.

Roe kicks at the trailer wall. "Fuck!"

"I'm so sorry, Roe." I study the flush of his cheeks and the blood smearing his knuckles, and I can't stop myself.

Violently, I pull him toward me until we are nothing more than a crashing together of limbs and teeth. I kiss him until there is no breath in my lungs, no oxygen coating my tongue. I kiss him because he is the one, good, *true* thing in my life, the thing that has always been there, waiting for me. I was just too stubborn to see it at first. Because, if only for a moment, I want to take away his pain.

His hands fumble in my hair, and then he pulls away, breath still hot.

"What was that for?"

"For not being a monster," I say. "I'll meet you at the church, okay? I gotta go home and—" I look down at the grass stains on my shirt, the mud drying on my shorts from where I sat on the earth in the cemetery. "Mrs. Denton will try to convert me if I show up to the church looking like I just made out with someone in the graveyard."

A lazy smile slips over Roe's face. "We're adults, Mila. Plus, you *did* make out with someone in the graveyard." He clears his throat, and a shade of effervescent pink blooms on his cheeks. "We did more than make out."

I can't help but laugh. Even for all the crazy, messed-up bullshit haunting the both of us.

"Yeah," I say. "We did."

"I also don't think Mrs. Denton will be there."

A sour taste floods my tongue, sobering me up.

Olive, dead on the floor, her chest ripped open. Olive, who won't get to be Blueberry Queen. Won't get to graduate college and become whatever it is she wanted to be.

She could have been anything.

And now...

Something pings softly against the windowpane and breaks the spell. My breath catches in my throat at the spindly black legs and the incandescent wings of a black fly.

Roe goes still. Are we just repeating history? Cursing ourselves to whatever Grandma Ruby and Cecil found, the torment that twisted them into so much pain, rot, and revenge, it made the bog go sick? Wrong as stomach bile.

Roe leans over and grabs my hand, squeezing tight, his skin warm.

"Mila?"

No. I shake my head. "I'm fine."

No. We are nothing like them. Roe is good. *Too* good. I take his hand in mine, run a finger along the rewrapped bandages, and press a kiss to his lips, then drink in the taste of him. Coffee and woodsmoke and the stale catch of weed. I pull away.

"I'll fill Agatha and Camille in on the way there. We'll figure it out, okay? You just get your dad into the church, and we'll go from there. Confront him, let him know we know everything. We'll get him to tell us how to undo the curse, and then turn him over to the police."

He nods and watches me make my way down the slip hall to the door beyond.

"Hey, Mila, just promise me one thing?"

I turn back to him, fingers on the latch. "Yeah?"

"Try to keep the church burning to a minimum today."

21

THE BLUEBERRY QUEEN

The parking lot is packed with cars shining like freshly unearthed beetles in the afternoon sun. It's surprising, with Olive's death, that the Sunday School Picnic hasn't been canceled. But that's how some people deal with grief, right? Keep calm and carry on.

Telling each other everything happens for a reason. That it's God's will. All things work out for good in the end. To all of which, I call bullshit. The God I believe in doesn't want Olive dead. The God I believe in is big enough to hold anger alongside His love. The God I believe in contains multitudes.

And so do I.

I pull my bike over and drop it at the roots of the willow tree outside the reverend's office window. Agatha and Camille do the same. I swallow hard, scrubbing the backs of my hands against my thighs until I'm sure I'll rub the skin into flakes.

Agatha and Camille know everything. I told them in hushed, hot breaths while they both blinked and yawned over mugs of poorly made coffee. Camille's reaction was how I expected: Confusion turned to denial; denial turned to anger and hot tears, with Dani's name on her lips.

Agatha, on the other hand, didn't bat an eye. Almost like she knew. When I pressed her about it, she shrugged and dug a finger into her chest.

"The bog isn't surprised, so I guess I'm not either," she'd said, and I took it for what it was.

The truth.

That's all it can be. As two girls pressed out into the shallow water by a mother who doesn't know how to love us right, the bog is all we have. I stare up at the church windows. My whole life, I have always known I am fatherless. It didn't matter who he was, I guess, or even if he existed.

And for Agatha, it was the same. She knew her father, Niall, for a time. But he left, just like mine had before him, just like Jed's had before that. It didn't bother Agatha and me.

But it bothered Jed. It *always* bothered him.

"There's Roe," Camille says, and I turn to face the road.

But he's not coming from there. Roe is stepping out from *inside* the church. I glance behind him, and when there is nothing but swinging doors, I bolt forward. My fingertips sink into his skin, and he winces when I pull him flush with the church's chipped paint.

"What were you doing in there?"

I think about the reverend, about his sharp white teeth, his dark eyes set behind those flashing spectacles—mirror images of the empty spaces in the bog worm's skull. A shiver runs through my bones. I press my arm harder across Roe's chest until a smile breaks out on his lips.

"Mila." His voice is soft, kind, loving, even. "You're kind of hurting me."

I step back, dropping my arm. "Sorry, I just—I'm just—"

He stops my words when they leave my throat, wrapping his arms around me and squeezing me until I might pop. But I don't mind. I could stay here forever and a day if he let me.

"I know. I'm scared too." He pulls back, his palms lingering on my shoulders. "But we're going to be okay. We can do this. Together." He fits his hand into mine. "I was talking with my dad."

I turn sharp. "What did he say? Fuck, you didn't ask him about—"

"No." Roe shakes his head and leads me back to where Camille and Agatha are leaning against the trunk of the willow. "I apologized for everything he's ever accused me of and asked if he'd like to talk more after the festival. So that I can"—he stops and winks—"attest for all my sins against him."

"Bullshit," I say.

Agatha perks up. "What's bullshit?"

I knock Roe in the ribs. "His plan. But it might just work."

Roe grins at me, and my heart flips in my chest. "It actually might. The real trick will be getting this one to listen."

He reaches for my waist and digs fingers into my sides. I can't help myself. Laughter pours from between my lips. I look up at Roe, there in the sunlight dappling down through the lithe willow, and can barely imagine any part of him that would turn into a monster.

Grandma Ruby's words fill my mind again—*but only in those who are like you.* Roe is nothing like his grandfather. He does not crave power or wealth or the souls of other human beings. Roe is wholly just himself—a soft-anger boy who lives in a trailer out in the bog. The one who feels too much of the world and tries to make it better, even if that looks like using boiled water to wash his dishes or making sure his coffee doesn't come from a can.

I want to kiss him, right then and there, even though the world feels like shadows choking me, wrapping around my neck like a black-gloved hand.

A dark speck buzzes above his left shoulder, beady eyes clicking in my direction, and my stomach drops to the soles of my feet.

"Roe—" My voice is vapor on wind.

"So, you two are finally hooking up? Bog-boy and frog-face? Sounds like the title of some shitty TV show."

My teeth grind to dust, and I turn. Simon stands in the sun behind us. His left eye has the appearance of raw hamburger, splotchy and red and smelling awful. His nose has been set right again, but the bones still appear crooked, stitches lining both sides. There are two scratches on his jaw.

A dour grin smears my lips. I hit him *good.*

"How extremely mature," I say, sinking deeper into Roe. "You know, I'm going to ignore the fact that you're still calling me the same thing you have since we were ten and say, instead, I'm sorry about Olive."

Simon's face blushes hot pink. "Uh, thanks."

Now that I think about it, I'm pretty sure those two scratches on his jaw weren't made by my punch. I take a step closer. "Must be really hard, having someone die who you loved so much."

Roe tenses against me. I am wading into untamed waters. But I was born into a bog that swallows people whole and spits back the bones. My mother's savage daughter. My grandmother's blood. The blood that created the monster, and the same blood that can end it.

I await Simon's reply. His eyes narrow into slits, and the wounded skin tightens on his cheekbone.

"You'd know, wouldn't you, Thomas? Seeing as how your brother is *dead*."

The roof of my mouth shrivels to ash. Roe's fingers clench down around my waist. Heat rises through me like a tidal wave, and all I can suddenly think about is sinking my fists into Simon's face until it is nothing but pulverized meat. Agatha's feet slap in the grass behind me, her hand on my shoulder, her head against mine.

"Don't do it, Mi," she whispers. "He'll get what's coming to him."

Simon's eyebrow twitches, and when he takes a step forward, the cords in his arm flex. His eyes are flames—bright orange, burn-the-forest-down flames—and I should be scared. I really, really should be, but I'm not.

Instead, I'm angry.

It boils in me like water on a woodstove, like the ocean in a storm. And then I see it, the wisp of black curls on the wind, coming toward us, moving closer, bringing a sound I know too well now.

My teeth rattle in my skull, and I wrap my fingers firm around Roe's. No one else appears to notice them, the flies. Simon looks behind him, blinking stupidly, and then turns back.

"Seeing ghosts now, Thomas?"

And there are so many things I want to say, starting with, "Go fuck yourself." But I don't. I keep my mouth shut and walk past him, taking Roe with me. Camille and Agatha quickly follow behind.

Rows and rows of tables set with mismatched tablecloths glint in the midmorning light, each one with flowers picked from the field beyond the cemetery. There are people everywhere, people I have no desire to see. They mingle through the tables, Kool-Aid cups and store-bought cookies from Phil's clutched in their claws.

Their whispers choke the air like gasoline vapors. Eyes dart our way, and greasy smiles spread on lips when I catch their gazes. The rage inside me is boiling acid, eating away at the lining of my stomach, but I keep my mouth shut while Roe leads me to a table on the outskirts of the field. I sit down beside him. Agatha and Camille settle in across from us.

Cruel laughter cracks behind us.

Mrs. Denton reigns over her little court of fellow churchwomen, all of whom are dressed in various shades of beige, with personalities to match.

Why is she here? Shouldn't she be at home, planning her daughter's funeral?

Her eyes snag on me, and the smile on her Botox-tightened face turns sour at the edges. I offer a demure little grin over the cup of Kool-Aid someone shoved in my fingers. Then I lift it over the edge of the grass and let the liquid pour. The facade cracks when Mrs. Denton's lip curls, and she turns back to her gaggle of faithful followers.

"What the hell was that for? Her daughter is dead." Roe's lips are pressed around a Coke can.

I shrug and wipe my mouth with the sleeve of my flannel.

"And yet, she's here. Plus, I'm not drinking any of the church's water. I'm just pissed. And sick of all"—I flap a hand at the people in the field—"this. I'm sick of the show, of people pretending like they care about each other. It's all bullshit."

It's all poison.

I reach for a can of Coke chilling in a cooler and chug until the brown liquid fizzes on my chin. Roe reaches over and slides the can closer to Agatha.

"Probably should lay off the stuff for a bit there, Mila." He grins, and I swat him in the shoulder, for a moment forgetting his dad is a monster who sucks souls.

It's poetic, really, that the reverend drinks souls through his savage lips. The same lips that preach eternal life are those that take it.

By midafternoon, I'm sweating through my flannel. The cooler of Coke cans has turned to a watery tomb, and I'm pretty sure a sunburn is quickening a march across the bridge of my nose. Roe tips back in his chair, and we watch kids bob for apples in big wooden barrels on the stage. Parents stand around, cameras and phones clicking. They shout and jeer and laugh when one of the kids snorts water out his nose.

"This is disgusting," Camille says, reclining into Agatha's lap.

I look at my sister, sitting there in the sun, dressed head to toe in black and lace and fishnets. Honestly, I don't know how she's doing it, because this heat makes me want to die. A flash of darkness moves in the corner of my eye, and I whip around.

Simon and the reverend stand on the far side of the stage. Their voices are hushed. Simon seems to be crying. His face is scrunched, the wound on his face reopened and bleeding. The reverend shoves him back, and says something I can't make out. And then Simon turns and walks away, disappearing beyond the stage.

Something is wrong.

I turn to tell Roe, but he's already looking in the same direction, his muscles tense.

"You just saw that, right?" I ask.

He nods and stands up from his chair.

"Saw what?" Agatha asks, gently pushing Camille off her lap.

"Probably nothing," Roe says.

"No." Agatha reaches out a hand to stop him and stands up. "I'll do it. I've been wanting to have words with Simon for a while."

She turns to leave, but Camille digs her fingers into Agatha's wrists. "Just, be careful."

Agatha smiles and bends down, brushing her lips against Camille's. "Aren't I always?"

"No." Camille laughs, kicking back in her chair. "That's why I said it."

I watch Agatha walk away, a dark drop in the ocean of beige and pastels, and I can't help but feel like I'm sending my sister into the belly of the beast. Simon is all fists, angry words, and leering eyes. It should be *me* going back behind the stage, to finish what I started when I punched him in the face yesterday.

I try to get to my feet, to follow my sister through the grass, but Mrs. Denton mounts the stage, and Roe grabs my wrist.

The word is on his lips like shadow—*no*—and so I take my seat. Agatha's blond hair disappears around the back of the platform. High-pitched sound rings out from the stage when Mrs. Denton's cream-colored fingernail pings against the microphone.

"Hi, folks. Sorry about that!" she chitters, a single white envelope clutched in one hand. "First of all, on behalf of the Credence Hollow

Sinner's Chapel and Reverend Byron, I would like to welcome you all to the fiftieth Sunday School Picnic and Blueberry Festival!"

The crowd cheers apathetically, and my eyes scan the tables for the reverend. I spot him lording over a spread of chocolate cream pies and lemon bars. My belly drops out from underneath me. The sun reflects off his glasses again, and the light almost blinds me.

We make eye contact. He smiles and takes a bite of pie. The whipped cream sticks to the top of his lip.

I spin away.

Another woman stands on the stage behind Mrs. Denton now—Mrs. Chartier, Dani and Camille's mom. There is a beige pillow in her hands, and on top of that rests the coveted Blueberry Queen crown. Made from twisted metal resembling vines and faux gaudy sapphires, the crown has always been something of a legend.

Every girl who has ever worn it has gone on to be favored in Credence Hollow—the girl who wins the college scholarships, gets the guy, and goes on to become church secretary, like Mrs. Denton. I can still remember the day Dani Chartier herself won the crown. Though, in her case, the next day, she turned up missing and was never seen again.

I look across the table at Camille, who is absentmindedly chewing on the beds of her fingernails. Dani has never asked me to talk to her sister for her, to let Camille know she is okay. And maybe that's because she's not. Because, even if the reverend is stopped, those souls will be forever trapped in the liminal space of the bog—floating in a limbo of in-between, like a flower trying to grow through rock, coins lost between cushions.

And so, I don't push it. I don't reach across the table and whisper some bullshit about, "Your sister wants you to know she's okay and she loves you."

Because Dani is dead.

And Jed probably is too. Maybe I just need to finally come to terms with that.

"Now, I know it probably seems strange, me being here. I'm sure everyone has heard the news by now. But the reverend assured me this is what Olive would have wanted. So, let's first raise a glass to my daughter." Mrs. Denton holds a plastic cup over her head and then drinks.

Everyone else in the field follows suit.

I lock eyes with Roe.

Bog water, he mouths.

Of course. I look around for the reverend, but he's nowhere to be found. Pain fizzles at the roots of my skull.

Mrs. Denton smacks her lips. "The time has come for us to crown this year's blueberry queen." Her fingers fumble with the cream-colored envelope, her nails shredding it open.

She pulls the paper closer, and I watch with unbridled satisfaction when the look on her face drops. There is silence in the field for a moment. The only noises are the heat bugs drawling out from the trees in the cemetery. And then Mrs. Denton clears her throat, and a laugh twists from her lips.

"Well, uhm, it would appear that this year's blueberry queen is Mila Thomas."

As soon as my name leaves her lips, the world around me seems to slow. All the colors blur together, turning to smears on the corner of my vision. Roe says my name, and his arm squeezes around my shoulders, jolting me from my chair. But everything is far away, as if I'm watching the scene play out on a screen.

The field silences. No one seems to be clapping except Roe and Camille, and when I try to stand to my feet, my legs shake beneath me. The feeling taking root at the base of my skull is pushing petals up the back of my head, a hot pricking breaking out along my skin. My fingers fumble with the pop can in front of me, knocking it over. The dark liquid bleeds out onto the tablecloth.

My eyes scan the crowd. Mom isn't even here.

Where is Agatha? She should have heard my name called and come.

Mrs. Denton repeats my name, and I turn for the stage. Each step is like walking through a fog. I clamber up the wooden stairs to the platform, trying to smile through the pain cracking through my mind like a hurricane. Already I can hear it—the voice pressing against my outer wall.

Mrs. Denton's face swims in front of me. She turns and smiles, saying something I can no longer make out. Mrs. Chartier holds the crown out, and I bend my neck. Metal vines dig into my scalp, and the weight of the thing sends pressure to my shoulders. I try to turn toward the crowd of weary, bog-drinking onlookers, but the feeling in my skull is overwhelm-ing, worse than it ever has been before.

I'm down on my knees before I can stop myself, and somewhere above me, someone is laughing.

It sounds gravelly, like rocks being tossed—

Someone shouts, but it's nothing next to the flood of noise cascading through my bones, making my teeth rattle and the layers of skin vibrate. It's like I am pressed inside a coffin filled with needles, and when I open my mouth to scream, no sound comes out. I drop on my side. The crown clambers off my head, and my body begins to shake there on the stage. I roll and hit the ground, but there's nothing I can do. No way to soften the impact. To avoid the cracking in my ribs.

Screams. Mrs. Denton shouts something into the microphone.

And then Roe's hands are on my face, my chin, angling me up to look at him, but I'm already on the ground, dirt grinding into my skin. The voices break out like fissures in my bone. Not one, not two, but hundreds. They reach up to me through the earth, from the water shushing deep below me. Their sound a wretched choir of pain and righteous anger.

He is coming, they say.

Look around.

He is already here.

And then Dani's voice, like a wisp of smoke curling and embracing my consciousness—soft, warm, familiar. *He has no eyes.*

The reverend. I try to get to my feet, to search through the maze of faces for his eyes blaring like twin suns. But I still don't see him.

He is gone.

Roe says my name and tries to drag me up into his arms, but all I can feel is the bog. I steady my fingers against the earth. The water courses through my own blood.

I am ready.

And I open myself up to the voices swimming below its inky surface. They break through me like water from a rock, like fire spitting up be-tween logs—Dani and Owen and Grandma Ruby—while the flies drone overhead. People start shrieking, getting up to run from the swarming insects, and all I can do is raise my hands to the heavens and smile. Because finally, the town will see the reverend for who he is, and I will be the one to show them.

Mila.

I turn my head to look at Roe, but his lips are not moving.

Mila.

The word comes through me again. It's Agatha's voice. But it isn't coming from around me. It's coming from beneath.

From the water seeping up to kiss my knees. There's a whiff of death to it.

Mila, he's got me. Mila, come to the bog.

22

THE GENERAL

Don't panic. You'll find Agatha. You can't panic.

This is what I repeat over and over in my mind while I pedal furiously toward the swamp. But even as the words melt against my tongue, I start believing them less and less. Simon is gone, the reverend is gone, and Agatha is calling out to me through the water, which means she could be dead. But I refuse to believe that. Refuse to let my sister be among the bones.

If the reverend has Agatha, he means to kill her. But he also might be trying to lure me into the bog, and if that's his plan, it's working.

My breath comes in short gasps. The pain is now rooted in my chest rather than my skull. It threatens to rip my heart to shreds right there in the red dust of the road. But I keep pedaling. I have to or else I might just jump in my truck and never look back.

But I can't lose any more of my family.

So, I don't panic. Don't let the feeling between my ribs overtake me. I will live, I will survive, and so will my sister.

My breathing only ramps up when I crest the hill toward home. Sharp stones kick up from the ground when I fling my bike against the porch. Roe and Camille are close on my heels. My eyes dart around the cabin, but there's no sign of Mom anywhere, except for her car parked haphazardly in the drive. For all I know, she's probably still passed out on the sofa.

Just where the reverend wants her.

Agatha, I tell myself. Agatha, Agatha, Agatha.

I turn toward the tree line. The cool breeze echoes from between the cedar trunks. She's in there.

"We can't just blast in there," Camille shouts, panic swimming in her voice. "We don't have any—I don't know—weapons!"

"Mila." Roe is behind me, his fingers sinking into my arm. "We have to think. We have to come up with a plan."

I wrench my arm from him and march toward the trees. "I already have a plan: rescue my sister."

He and Camille have no choice but to follow me.

The woods are dark and quiet. Waiting on the brink of something with bated breath. The only noise is the gentle hum of flies. They're everywhere—hovering in the branches, caught up in the weak rays of sun, buzzing around the undergrowth at my knees. For a moment, I wonder if they're meant to warn me again, to tell me to open my eyes and look around, see the reverend for who he truly is. But while we continue through the woods, the flies part. Like they're making paths for us, leading us through the trees until we empty out onto the shore of the bog.

The air swims cool here, even with the sun beating down against the dark surface of the water. The stench of death fills the air, and I gag when I see the source.

Bones. Everywhere. Spat out onto the shore in piles, in grotesque heaps of human remains. The consequences of Grandma Ruby's curse. Her bitterness. People always said the bog was different, acted strange. And now I know why.

Camille yelps behind me. Roe tries to quiet her, but all I can do is stare at the bone meadow stretching before me like the unearthed grave it is. The bones glint in the sunlight, covered in weeds and muck, growing algae along their ridges and pores. Rage like a blade slices across my chest.

I scream.

I scream out my anger and pain. I scream out my terror and the unending grief threatening to undo me, there between the bones of all those the bog has swallowed. All who the monsters have taken. Those nameless hundreds who will never again feel the sunlight on their skin, who will crack against my skull day after day with messages for loved ones.

And though it seems impossible, every inch of the bog runs through my veins. Its anger, its rage, floods through me and explodes from my raw and screaming tongue. I don't care if the reverend will hear me, if he tries to tear me limb from limb, because I am just a girl with enough anger spilling from her pores to douse the entire town. The bog rushes up to meet me, and I speed for the shores, kicking up bones as I go. There is no stopping me now.

There is no stopping the bog.

I leap across the water. The spits of land quake beneath me, and I let the energy soak into the soles of my feet. Roe cries my name, but I don't turn around. Every inch of me quakes with the need to rid this place of the reverend, once and for all.

And then it comes again, a voice, up from the water like a whisper on wind.

The cabin, Mila. He's in the cabin.

I scan the bog for the old family cabin. It sits half shrunken in the shallows, lined with moss and corpse finder mushrooms, like some macabre gingerbread house.

"Mila!"

Roe scrambles toward me through my haze, over a scrap of muddied grass and cattails, Camille close behind him. The wind picks up, swirling from the western banks and bringing with it the thick smell of death and rotting bones.

"The cabin!" I shout. "They're in the cabin."

And then a flash of movement catches in the corner of my vision.

Someone hidden among the reeds.

I narrow my eyes and make out a body—dead or alive, I can't tell. But it's there, and no matter the consistency of its soul, it's watching us. Roe reaches me, and the water gathers around our ankles.

"We need to make it across the water to the cabin." My voice now fights with the wind spewing at us from the shore.

Roe's face swims with sick, the color leeching from his cheeks, and I can only imagine what is coming up at him from the water. I reach for his hand, folding his fingers into mine.

"We can do this," I say. "You and me. Not alone."

And then, behind us, comes a scream. A god-awful sound turning the blood in my veins to hot ash.

It's Camille.

Hair whips my face, and I scramble for it with bog-wet fingers. She clutches onto a thick carpet of moss, her fingers scrambling, hanging on for dear life. Her body bobs violently in the water. There are ripples in the darkness, sucking at her while she chokes on the bog.

No. No, no. I will not lose another loved one to this wretched place.

Without waiting for Roe, I leap across the water, fingers and feet flailing. My hands grip reeds, the thin cellulose cutting my skin. My blood mixes with the swamp like oil and vinegar. And then icy fingers clamp around my ankle. I hear the voice. The same one I heard only days ago. The wrong name on its lips.

Ruby, Ruby, Ruby.

And I recognize it now; I have heard it screaming, if only in my mind.

Cecil Byron. Who wandered out on a ripe June night and let the bog take him.

The rage inside me bursts like the white light energy at the center of a shooting star. I erupt from the water, kicking and scraping my hands on the reeds.

This is the end.

The final moments of all the pain our two families have caused.

But when I look up, Camille is still screaming in the water. The rage in my blood turns to ice.

Slick, anemic hands wrap around her torso, desperately trying to drag her beneath the waves. And then slowly, like a snake from a basket, a head emerges: shoulders, the arms and torso, and those eyes blazing like dying stars.

The reverend.

He blasts from the water, folding Camille into his beastly arms. His skin crawls, turns snow-white and hard. His fingers lengthen, sharp nails thin and crystalline. Fear roots in my belly. He holds Camille, pale muscles bulging. His clothes are stripped away, and he is nothing but the worm. Humanoid, yet ruined. A fallen form of life.

Camille's cry stops in her throat. There's nothing I can do. I am helpless in the water. And I let that feeling fill me, let it seep out into every cell in my body until I am nothing but a vessel of righteous fizzling anger. Nothing but a girl with bog water pumping in her veins.

The reverend rises from the water, his skin stretching, pale and sickly and snapping with phlegm.

Roe's hand presses on my back, warm, trying the best he can to keep me safe.

And then another roar echoes across the water. I turn toward the cabin. Though I see nothing, I know something is wrong. Agatha is going to die. I clench my fists at my sides, let the bog fill me until I am near bursting, and turn to face the reverend and his milky eyes.

"Let her go!" I shout against the wind. "I know you. I know what you're doing! Feeding the whole town this swill so you can take their souls at any time you please. You think you can just steal the thing that makes us human so you can do what, grow immortal? You're sick!" I take a deep breath. "No more bog. No more monster. Just you. It's over, Reverend Byron."

The pale face cracks, and his pink gums bleed out against slimy skin. "Oh, it will never be over, Mila."

The voice is worse than I could have ever imagined—sucking mud, sharpened rocks and tearing flesh, sand and salt rubbed into a wound. It shakes me to my core and rattles my teeth. If I open my mouth, they will fall like bloody pearls into my palm. I look back up at the reverend, study the peeling scalp of stringy, muck-caked hair, the soulless eyes, the lipless tear of a mouth. Groping hands, always reaching.

And I smile.

Men are so afraid of queens and witches. But I am something more savage, wilder than the dark, the cold, the fighting wind.

I am a girl with nothing to lose.

And so, I spread my arms wide, allow the bog to pool up against my toes, caress the roots sinking beneath me, and I let the voices in—every single one of them who has ever felt the power rush from their lungs, their heart, their soul.

I am filled with every emotion, every broken spirit, every vengeful, raging cry breaking out from skeletal teeth. My body contains multitudes. And I let it all out in a scream that cracks against my lips and twists from my throat, raw and bleeding. The sound buffets the air around me like a shot from a cannon, and Roe cries out in pain. He falls to his knees at my feet.

But I don't stop. *I can't stop.*

Every ounce of rage and anger I've felt toward the reverend, toward this town, toward the fact my brother disappeared into these trees three years ago and never came back, winds me up and spills out like a forest fire. The reverend cracks sideways, his lipless mouth open in a shout of agony when my battle cry rattles his bones.

Yes, yes, I can feel it. The power like a set of wings encases me, wrapping me up and breaking against the back of a man who craved so much power, it changed him into a thing—a monster doomed to squirm across the earth without a soul.

But then the reverend starts to straighten—sinuous limbs pulling up at odd forms, like a puppet connected to unseen strings. His eyes blaze toward me, so hot they might melt my flesh. Camille's cries cut through the air.

He's crushing her, folding her like a rag dog until all her bones snap at wrong angles.

And I do the only thing I can think of.

My toes barely brush the sharp reeds when I leap across the water and throw myself against his clammy hide. My nails scratch along thick and corded skin, but they are nothing to the density of him, the strength. Screams rip from my throat while I beat my fists against his spine, trying to free Camille. Hell, trying to free myself. His hand tightens around my waist, my rib cage, squeezing until I will burst right there in the bog—nothing to identify me but a pile of viscera spilled out like red paint on dark canvas.

Through blurry, bloodshot eyes, I see Roe, sprawled out in the water-choked reeds, his face turned toward me. Twisted in agony, he is almost unrecognizable. His mouth is open, but I can't hear him, can't touch his skin and tell him that it's going to be all right. I squirm in the reverend's hold, trying to get near enough to Camille to say Dani loves her—to tell her Dani will be there waiting for us—but something stops me.

A flash of movement in the shallows again, and then someone emerges. My chest cracks in half.

A young man with dirty blond hair falling to his shoulders and eyes as blue as cornflowers charges from the reeds, leaping across the bog.

He knows the paths.

He taught them to me.

Tears pool in my eyes. The breath catches on hooks in my throat while my lungs try and expand in a chest that feels broken.

Jed. *My* Jed.

The reverend's grip tightens around me, but I don't care. I barely feel it while I watch my brother cross the bog, his golden hair shining like wheat in the sun. And then the breath rushing up from my lungs escapes my lips, and I'm screaming his name over and over. Hot tears spill down my cheeks.

"You!" the reverend roars, and he flings Camille aside.

Her body crashes into the water.

Jed plants his feet in the reeds, and then, in a moment, our eyes meet. Every ounce of rage I have ever felt melts because my brother is alive.

"Why don't you tell her?" Jed cries above the tumult of wind and roiling heat. "Why don't you tell her the truth?"

I stare at my brother, noticing the jagged, rusty knife clenched in one fist. The reverend holds me out over the water, letting my feet dangle inches from the snapping surface. Cecil's ghost is down there, I know, waiting to drag me under, to add my bones to the legacy he built with my grandmother.

"There is no truth," the reverend says.

"Jed." The name feels almost false on my tongue, like if I say it too loud, he will vanish into smoke.

He grins lopsided up at me, and though the years have changed him, he is still the same brother who wrapped me up in those strong arms and told me everything would be okay.

Jed brandishes the knife. "Tell her, or I swear to God, I'll run you through."

Heat cracks out on my skull, and Agatha's voice echoes in my ears. *Mila, he's going to kill me.*

But that's not possible. I scratch bloody nails across the reverend's arm. The bog comes up to meet me again, and a scream rips from my throat. The reverend's grip loosens, and I drop to a clump of cattails, the water soaking into my shirt.

"Jed, now!" I cry.

He leaps across the water, sinking the blade into the reverend's ribbed, white neck.

The sound of stone cracking erupts from the monster's throat. He sinks beneath the water. Jed falls to the peaty soil at my side, grinning widely.

"Hey, little sis. I've missed you."

23

THE SONS OF TITUS BYRON

I quake in the water, a hand pressed in the reeds to steady myself.

Jed. How is it Jed?

My head reels with the idea that my dead brother is *alive*. Even though I've tried to believe it for years, even though I heard his name spilling from Olive's lips last night, I can't truly wrap my mind around Jed standing in front of me now, with a hand outstretched and a smile on his lips. I'm scared if I touch him, if I open my mouth and say his name again, he will disappear before me like smoke, like some sick, twisted illusion.

So, I push myself to my feet and punch him.

And when my skin meets his, when his cartilage crumples and his bones shift beneath my knuckles, something inside me bursts hot, like a ruptured balloon, and angry tears stream down my cheeks.

"Damn, Mila." Jed rubs his jaw, feeling for loose teeth. "I see your usual way of dealing with things hasn't changed."

He grins, ruby dripping from his nose. I fall against him, his blood warm and sticky on my fingers. He doesn't get mad, doesn't yell or push me away. Jed just envelopes me, smelling like wet sand, mud, and worn, patched denim. And for a moment, the world feels a little okay. Like we might all survive what will undoubtedly return from the bog's bitter depths.

"Where the fuck have you been?"

He laughs softly. "Here. I couldn't stay home, not until I knew I wouldn't turn. Not until I knew you and Mom and Aggy were safe. From me."

A sob breaks from my throat. Water is pooling up around my calves. If we stay here a second too long—a moment, even—the bog will come up to swallow us, and the ghost in the water will drag us down.

"We need to get to Roe and Camille and Aggy," I say, clutching the seams of his jacket.

He nods, and there are tears in his eyes. "We know the paths."

The words crash into me like a thousand weights because I have waited the last three years to hear him say them again.

"We know the paths."

I take his hand in mine, leap across the water to where Roe still lies prostrate in the moss, and brush my fingertips hurriedly across Roe's brow.

"Roe, we need to move." My voice is quiet, rushed.

I dare a quick look back at the rippling, black water. I doubt Jed's blade did much against the scaly hide. The reverend won't stay down there for long.

Roe whimpers under my palm, his eyes shifting beneath closed lids. I try to pry him from the ground while the water seeps up to stain his shirt.

"I can feel him," Roe whispers, breath hot against my skin. "I can feel him down there, Mila. My...my dad." He turns his face to look at me then, pain swimming palpable in his irises like oil in a puddle.

"I know." I do my best to keep my voice gentle when my insides feel anything but. After pulling Roe up, I brush plant remains and mud from his shoulders. "Look at me." I slip a finger beneath his chin, pulling his eyes to meet mine. "You have to fight how he makes you feel. He's hurt you and made you feel worthless your entire life. But he's wrong on so many levels, and you've got to fight him. Because if I don't have you—" A choke fills my throat, and I turn back, watching Jed help Camille from the patch of bloody reeds she is on. "I might not have anyone else."

Roe struggles, following me to his feet. He looks broken. All the soft anger has turned to piles of smoldering ash and melted ice. I lift one of his hands in mine, unwrapping the bandages around his knuckles, where the skin is raw and open. He winces, but I drop the bandages one by one to the water curling around our toes.

"Let him see," I whisper, pressing my forehead against his. "Let him see the pain he's caused."

Jed splashes in the water. He's nearing the cabin with Camille tucked loosely against his shoulder. I turn back to the churning water, setting my eyes to the place where the reverend slipped beneath the waves.

Agatha, are you still in there? I hope the bog will act as a conduit, bringing my words to my sister's ears.

Yes, but he's here, Mila. You have to come now.

Right, well, that does it. I just got one sibling back from the dead, and I'm not letting my other go to an early grave. With Roe's arm looped around my shoulders, I turn us toward the shore.

"We're going to have to jump," I say. "Can you do that?"

He nods, and I suck air into my lungs, bracing myself for the leap across the water.

But it never comes.

The bog tremors beneath our feet. Roe crumples beside me, his knees hitting the water, head cradled in his palms. This place—this pain is too much for him. My heart pounds in my chest until I'm almost sure it will burst right out of its confines of ribs. I'll find it beating in my hands. Without waiting for Agatha's voice or Jed's, I pull Roe tight against me. My feet hit the path toward the cabin that Grandma Ruby taught me so long ago.

I drop Roe to the sand. He is coughing and spluttering, but my mind is no longer on him. Jed kneels over Camille, pumping her chest with a fist. Bog water dribbles from her lips, which are thick and choked with weeds. Roe's hand slips into mine.

"Mila." My name is cracked on his lips, and his eyes are round as saucers in his pale face. He points toward the cabin.

"What is it, Roe?"

He falls against me, every inch of his body limp and heavy. "He's in there. They're both in there."

Agatha. The reverend.

My feet push through the sand, running, so fast my chest is burning. Roe's hand breaks from mine, and his knees hit the ground. Then Jed is standing in front of me, blocking the way, a firm line set on his lips. He grabs me by the shoulders, hands like immovable boulders.

"You can't go in there," he says.

"I have to, Jed. Agatha's in there. He's going to kill her." I push past him, my feet squelching in the mud.

His hand grips my wrist, pulling me back. And I see it then, there in his pupils—the fear, the pain reflecting the anger seeping from my soul.

"You don't understand what's happening."

I rip my hand from his, eyes flashing. Heat blazes a trail down my breastbone.

"You left," I spit. "You left and I had to pick up the pieces. And for what, Jed? Why did you leave?"

He pulls me in closer until I am beating heavy palms against his chest, tears bleeding from my cheeks and wetting the cotton of his shirt. His warm hand comes to smooth my hair, his chin resting on my head.

"I tried to tell you, Mila. Don't you remember?"

I'm a curse.

The words swim in my mind, cold and bitter.

"But why?" I sob against him. "You never explained. I watched you talk with Grandma Ruby the night before you slipped away into the bog. I thought you would come back. I stayed up all night waiting, but you never did. And I never knew why."

His palms are on my cheeks, pulling me to look up at him, to stare into his blue eyes that glint like snowmelt pools in the sun. And then I see it, deeper, the way they almost seem to glare too bright, too hungry.

Three sons, Simon had said. *Three.*

My gut swims, claws raking through my viscera, peeling back my skin and revealing nothing but dust beneath.

Three sons.

Mom never told Jed and me who our dads were. *It wasn't necessary to know*, she used to say.

But maybe that's because the truth was too awful to face.

I reel back on my heels, dry heaving onto the sand. Roe shouts my name again, but it's too much. My palms crash into the grit, and my stomach empties itself of the fizzy pop, burning and acidic while it coats my tongue. Jed is on the ground beside me, his palm on my back. I twist my face to look at him and see it there again, in his eyes—the reverend.

"Is it both of us?" I ask. "Are we both...*his?*"

Jed shakes his head. "No, only me. I found out that night. Grandma

Ruby told me the whole story. About him and Mom, how they'd loved each other in high school, how she hadn't known about the Byron curse until it was too late and Grandma couldn't protect her. How he'd abandoned her when she'd told him about me because his wife was already pregnant with—"

"Simon." The name presses inside my mouth like the wholeness of a sour apple. I gag on it, spilling silky vomit into the bog.

Jed's fingers brush through my hair, pulling me back to face him. His eyes are soft, puddled, and filled with three years of regret. Three years of fear the reverend would find him.

And then it all clicks.

The conversation I overheard in the confessional.

I thought Simon was talking about the monster, but he was talking about Jed. And if he knows my brother is still alive, that means he knows everything.

He is a monster.

I snap up, eyes scanning the bog.

"Mila, what is it?" Jed falls back into the sand.

But before I have time to tell him, before I let my suspicions take root, the door to the cabin cracks open, and Simon walks out, dragging Agatha by her hair. Red blood courses from a wound on her leg. I want to launch myself at him, but hands wrap around both my wrists. When I look back, Jed and Roe stand ankle-deep in mud.

I want to scream, tell them to let me go, but I am motionless, triangulated between the three sons of Titus Byron.

"Well, well, well, if it isn't Jed Thomas, back from the dead." Simon's lip curls back, revealing white and glinting teeth. "Come to rescue your baby sisters."

"Come to set some wrongs right, Simon." Jed's grip is still firm on my arms. "Want to tell them what you did with Olive?"

Simon opens his mouth, and a laugh cracks on his teeth. "Olive had what was coming to her. And what do you know of right and wrong, Thomas? Dad tried to teach you. All those days, I'd find you both behind the church, talking. He was trying to teach you what you could have become. But you were too weak, just like Roe." He jabs a finger into the air, eyes like narrow slits. "Such a fucking disappointment."

I snort. "I think the real disappointment is the son who abused his girlfriend like she was a sack of meat. Did you ever once look at Olive and feel love, Simon? Or is it only possession?" Anger laces every word.

A thin, warning growl slips from Simon's mouth, and his fist tightens on Agatha's curls. She winces. Her body is covered in scratches, rips in her tights, her clothes dripping with blood and bog water. Somewhere behind us, Camille heaves in a breath, my sister's name on her tongue.

"Don't you get it, Mila?" Simon's voice is like ice on rocks. "Don't you see? It's only ever been about possession." He wrenches Agatha's neck back so her eyes meet his. "About power. Olive would have helped me, but the bitch got away. He helped her."

Simon points at Jed.

A pinch of heat grows on the back of my neck, and the thin whisper of a voice curls through my ears.

I curse you now, to walk soulless on the earth for all generations to come. But only in those who are like you—who take advantage, who crave power.

I smile. The grit of sand lingers in my teeth. *Grandma Ruby.*

"Is that what happened?" I watch Simon's skin begin to coalesce into cords of white sinew. Transforming. "Both of your father's real picks turned out to be disappointments, so he turned to you? The big, ugly brute of a son he knew would crave the kind of power needed to turn you just like him? How long did it take you to understand what was happening? How many nights did it take of you waking up, covered in blood and bog water, to realize he was turning you into a monster? Making the outside match your inside?"

Roe's grip loosens at my words because he's starting to see it too. The monster isn't just his father—it's his brother. A whole rotten legacy of ravenous men whose blood runs through his own veins.

Simon's laugh rips through the air, and he takes another step toward us, dragging Agatha like a rag doll.

"You think I was his *last* choice?" Simon sneers. "You think that I didn't want this?" He lifts a hand into the air, and the slew of white drips in cords down his wrist. It grows up his arm, hardening the skin to bristled epidermis. It spreads across his face until all the features there have turned to marble, leaving only the beacon-bright holes in his head. The lipless mouth rips, flesh pulling flesh like strings, revealing glinting, sharp teeth. He smiles. "Oh, Mila. This is all I ever wanted."

He's gloating, and I want to tear him into shreds. Slash him into a million pieces and scatter them like ashes on the wind.

I want to burn him *down*.

Simon lets go of Agatha and takes a step closer, and that's when I pounce. My body collides with his, cold flesh against hot, angry skin. I throw him to the ground. He's smaller than the reverend, but the air is still knocked from my lungs when he flips me over and presses my back into the wet sand.

The smell emitting from his shredded mouth is like fish intestines left to bake in the sun. I gag, and a thick wad of saliva drips down the back of my throat. Simon's face is inches from mine, breath hot and humid on my skin, his fingers curled at the edge of my jaw.

"Want to see how it works?" His voice rattles like the end of a snake tail, spittle flying in my eyes. "Want to taste death, Thomas?"

For a moment, I entertain the thought. What it must feel like to have eternity wash over me in waves, rubbing me as smooth as river stones. But the last thing I want is to become another voice, another dead thing drifting through the in-between of the bog.

I don't want to die.

Roe and Jed are behind us, frightened.

I *won't* die, not when there is so much to live for.

As if they hear my thoughts, a swarm of flies curls up from the outer reaches of the swamp. Their wings send the familiar noise bouncing across my skin. Simon's head swivels, stringy, wet hair whipping my face. I bend my legs up underneath him and knee him hard in the belly. Air rushes cold from his lungs, and I pin him back beneath me, one arm pressed against his scaly throat. Jed and Roe are at my side, swifter than the wind. The flies swarm heavily, blinding Simon. He shouts and roars and tries to bat them away.

The trees all around us begin to shudder, and the bog ripples and quakes. The anger rushes through the ground beneath me—the vengeance—and when I look up from the monster thrashing in the muck, Agatha is on her feet, beaten and bloody.

But her mouth is open, and she's screaming. Bog water empties from her lips, her teeth like incandescent pearls in the high sun. Simon flails, his eyes blinking wildly, like a dying flashlight. He roars against Agatha's bloody screams.

"We have to get him into the cabin!" I cry to Jed above the din.

He nods and looks at Roe. They each take hold of Simon's scaly, thick arms, dragging him toward the cabin. Agatha follows us, her siren cries like a funeral procession. Simon's claws sink deep into my skin, hot as freshly forged spikes. But still we run, through the shallows to the crook-ed door.

Simon is too fast, too slick. He breaks free of his brothers, and before I can stop, before I can think, my temple is cracked against a rock like the shell of an egg and Roe is enveloped in shadows.

What I witness nearly has me spilling more sick into the shallows at my cheek.

Simon writhes with Roe in the mud, except he isn't Roe anymore, not truly. Every feeling, every emotion he has felt from the bog, knits together across his skin, like the rugged pattern of a quilt. And though he isn't a monster, the bog changes him, turns him into what has always lived inside him—anger.

"No!" I scream.

Agatha's steady hand is on my shoulder, and Jed is pulling me back.

The brothers battle, a screaming melee of tooth and claw and burning eyes. Roe's hands rake against Simon's torso, red welts bursting in their wake. The skin on Roe's knuckles breaks, and the blood pours hot. His fists sink deep into Simon's corrugated skin.

"We have to stop him!" I shout, scrambling, my vision blurry and thick.

Simon's eyes swivel toward me. One hand crushes Roe's throat, and he smiles. The sound of rending flesh fills the air. Simon's not even human anymore, not really. Part man, part monster, but worse than his father before him or even his grandfather. Simon is not just a man who craves power; he is a thing of death. A creature bred by eons of white men who have never had to answer for anything in their entire lives. Men who have never listened and never cared to do so.

He drops Roe's shaking limbs to the reeds, turning on him with only one thing in those soulless eyes.

Death.

I lurch to my feet, wanting to kill him, to separate him limb from limb and burn his body until he is nothing but dust, left to be forgotten. But Agatha pushes me to one side. The bog water still runs from between her lips, and when she opens her mouth, flies pour forth, blinding Simon while she shepherds him toward the cabin. They buzz around his skull, drawing him like smoke to a fire, and that's when I notice the matchbook in Agatha's hand.

I wrench myself free from Jed and throw myself at the monster. The cabin's door is inches away now. My feet stumble over rock and water. I press toward Simon until I can hear his heart beating, feel the ice of his scales, taste the tang of his rotten breath on the wind. Roe and Jed scream my name, but it's too late. If killing Simon takes my life too, I will gladly give it up. I find Agatha through the swirling cloud of whisper-wind wings and nod.

Light him on fire. Even if I'm still inside.

She nods, and I crash through the door, pinning Simon to the rotting floorboards beneath.

"No more," I whisper into his ear. The flies buzz all around us. "It's over. You will never touch Agatha again. You will never touch me again. You will die here alone, powerless, without a soul, Simon Byron, because that is what you are—pitiful and alone."

I feel the blaze before I see it—crisp orange light licking up the dry-rot wood like sunrise against a forest. The smoke billows toward us, and the wet sound of Simon coughing, choking on his own blood, pours from the wound in his face.

What if I will die here, where it all started? Where Grandma Ruby took the bog into her hands and made it sick. Cursed us all, even if that wasn't her intent.

The flies in the cabin sizzle and pop, and then a hand reaches through the swirling shadow. I can't see who it is, but they are pulling me up, up, up out of the pit. My tongue tastes fresh air and muddy water, and for a moment, I am free again.

24

THE GNASHING OF TEETH

I look up through the haze; it isn't Jed's eyes I see, but Roe's. For a moment, I want to smile, to say, "We did it." Return everything back to normal. But then I remember: The reverend is still out there.

I lurch to my feet. The air in the bog swims with thick, choking smoke. I cough and drag it into my lungs. My fingers fumble with Roe while I lean into him, trying to get away from the burning cabin.

"Jed," I croak. "Where is Jed?"

Agatha and Camille stand at the edge of the water. Camille is crying into my sister's shoulder, and Agatha smooths her hair. I look back at Roe. His throat is swollen and bruised, purple standing out against the tan, like an oasis in the desert. There is nothing beautiful about the way his face is pinched, the way the truth lies delicately on his tongue. Like he's afraid that if he tells me, I might crack along the fissures running through me like veins.

"My—my dad," Roe chokes. "He took him while you wrestled Simon into the cabin."

My skin flares hot, and I scan the bog. But there is nothing, no one, except the four of us standing stalemated in the shallows.

No. I will not lose him again.

Agatha shivers, her leg losing blood. "He said the church is the holiest of holies. Where the water touches hallowed ground."

The words swim through my mind, thoughts scattering on the wind. I clench my fists and grind my teeth until they've turned to bone dust.

There are tears in Agatha's eyes when she takes Camille's hand. All that was left of the bog inside her is now gone.

"What does he mean, Mila? What's he going to do to Jed?"

And I know why the bog has left my sister. It surges through me like a storm, crashing against my skin.

End it, it says. *End it now. Use us.*

And then Grandma Ruby's words—soft, sincere, full of repentance. *Your time has come, child*, she says. *To end the misery I created. Use your gift.*

I drop Roe's hand and push through the water toward the far shore, where the bones lie scattered, spit out by the bog.

Set us free, set us free, set us free.

"Everyone get behind me," I say.

My skin crackles with electricity. All my life, I have been afraid of this power. That first time, with Roe last summer, I thought I killed the thing I had raised. But instead, I had brought peace. Like I did with Owen.

And now...

Now you all will rest. Just help me one last time.

The voices undulate. I reach the sand and bend down. The others stay behind me. I skim my fingers across a single bone. It starts slow at first, like hoarfrost creeping along a rose. But then the flesh blooms. Tendons spit up like roots, brown skin grows over, and soft lips burst in a grin.

"Oh my god, Dani."

The body surges to new life and crashes toward Camille, wrapping arms around her.

"Holy shit," Roe says breathlessly.

Dani Chartier pulls away from her sister and takes me in with pale, milky eyes. "We're here, however you need us. And then you'll let us go?"

I nod.

Dani. After all these years. She wraps Camille back up and places a cold kiss on her sister's forehead.

"I never left."

Then Camille is weeping, Agatha is crying, and I am moving through the bog, doing the one thing I have been terrified to do my whole life.

I raise the dead.

❦   ❦

The trees on the roadside shudder and shake while we pedal our bikes toward the church. Dani and the rest of the dead are on our heels. Their bodies are broken at strange angles, bones slipping through skin, that gaping hole in their chests where the worms reached in and tore out their souls. There are so many gray and sallow faces I know, and some I don't. People who fell between the cracks. Who died ages ago when Cecil first tried to create for himself an immortal soul.

The bog runs beneath us, shushing under the town. The roots below conjure its anger to match the gathering clouds above our heads, the dark tendrils like ink drops in the sky. When we reach the church, the field is deserted. Only empty chairs at empty tables, empty cars, tablecloths flapping in the chilling breeze. My tires skid on the gravel, and I throw my bike down.

I glance over at Roe. "Ready?"

He nods.

Before us, the dead wait for instruction. *Dani* waits.

"Roe and I will go in alone, figure out where Jed is and what the reverend's plan is. If there's anyone else in there, I'll need Dani and the rest of you to help me clear the church. We don't know what the reverend will try."

Agatha limps up to me and presses something into my hand. The matchbook.

"Camille and I will stay out here." She looks down at her bloodied leg. "Not that I'd be much help anyway. Just—" Her gaze matches mine. Cold. Hard. Determined. "There's only one match left, Mila. Use it well."

I nod. "Right, let's go."

I grab Roe's hand and fling open the doors to the church.

The smell of decay floods my nose. All along the once-white walls of the church, green-gray algae grows in clumps, spilling water down to the seeping floorboards. Not only was the reverend filling up his parishioners with the bog, he was saturating his church. One day, he hoped to take their souls all at once. No more need for the shores of the bog when he could bring it inside his house of sin.

"Roe." My voice is shaky, strained. I try to swallow it. "Look, I don't know what's gonna happen in there, but if your dad tries to hurt Jed, I—"

Roe stops my words with a kiss. He tastes of salt, bog water, and earth, and I don't let go, not until he steps back for a breath. His eyes stare hard into mine.

"Do whatever you have to do, Mila. That thing isn't my dad anymore."

My chest grows tight. I nod. Right, whatever I have to do.

I motion toward the swinging doors at the top of the stairs, and we make our ascent, the pink carpet squishing under our feet. "Let's go."

Roe takes my hand. We reach the landing before the door—he is so good, too good to have a father like Titus Byron.

And Simon. For a moment, when my fingers press gently against the moist rot of the swinging doors, I wonder when exactly Simon Byron lost his soul. Was it all the times I caught him leering at me with hungry eyes? Or was it even sooner? Did the curse my grandmother create prey upon a boy who was born to a monster, a boy who felt he had no other choice?

Roe comes up behind me, and his fingers slip over my own. I turn to face him. No matter how Simon lost his soul, it was his choice that led him to a fiery end.

Choices Roe and my brother will never make.

"Together," Roe whispers.

"Together." I push open the door.

Bog water floods the sanctuary, pooling around the pews and making the floor sag beneath our weight. An amalgam of sulfur, peat, and rotting skin permeates the air. I blink against it and hold my breath, then look around.

The pews are not empty.

Every person I know who has ever stepped foot inside Sinner's Chapel now clogs the pews. Even my mother, her eyes vague, staring ahead. A sound slips from my throat. Grief, maybe. Anger and fear. The thick scent of rotting plant life chokes my nose and throat, and my fingers squeeze around Roe's while I try desperately not to retch.

The people don't move. It's like we're not even here. They just stare ahead. Roe grabs my waist when I stumble and catch myself on the wall.

"Mila, the altar."

My eyes are hazy, but I look past the rotting pews, the people—breathing, but in some sort of trance. Water drips green from the ceiling.

The reverend, the monster—lithe with its corded flesh covered in bog mud—bends over the dark stained wood of the communion altar, all teeth and scales dripping with gray-green water. Jed is laid out like a sacrificial lamb, blood seeping down his temple like wine. My heart drops to the soles of my feet and drums an unsteady rhythm into the water pooling around my ankles.

Roe's fingers clutch my arms. Jed's eyes flutter open, bruises already forming on his skin. The monster's face tears, teeth glinting, and I grab ahold of a pew to center myself.

"Stop!" I shout, scrambling down the aisle.

The water grows thicker, deeper. Roe pulls me back, but I wrench away. I will not be held back anymore. The bog comes up through the floor and floods my veins.

The reverend turns his sickly face to me, shapeless eyes glaring. "You cannot stop the power, Mila. You cannot keep me from what I have deserved all these years. Roe was never going to be what I needed him to be, and Simon was too greedy—too angry—to see past his own petty arguments and do what needed to be done for the greater good. And now that he is gone, your brother will take his place. I will not let my legacy die out."

He draws a single fingernail down Jed's chest. My fingers grip tighter on the pew beside me.

Wait, I think to Dani. *Wait.*

"And what is that?" I ask, my voice breaking on my lips. "What is the greater good?"

The reverend's smile widens and cuts into his face like a dull knife through raw meat. "Salvation." The word curls from his lips like vapor. "The Lord gave my father a gift that day in the bog. *He will change our vile bodies to be like His glorious own.* Don't you see, Mila? Your grandmother's words were not a curse. They made us gods."

A laugh twists sharp in my chest. I step closer to the altar. The water of the bog vibrates around my legs. "You call murdering and stealing innocent souls salvation? A gift? All Grandma Ruby did was reveal the sickness that was already brewing in your bones."

The reverend's head quirks at this, and water slips off his slick hide like syrup. His grin widens, and one fingernail sinks into the bare skin of my brother's throat. Dani's mind presses against me.

It is not yet time.

"And what is innocence to you, Mila?" the reverend asks, when another surge of power pushes me forward. "For all have sinned, have we not? For all have fallen short. I give them all everlasting life, there in the bog, and from their life comes my own eternal water of life."

He wrenches Jed up from the altar, pulls their cheeks flush together, and snicks his teeth like something hungry.

"Who will it be, my son? Your first taste at immortality. If you do not become this, God's wrath will punish us both. We will shrivel to nothing. Pick one and find eternal life."

Jed's eyes shake in their sockets like a death rattle.

"No one deserves to die," he says. "Except for you, maybe."

The reverend's hideous, soulless eyes blink brightness into the gloom. His head rolls back, and his mouth opens. The sound I heard on the road—like rocks tumbling, of hail hitting water—pours from his gory lips. It splits along his skin like cracks in a stone wall.

He isn't made from bog and blood, not really, not in the way I am. Not in the way I can sense the water deep in my bones. The reverend is comprised of something else—from rotted love, from decay and curses made on quick lips. He is made from death itself.

"Oh, my child," he says, voice thick and snapping with phlegm. "Don't you get it? Everyone deserves to die. To be born again."

He pounces, muscles in his arms and legs coiling, nails like flashing iron toward Jed's throat. The bog inside my veins awakes.

Now.

I scream, mouth ripping open. The sound pours bloody from my throat. The bog pulses in my blood, turning it to muddy water. I raise my arms, and the moisture in the sanctuary comes to meet me when I press forward.

In this moment, I am not my mother, so afraid of her past that she let it haunt her. I am not my grandmother, blind with heartbreak and malice on her lips. Nor am I my sister or my brother, or anyone who has ever come before me.

I am the bog.

I am the bones spit back in the shallows, drinking in the sun.

The voices swimming in the depths, the ones who have been trapped for so long.

Too long.

I am myself.

The dead flood into the sanctuary, moving people from the pews. The reverend's eyes widen, and a scream tears from his white throat.

In a blur, Roe rushes past me, spitting water. He tears toward Jed, slinging him up in his arms, and pulling him down from the altar.

But the reverend is mine.

He has always been mine.

I push the water toward him until he is nothing but undulating, wriggling flesh behind a curtain of crystal. His mouth drips with blood, eyes blinking. He scrambles back against the wall. His voice is hoarse with his screams, his cries for mercy. But there is no mercy left. Not in the bog, and not in me.

Not for the man who has opened his mouth and swallowed souls whole.

I do it for Grandma Ruby. Do it for Jed. For Dani and Agatha and my mother, who clings to a bottle because of this monster. This *worm*. I do it for all those in Credence Hollow who have felt the curse of this man, the evil that permeated the water beneath our feet for far too long. All those dead around me.

A gentle buzzing warms my ear, droning two words, over and over and over.

Look around, look around.

And when I do, the flies, hundreds upon thousands of them, fill the sanctuary like some biblical plague. But they are not a threat. I see that now. They have only ever been a warning.

Look around, they say, and so I do. The bog surges under one hand, and in the other, I hold Agatha's matchbook. This church is old, even more so than the town itself perhaps. A place of worship turned to a house of pain, condemnation, and death. And that is what it will always be.

I peer into the reverend's eyes, the smile light on my face. My fingers free a match and strike it against the rough wood of a pew. The scent of red phosphorus floods the air.

"Mila." The reverend's voice is weak, watered-down. He cowers against the wall of the church, nothing more than a pale and frightened man now. "Please."

I crouch, the water still streaming from one palm. "Why?" I ask. "Why did you do it? You could have stopped it. You could have been like Roe."

His eyes shift past me, to where his two remaining sons stand. "Roe is a disappointment."

And in the end, those words are the things that send the match from my hand. To know, even in his last moments, Titus Byron thinks his beautiful, gentle son is a disappointment. The softest boy I've ever known. The boy who carries the world on his shoulders. The boy who kissed me like he thought the world was ending.

Because maybe it is.

I drop the match. The poisoned water ignites beneath me, licking up the walls. The screams fill the sanctuary. But I don't wait. I turn and race down the steps, following Roe and Jed out while the dead save the living from the flames. We empty out onto the grass beside Agatha and Camille and watch the fire and water burst from the stained glass, the chimney, and the steeple.

It won't be standing come morning.

25

THE PATHS HOME

I stand in our home's driveway, watching Camille and Agatha disappear into the pines, their hands held tight. They leave for college in a few weeks and have decided to make a grave for Dani before they go. Just something simple—a circle of stones and a place to lay flowers and crowns of blueberry leaves. It's what Dani would have wanted.

Peace.

The congregation doesn't remember their dead loved ones. The bog water and the reverend's power were too much. It hypnotized them. All they know is one moment they were crowning me Blueberry Queen, and the next, they were standing outside Sinner's Chapel, watching it burn to the ground.

For the best, I think.

Behind me, the door slaps open and shut, and feet echo on the porch. Roe bumps me with a shoulder, the smoldering end of a joint held in his lips and a mug of coffee in one hand. Its bitter scent floods the air, and I lean deeply against him, drinking in the smell of it all. He is solid and warm and *here*, and that's what matters most.

"Where's Jed?" He hands me the mug.

"Upstairs, helping Mom clean out the shower drain. I don't think he's left her side since we got home," I say and then smile. "It's like so much has changed and then again, so little."

Roe nods and softens against me. There are no more bandages around his knuckles, no more hurt to keep inside. He offers it freely now, to the world around him. To those who only want to help him heal. I slip my hand into his, rubbing his skin with my thumb. It will take a while for the scars to disappear, but isn't that just the way? Our minds and bodies restore at different speeds, and it's a beautiful thing. A kind of growth, I guess.

"How are you holding up?" I ask, taking a sip of coffee.

His breath shudders out of him. It is cruel and painful to remember who his father was, his brother, but there is a sense of relief too. Like the world isn't his to make whole anymore.

"My lawyer wants me to sell the house, and I think I will. There are too many bad memories in that place for me to keep it."

"Hey..." I reach up and pull his face down to meet mine. "I'm here. Whatever comes next, we're in it together. I quit my job this morning and broke my lease. Told Denise I'm staying here."

His eyes light up at this. He blows another puff of smoke into the air. "Oh, yeah?"

"Yeah. Figured maybe I could get a job at Phil's for now. See what else comes up." I stretch up on tiptoes and slip my lips softly against his. "I'm not going anywhere. The bog is my home."

We turn our faces toward the tree line when a breeze kicks up from the bog beyond. It caresses the back of my neck, an odd sensation curling around my skin. I open my mind to it, to the voices. Only twice since the burning of the church have I heard them, but this is different. There is a gentleness to the sound, a gratitude, a sense of peace.

They are free.

The bog is free.

The town is free from the monsters that prowled it during the day, with human flesh over slimed, putrid coils of skin.

I turn my ear to the voices.

And they are singing.

Autumn comes quick upon the bog. Kissing the water with lacy ice, weighing down the heads of cattails with hoarfrost. Soon, the depths will lie beneath a sheet of glass, a reflection for the sky above. But not yet.

Today, the bog flexes, reaching fingers beneath a town finally ready to heal. It feels the family in the cabin—mother, son, two daughters—while they press forward together, washing themselves in forgiveness and love. It also senses the man with broken knuckles who has decided to set his pain free.

Because he himself is unbound, the bog rejoices in this freedom now flooding its banks. No more sorrow, no more death, no more swallowing of bone and blood. And so, the bog sings, the voices beneath the waves no longer caught, ready and able to move on, thanks to the girl who broke the curse. The bog opens its throat, and the notes reach up to the heavens, like a honey-tongued choir when peace enters their souls.

The girl on the porch, wrapped in a quilt and clutching a mug of coffee, hears them and smiles. She has found a sort of freedom too. The kind that comes from deep within, the kind that will finally let her spread her wings and be who she has always wanted to be, unhindered by pain, by the greed and ambition of men who wish to rule her. For she will rule herself, knowing wherever she may roam, whoever she may become, she can turn back to the bog and rest in the knowledge there is a firm foothold among the cattails and peat.

That there, in the bog, she knows the path home.

ACKNOWLEDGMENTS

The idea for this book came like a thief in the night. The process of actually writing it, however, was like grinding bones to dust. I agonized over it for years, terrified I would never be able to tell the truth with justice. What is the truth, you may ask? My brother's name was Jed. And I have carried him with me my entire life. I wanted to tell a story that immortalized him, that spoke to what he could have been, *who* he could have been. And everything crystalized the moment my mother sat me down and said, "Write about it." So, I did, and Jed, this one is for you. It has always been for you.

It's also for my mother, who is strong beyond her own knowing. Thank you for your patience, your dedication, your love, and for being my biggest cheerleader. There are so many times when I look at you and think, "If she could get through that, then I can survive this." I love you, Mumsie. You are power and strength embodied. Last, but certainly not least, it's for my grandma, my Oma. Not only is she my biggest source of inspiration and spiritual guide, she is the mirror I look into, holding a place on a pedestal I can only hope to achieve someday. She will laugh at this, I think, but if you know my Oma, you know I have only scratched the surface on the majesty of this woman.

Unmeasurable thanks to my agent, Amy Giuffrida, who believed in me even when I didn't believe in myself. Thank you for everything. To my editor, Amanda Chiu Krohn, along with Ashlyn Inman, and the entire team at Turner Publishing and Keylight Books who saw the diamonds beneath the bone dust. Special thanks as well to Lyndsey Smith of Horrorsmith Editing.

To my sister, Emma-Rebecca. You are strength embodied and I love you. To my baby brother, Ty. Thank you for that late night in spring of 2024, when you wrapped me up in your arms when I thought the world was falling apart around me and whispered, "You took care of me for so long. Let me take care of you for once." I love you. To my Opa, thank you for being a rock and cornerstone in my life. And thank you for telling me the stories of the old family swamplands. To Dad, who taught me to put my nose to the grindstone and never stop moving.

To the A-team. Thank you for all your support and your screaming and cheering in the Slack group and the way you flock to the chat every time our agent makes a vague Twitter post. You all bring me joy.

To my early readers—Annie Bayer, Erica Rose Eberhart, Zeyneb Holdridge, and Amanda Linsmeier. Thank you for your guidance, your enthusiasm, and the late-night email notifications I would get from you all, screaming in the comment section of my Google doc. Sorry (not sorry) I gave you nightmares.

To Hannah Whitten and Skyla Arndt. You have both cheered me on from afar, and I am so grateful.

To my best friend, Amanda Havill Adgate. We have weathered so many storms together and apart. Thank you for your light, your support, and for loving Mila—and me—through so many drafts. To Jenny Adams, Mire Marke, Ahnna Reyes, and Andra Mae Johnson. Thank you for being there for me through every step of life and cheering me on.

To my eighth and ninth grade English and French teacher, Madame Roberta Santoni. Thank you for inspiring me, believing in me when I was so young, and for always creating a safe place for me in your classroom. Your kindness and protection for that strange, gangly, redheaded creature who sought you out as a haven in the dark places will never be forgotten.

To Hunter. Thank you for loving me and dreaming with me. You're magic.

And lastly, to J.R.R. Tolkien, who not only taught me how to weave worlds into existence, but also showed me how absolutely freaking terrifying bogs can be. Don't follow the lights.

ABOUT THE AUTHOR

AUTHOR PHOTO BY VIXEN GALORE STUDIOS

TEAGAN OLIVIA KING grew up in Michigan's wild Upper Peninsula but traded in the stormy shores of Lake Superior for the windbeaten sandbars of Lake Huron. She holds a degree in creative writing from Northern Michigan University and is the author of several works of short horror fiction. She lives in an old farmhouse with her beloved, a rescue pup named Remus, a black cat named Chester (who may or may not harbor the soul of some long-dead deity), and probably some ghosts.

www.ingramcontent.com/pod-product-compliance
Lightning Source LLC
Chambersburg PA
CBHW031943010726
47493CB00007B/2048